Best Wish
Freddie (Remza
2018

SHATTERED BANGLES

FREDDIE REMZA

Outskirts Press, Inc.
http://www.outskirtspress.com

ISBN: 978-1-9772-0392-2

Outskirts Press and the "OP" logo are trademarks belonging to Outskirts Press, Inc.

ACKNOWLEDGEMENTS

I would like to express my appreciation to Ashish, my brilliant *Overseas Adventure Travel* (OAT) guide who shared so much of his country. I arrived home not only with knowledge but with a deeper appreciation for India, its people and its culture.

Special thanks goes to my travel friend, Terry Clift, who took the proverbial leap of faith and consented to come on this crazy trip with me when so many wouldn't. She was the perfect travel companion, and walked away knowing she had the experience of a lifetime.

Many thanks to my husband, John, who has no problem turning me loose to research the settings of my stories. He's lived through the writing of six books which is no easy task. Always supportive and pushing me forward.

My thanks to Beth Pullman who called to my attention the serious problem India has with acid attacks. I knew I wanted to write a story set in India but didn't know exactly what to focus on until that afternoon conversation we had weeks before my departure.

Lastly, to all the women from *Sheroes Hangout*. The warmth and affection you showed as I visited your café will never be forgotten. I left never to be the same again. God bless you, my sisters from India, and all that you do for each other. Thank you for teaching me how we can all bounce back when times look dismal. You ladies are amazing!

Freddie Remza

Hope is the thing with feathers
That perches in the soul
And sings the tune without the words
And never stops at all.

Emily Dickinson
(1830-1886)

CAST OF CHARACTERS

Allison

Allison Wagner—Journalist and editor for a documentary film company
Wesley Gerhart—Allison's boss
Lan, Ashwin—People from "The Stolen Brooch"
Abha—Receptionist & Secretary at the Delhi newspaper
Mr. Arun—Editor at the Delhi newspaper
Jay—Abha's fiancé
Arpan—Sikh guide at soup kitchen
Detective Mahor—Detective
Riya—Assistant editor of the Delhi newspaper
Vihaan—Copy editor of newspaper

Kasi

Kasi Beckham—Victim
Lina—Kasi's cousin
Lalit Joshi—Kasi's brother & plastic surgeon
Keith Beckham—Kasi's husband
Rani—Lalit's wife
Hari Chubney—Ex-suiter of Kasi
Dr. Kalawat—Lalit's partner & Kasi's doctor
Yash—Police officer

Lynne

Lynne Fenton—College student & intern at Mukta Cafe
Abby, Sara, Trina—Lynne's college friends
Maruti—Presenter at college
Debbie Fenton—Lynne's mother
Chandra—Supervisor at Mukta Café
Shelby, Kimberly—College exchange students on plane
Naomi—Intern from Israel & Lynne's roommate in India
Parvati—Acid victim & greeter at Mukta Café
Kiri—Acid victim & accountant at Mukta Café
Jaya Gowda—17-year-old acid victim
Deepak—Kiri's abusive husband
Dr. Lalit Joshi—Jaya's doctor & Kasi's brother
Kumar—Kiri's son

PROLOGUE

The nurse drew the curtain to prevent the light from bothering the young woman. Confused and terrified, the woman described being dragged from the car into some building. She screamed, but he put a rag over her mouth allowing only muffled sounds. She punched, but he tightly secured her hands with rope. She kicked and squirmed, but he bound her to the bed. She pleaded with him, but he laughed. She reasoned with him, but he would see it no other way.

She was to be his wife, but she backed out and left with someone else. To him, that was an unforgivable embarrassment, and the humiliation never lessened. He tried to go on, but there were constant reminders. At first, people inquired. He saw the puzzlement on their faces. Eventually, all conversation stopped, and all he received were pathetic nods. He knew they wondered. His family insisted he must have done something wrong. After all, she agreed. What changed her mind? He didn't know. Anxiety built up. The pressure of life weighed heavily upon him. He snapped.

She resisted until her spirit weakened. Then she withdrew and obeyed.

Chapter 1

LYNNE

(Thirteen months earlier)

QUICKLY SHOVING HER notebook into her backpack, Lynne hurried out of the dorm, crossed the quad, and into Jeffers Hall just in time for her World Issues class. She slid into the seat next to her friend, Abby. "Have I missed anything?" she whispered.

Abby smiled and nodded her head towards a woman sitting up front dressed in a yellow sari. "No, Doctor Bailey is just about to introduce a guest speaker."

Lynne put her purse down on the floor beside her desk and looked towards the Indian woman. At first, she noted how pretty the young woman was until she turned her face towards the window, and Lynne noticed severe pot marks and scars on a disfigured face.

Professor Bailey stood up and said, "I would like to introduce someone who has become a good friend of mine. This is Maruti. I've invited her here to talk to you about India and the situation there affecting women and young children."

Maruti stood up and walked over to the podium. "Thank you, Doctor Bailey. I am most happy to be here to share with your students what the situation is like for many young women in India. I suppose you might be wondering about this."

She pointed to the right side of her face. "You have an expression in America that I learned. It is 'address the elephant in the room.' Is that right? So I will start off by telling you what happened to me. Have you ever heard of the acid attacks taking place in India? It's quite frequent with approximately 1000 assaults in India each year. Well, I was a victim of such an attack. Some attacks are by strangers, but most are out of revenge or rage. It could be anything from a rejected marriage proposal, a relationship not approved by the family, a jealous husband suspects that his wife was involved in an affair, or a spurned sexual advance. With me, I just happened to be in the wrong place at the wrong time. A man I had never seen before threw acid in my face as I was leaving a train."

Maruti had everyone's attention as she continued her story. "Many attacks in rural areas go unreported. The government tends to look the other way as though a crime never happened, and police and the judicial system often are unwilling to take the time or make an effort to pursue reported attacks."

Lynne raised her hand. "Maruti, isn't this punishable in your country?"

"The situation is growing, forcing the government to acknowledge that harsher laws should be in place. There is a fairly new law stating that acid violence is considered premeditated."

Abby said, "I would think so. I mean, how many people carry acid?"

Maruti nodded in agreement. "You're quite right. The perpetrator needs to purchase the acid and then stalk the victim; all leading evidence that the attack was deliberate."

Another student, Patrick, who sat in the front row asked, "What happens after they are caught?"

Maruti sighed. "The Criminal Law Act of 2013 states that anyone convicted of such a crime is sentenced as little as ten years."

Abby shook her head. "That doesn't seem like enough time."

"Exactly," Maruti agreed, "after my attack, I had six operations. This attack was damaging, but so many other women have had much worse. In one case, a husband doused his wife with acid as she slept because he was sure she was having an affair with a co-worker. The acid ate into her eyes, ears, nose, and mouth. She needed many reconstructive operations since her eyelids and lips were burned off and her nose melted closing off her nostrils."

"Oh no," Lynne whispered under her breath as she covered her face with her hands.

"You see," Maruti continued, "often the thinking behind this is to disfigure the woman so that no one would want her. This woman is also partially blind. Not only was her livelihood taken from her, but her family and friends distanced themselves leaving not much of a support group. As for myself, I was fortunate because my family has been very supportive."

"Where do they get the acid?" asked Patrick.

"It could be something as simple as toilet cleaning liquid or as dangerous as nitric, sulfuric or hydrochloric acid. These are all available in stores. Laws have recently been passed in India that regulate the sale of these acids. Buyers must provide a photo ID as well as their name and address. Stores don't always enforce these regulations while others aren't even aware of them."

When the class ended, everyone quietly walked out of the room—no one spoke. Each person was deep in thought trying to process Maruti's story. Lynne sat in her seat and stared at the door. She motioned to Abby to wait for her outside of the classroom, slowly got out of her chair, and walked over to Maruti who was preparing to leave the room.

"Maruti, I'm deeply moved by this problem. Does India give you any assistance?"

"Well, the court directs hospitals to treat survivors with some government assistance."

"What about the psychological effects? Surely, you had to deal with that yourself."

"May I ask your name?"

"Oh yes, it's Lynne. I hope I'm not keeping you from something. I'm just bothered by your story and want to know more."

"No, you're not. I want people to be aware of what's going on. The laws are important, Lynne, but a cultural change is also needed. Women need to be respected, and their rights acknowledged and enforced. This change needs to be a grassroots' movement starting with educating children from an early age."

Lynne nodded. "I agree with you, but it seems that this offense against women should be right up there with rape."

Maruti smiled in agreement. "You know, as bad and offensive as rape is, an acid attack can often be worse because there is just no escape from the visual disfiguration. I am subjected to humiliation every day. I see people staring at me, and I know they are curious. Every time I look in a mirror, I'm reminded of that day in the train station. Here, let me give you my card in case you want to contact me."

"Yes, I may do that. Thanks for coming to talk to us." Lynne accepted the card and left the room to meet up with Abby.

"I need to find out more about this situation, Abby."

They walked over to the student union to meet up with two of their friends for lunch and wasted no time telling Sara and Trina everything. Sara mentioned she saw something about India on a poster.

"Are you talking about the poster referring to some woman's program?" asked Trina.

Lynne sat back in her chair. "So where is this poster?"

"Right outside the Psych office," said Trina. "I believe there's a brochure on how you can volunteer and get credit for it. If you're interested in being an advocate, you should check it out."

"I don't know. Not sure how my parents would react to me going to India."

"You might be able to sell it to them by counting the experience as part of your required internship," suggested Trina.

"Yeah, plus get credit for it," added Sara.

"Sounds possible; just not sure how to make it happen."

Abby moved her finished salad towards the center of the round table. She rubbed her forehead as she glanced around at the other students in the room. Lynne recognized this look. It was something Abby always did when trying to come up with some new idea.

Sara smirked. "Uh oh, I think you're in trouble now. Abby is coming up with some sort of plan for you."

Abby smiled. "Okay, let's concentrate on that required internship."

"What about it?" asked Lynne.

"From what I have seen on the news, women in India are starting to speak out against the abuse thrown their way," said Abby. "I mean, not just acid throwing victims but also rape and forcible marriage at an early age—stuff like that. I can only imagine the psychological hang-ups these women might have, and I would guess could use therapeutic help. What a fantastic opportunity for you to not only have a unique experience but also help victims from overcoming these physical as well as emotional scars."

The following day Lynne found herself standing in the outer office of the Psych Department. She had difficulty sleeping that night unable to get Maruti's story out of her mind. It didn't help having her friends encourage her to follow her heart. All of that made a significant impression on her, but was she sticking her neck out too far?

"Can I help you?" the woman sitting at the desk in the outer office asked.

"Oh, yeah . . . well, maybe. I heard you had information on volunteer internships in India."

"India? Oh, wait. Are you talking about the Mukta program?"

"Mukta? I don't know. Exactly what is that about?"

The receptionist stood up and walked over to the opposite end of the room. She took a brochure nestled in a packet that hung on the wall and handed it to Lynne. "Are you referring to this?"

Lynne looked at the glossy pamphlet. On the cover was a painting of a woman with splashes of red, blue, and purple surrounding a troubled face.

"Can you tell me about this?"

"I don't know a whole lot about the program because it's something new that recently came to us, but there is a website you can go on to get more information." She pointed to the information at the bottom corner of the brochure. "This could get you started."

"I was thinking about using something like this as one of my internships. Do you know if this would qualify?"

"You probably should talk to your advisor about that. As I said, I'm not that familiar with the details."

"Okay, thanks," Lynne said as she took the pamphlet and headed towards the door.

"Good luck with whatever you decide."

Lynne smiled and walked out into the corridor. She found an unoccupied bench, sat down and opened the brochure to read the contents. "What am I thinking?" she muttered under her breath, as she found herself seriously abandoning her original plan to work with kids in an after-school program. "That would undoubtedly be less of a hassle than this crazy idea of going to India. Just the logistics of getting there is overwhelming." Lynne stuck the brochure in the pocket of her jacket and headed towards the library. Finals were approaching, and she needed to study.

Lynne never mentioned the India project to her parents. She did not give it any more thought until three months later when she and her friends showed up at the beach condo for spring break. When Lynne hung her jacket on a hook, she felt a bulge in the pocket. Looking inside, she pulled out the brochure on Mukta's Cafe.

"I forgot I put this in my jacket," she thought to herself. She threw it on the dresser, turned to join her friends, and then noticed a decorated plaque on the wall that said: *Peace Starts with Yourself and Grows.*

Maruti's image immediately flashed before her. Yes, Maruti was a victim, but she didn't use it as a crutch, although she certainly had the right to do so. Instead, she left her comfort zone to reach out to others in need; and perhaps by doing so, she helped herself. Lynne had good intentions in researching this women's program in India with the possibility of becoming involved, but life got in the way. Besides, the whole process of making this happen overwhelmed her. Then there was the after-school program which was undoubtedly a path of less resistance.

"Hey Lynne, where are you?" yelled Abby from the outside balcony.

Lynne joined the three girls who were dressed in their bathing suits and heading for the beach. "I need to change. Go ahead without me, and I'll meet up with you in a few minutes."

After they left, she sat down on the rattan chair and looked down at the inviting beach below. An elderly couple strolled with their backs hunched over and eyes glued to the sand. The lady stooped to pick up a shell and placed it in the bag the man carried. Seagulls flew overhead with lightning speed and coasted to the hardened sand. Garbage cans, some overturned by the wind, were positioned every twenty feet. Tracks left over from the morning clean-up crew were still visible along with the letters 'MARRY ME' inscribed in the sand. A three-year-old child raced towards the water and playfully jumped into the tidal foam. It was clear that this was his first encounter with the ocean. Lynne could not recall her first time at the beach. As long as she remembered, the ocean was part of her life. The little boy's mother grabbed her phone and took several photos recording this milestone. What a lucky little guy to have this moment taped. First- time experiences can never be replicated because the element of surprise is no longer possible.

Lynne wondered if the awe this child experienced could be similar to the day she, herself, first viewed the Grand Canyon one year ago? She remembered walking along the road filled with excitement and anticipation. After all, she had seen many photos of the canyon in books, posters, and movies. Lynne knew what to expect or sort of thought she did until the earth suddenly opened up before her. Never will she forget the element of surprise that rushed over her as she looked down upon the reddish canyon below. Nothing could have prepared her for that.

Lynne's world differed from the crowded shores of the Ganges. Arranged marriages were common; rare was the choice of a marriage partner given to young couples. The forgotten brochure, the decorative plaque hanging on the wall, the stirring she felt inside—Lynne was big on signs. Could these all be part of her subconscious mind directing her towards India?

Lynne walked back into the room and grabbed the brochure. *Why are some people born into a comfortable situation while others experience an environment of extreme poverty?* Fate, determination, luck or lack of it—all factors that play into one's life.

According to the pamphlet, Mukta's Hangout is a café enabling acid victims an opportunity to not only gain employment but to start healing from the inside. The brochure described them as "courageous women with scars."

Quickly changing into her suit, Lynne headed towards the beach to join her friends. Selling this idea to her parents would not be easy. She knew it was essential to learn about the program and prepare for their questions. Safety would be a big issue. Lynne needed to start preparations working towards being accepted, figure out how she would get there, determine where she would live, and learn what her responsibilities would be. As for an internship, it appeared this organization was in its infancy stage so she questioned how organized they would be. Then again, the challenge of being on the ground floor excited her. The raw, enthusiastic emotions that bubbled up inside, assured Lynne that there could be some merit in making all of this happen.

Lynne stepped out onto the short boardwalk leading to the beach. The sun was hot, but it felt inviting after going through months of a New York winter. She'd have to figure out India's weather in January. So much to know. Will she need a visa? What's the appropriate clothing over there? Traveling to Asia would be a first-time experience. She could not remember her initial reaction to the ocean, but her first encounter with India will undoubtedly make a profound impression. She was sure of that. By the time she reached her friends, Lynne had convinced herself that making the trip happen was what she needed to do, and she couldn't wait to tell them her decision.

"Lynne, I don't know if I like the idea of you going to India. I don't feel comfortable with it," said Debbie Fenton.

"That's because you don't know anything about the trip, Mom. Before you form an opinion, sit down and let me explain what it is I'll be doing."

Lynne's mom sat down at the kitchen table not wanting to hear about her daughter's plans. She knew Lynne could be convincing when she wanted to do something. There was no stopping her, and she worried this was one of those times.

"Lynne, this trip is not inexpensive. I'm not sure we can afford to send you."

"I have it all figured out. In addition to lifeguarding at the community pool this summer, I got an evening job waitressing at the country club. Tips are quite good; if I do weddings, I can make out quite well. I figure I would apply those additional wages towards the trip. I also spoke with the work-study person at school and was offered a job in the mailroom next semester."

"Won't that be too much?" asked Mrs. Fenton.

"No, it averages about two hours a day from Monday thru Saturday putting mail into mailboxes of two residence halls. Most everyone uses email, so there isn't that much to deal with—probably a couple of large mail bags to sort through. Then I'm on call in the mailroom from 4:00 thru 5:00 handing out packages. It's quite flexible, and I can arrange my classes around these times. I won't be making a ton of money, but I think enough to buy airfare to Delhi. You know, otherwise, I would just be hanging out with my friends. I also thought instead of gifts, everyone could give me cash at Christmas. What do you think?"

Mrs. Fenton gave her daughter an anxious look. "Okay, I'm coming out with it. I worry about your safety."

Lynne nodded her head. "It's as safe as any place anymore, Mom. Really—you can't limit yourself because of fear. If that were the case, we would never leave the house."

"But it's so different there and so far away."

"About a fifteen-hour plane ride. As for different, that's what I like about it. That's what makes the trip appealing. I'll be exploring a whole new culture as well as being a conduit in helping women overcome the abuse they've received. I will be doing something worthwhile."

Lynne's mom stood up and walked over to the sink. She rinsed out her cup and put it into the dishwasher.

"Mom, aren't you going to say anything about what I told you?"

Mrs. Fenton turned towards her daughter and saw the determination in her eyes. No way would she have had those kinds of opportunities when she was a college student. The world wasn't programmed to have young girls even think of traveling to Asia as a possibility. Take your classes, earn good grades, graduate, get married and go to work was the standard protocol. In a way, Mrs. Fenton felt a little envious—so many more choices for girls today.

"Give me some time to think this over, Lynne. You spring this on me and then expect an immediate answer. It doesn't work that way. By the way, would you be going by yourself?"

"Yes, but there will be someone picking me up at the airport. I've already contacted the organization, and they are excited about me coming."

"When would you be going and for how long?"

"In my senior year I have to do two internships, and this would be one of them. I actually would be leaving right after New Year's Day for twelve weeks."

"How do you know the university will approve this as one of your graduation requirements? Have you checked that out with your advisor?"

"I did. She thinks it's a fantastic opportunity with the hopes I will report back with information making it possible for other students to pursue the same assignment. I'm pretty much going to be part of a groundbreaker putting this together."

"What do you mean?"

"This woman, Chandra, will be my supervisor over there. She's the café's head administrator. I've spoken to her the past few weeks. She believes I could be helpful in counseling acid victims allowing them to feel comfortable enough to come out of seclusion and spend time working at the café. She also told me there was another university student from Israel who will be there at the same time. She's contacting her to inquire about sharing living arrangements."

Mrs. Fenton stared with disbelief at her daughter. "So you did all of this planning and made the necessary arrangements without even once discussing it with us?"

Lynne sighed. "I know I should've brought it up sooner, but I wanted to feel certain this is what I wanted to do. Also, I was unsure if the university and the Mukta program would approve the internship. There were a lot of loose ends. I needed to tie them up before I presented all of this to you and Dad."

Mrs. Fenton walked over to her daughter and hugged her. "I guess I have to start accepting that you are growing into a young woman and need to start making some decisions on your own," she quietly whispered in her daughter's ear. "Besides, I've learned since you were a little girl that if there was something you wanted to do, there was no stopping you. I'll speak to your dad about this tonight when he gets home from work. I'm sure he'll have a lot of questions. So be ready!"

"Thanks, Mom. I knew you'd come through for me."

"Lynne, are you sure this is what you want to do? You do know that things would be far less complicated if you just let the university assign an intern placement somewhere close by."

"I've thought about this for several months now. I even tried to talk myself out of going; but the more I've learned about the program, the more excited I've become. Besides, it's only for twelve weeks—not a forever thing."

Debbie Fenton smiled and nodded. Hearing those words revved up a new fear inside her. Lynne was her only child, and she never considered having her live far away. After all, had she not prided herself on raising her daughter to be independent and self-reliant? It suddenly became apparent they did too good of a job. What if this assignment changes her—makes her want to stay? She shook her head to free herself of that notion. No sense to start worrying about that now. Regardless of her feelings, she recognized this was her daughter's life. It was time to let go.

Chapter 2

ALLISON

ALLISON WAGNER WASN'T new to this type of journalism. It might appear to be exciting to the average person, but traveling to a developing country had its problems. Circumventing the language, cultural differences, transportation issues, and strange sounding names of the food she ingested were only a few roadblocks she had to master, but she loved it. There was nothing more thrilling than embarking on a new assignment.

It had been a year since her last international trip which was to Thailand. She deeply regretted the mistake of letting her emotions get away from her by mixing business with her personal life. She saw it coming and allowed it to happen. Deception, foolery, naivety—call it what you'd like; she swore to Jim, her managing editor, it would never happen again. Since her return, Jim was in and out of the hospital several times until he passed away. His initial heart attack led to two more with the last one being fatal. It wasn't easy accepting his death. Throughout her years of employment, she learned a lot from him. He was more than a boss—he was a mentor, a friend, and a father image. He was missed.

The agency hired another person to take his place. He was new to the staff, a recruit from another agency. Wesley Gerhart had the qualifications needed for the job. He had successfully produced several TV documentaries with a competing agency. Although much younger than Jim, he was more conservative in personality which made it more difficult for Allison when pitching a new idea. After three months of haggling back and forth, Wes agreed to Allison's idea of doing a story about various social issues surrounding India and how they mainly affected women. Inspired by the recent women's movement, she was packed, ready to go, and waiting at JFK to board the plane for New Delhi.

The airport remained festively decorated with Christmas trees, red and green garlands, and Chanukah banners. People sat with heavy coats, but there would be little need for them. India was warm in January. She opened her laptop and typed a few notes reminding herself of items she needed to take care of once she arrived. For the most part, she was ready.

It had been practically a year since the Hollywood award ceremony when they won first place for the 'Best Foreign Documentary' which Allison helped write and produce. Every time she walked into the conference room, she winked at the statuette that stood on the shelf inside the locked case. Lan, the young Vietnamese girl Allison met while in Vietnam, made the evening particularly exciting. It was incredible how Jim was able to pull that off by surprising Lan with a trip to California so she could be present for the evening's award ceremony. Nothing in Allison's career could possibly top that.

Allison managed to stay in touch with Lan who lived in a Safe House in Bangkok counseling young girls who were victims of the sex trade. The bond that was established between the two young women could never be broken. Having the opportunity to reconnect when she was on assignment in Thailand was an extra bonus. As for her Thai guide, Ashwin, she didn't have any further contact with him, even though he tried to reach out to her on several occasions.

Whenever she fell into a low, Allison would say, "It is what it is." Five small words, one short phrase—worked like magic. She owed it all to her therapist whom she visited upon returning to New York from Bangkok. Sometimes you just need someone who will objectively listen to get those frustrations and fears out in the open. Only then can you bundle them up and heave them as far as they will go.

Allison took her seat in Business Class which was one of the perks earned after winning the Best Documentary Award for 'The Orchid Bracelet.' An attractive young woman dressed in a beautiful blue sari sat next to her. They nodded to each other, realizing they would be spending many hours together as they crossed the Atlantic to India. Allison felt relieved to see that her seatmate was a female since it crossed her mind that the last time she shared a plane seat with someone, trouble followed. She will never be so casual about her unattended carry-on luggage again. Truth be told—a little paranoia had made its mark as she squeezed her bag under the seat in front of her.

Allison turned to the woman of obvious Indian decent and greeted her with a smile. "Are you returning home?" she asked.

The woman nodded. "I live in New York now but going back for my cousin's wedding."

"What fun! Will you be there long?"

"Yes, I will be visiting for three weeks. I haven't seen my family for over two years—very excited to return."

"Does anyone in your family live in the United States?"

"No, my brother lived in America while attending

medical school, but decided to return to India after graduation. He's a plastic surgeon," she said proudly.

"I see. So your brother's practicing medicine over there?"

"He said there are better opportunities for him in America, but he thought he would be more useful to the people in India."

"I find that quite commendable," Allison said, noticing the woman kept turning and twisting the several rows of bangles wrapped around her wrist. She wondered if this was a habit or a sign of anxiety.

"You have a beautiful set of bracelets."

The woman raised her arm and gave Allison a closer look. "Thank you. I've had these since my wedding."

"Really? Is there some kind of symbolism with the bracelets like there is with a wedding ring?" Allison asked.

"Yes, it is customary for brides to wear bangles. Mine are made out of glass which signifies the long life of our marriage. If any of the bridal glass breaks, that is bad luck."

"Is your husband on the flight with you?" asked Allison.

The girl looked away for a moment as though she didn't want to talk about it, but then said, "He didn't come with me. My brother will be picking me up at the airport when I arrive."

Allison wondered why her husband didn't come with her but decided it was best not to ask. "Well, the bracelets certainly are beautiful—do you always wear them?"

"When I was first married, I chose the smallest possible bangles. I had to put them on with oil because they barely fit over my knuckles. So, since then, I've gained a little weight, and now they are always on." She gave a slight giggle and twisted the rows of bangles to show how little room there actually was.

"Why do they have to be so small?" Allison asked.

"By wearing such a small size shows our life will be full of love and affection. This is important to me because my marriage was not arranged by our parents, you see."

"It was a love marriage?"

"Uh huh, my family was not happy about it. At first, my father would not speak to me. He wanted me to marry this older man from a neighboring town, but I refused. I wasn't attracted to him. I didn't care if he had his own business. I just didn't want to marry him. I kept resisting, but my family thought I would eventually come to my senses. It was around that time I met my husband. He was working in India for an export company but then had to return to America. I saw him on the side, so it came as a surprise when I announced I was joining him as soon as my visa came through."

Allison started out on this journey with the idea of learning first hand as much as possible about the place of women in India's society. Little did she realize that would start happening before leaving the airport runway. She nodded her head in agreement. "I think that didn't go over well with them."

The girl looked down at her bracelets and kept twisting them around her wrist. Was Allison approaching territory still too tender?

"I wanted them to come to America to be at my wedding, but my father refused. My mother wanted to come, but my father would not allow it. Only my cousin came. That is why I wanted to be at her wedding."

"Is this the first time you'll be seeing your parents since you left India?"

The girl stared out the window. Allison sensed her nervousness and decided to change the subject. She pointed back at the bracelets. "Why so many different colors?"

"Each color stands for something. See this red one? That shows energy. The green is for fertility and good luck. I think green is the color of luck for many people, right?"

Allison thought of the 4-leaf clover. "It is. The Irish consider the green shamrock as a symbol of luck. Tell me about the silver and gold bangles."

The girl pointed to the silver bangle. "The silver means strength and the gold represents prosperity. Let me show you something." She opened her purse and pulled out a small bubbled-wrapped package.

"Look here. I bought these for my cousin. Her mother and future mother-in-law will also give her bangles of a variety of colors, but I chose these white and orange ones."

She handed them over to Allison. Being very gentle with them, she carefully turned the several rings of orange and white to see the overhead light of the plane dance upon the sparkly glass beads.

"They are beautiful," Allison said handing them back. "Why did you decide to give her orange and white ones?"

The girl carefully rewrapped them and slipped the bangles back into her purse.

"White is for new beginnings, and orange is for success. I decided on those two colors because I think they are good for a marriage, right?"

What started out as small talk for Allison had now generated into pure curiosity.

"Yes, very much so. What about happiness? Do you have a color for that since it's also important to be happy?"

The girl's smiling eyes darkened. "Yes, happiness is important. That would be yellow."

Allison looked down at the bracelets but did not see

any yellow ones. She tried to hide her thoughts, but the young woman picked up on it.

"My yellow bangles broke several months ago," the girl said.

"Oh, very sorry about that. Do you plan to replace them?"

"No, what happens, happens—right?"

Allison agreed but thought that was a strange response. What happens, happens? She didn't want to be nosey, but she just couldn't resist asking. Maybe it was the years of probing and getting to the bottom of a story that did it. Nevertheless, she came right out and asked how they were broken.

"I'm not too sure because they broke while I slept. I do remember having this awful nightmare that made no sense."

Allison was now intrigued. "What was the nightmare about?"

"It's a little crazy, but I remember being stuck in a corner and not being able to move. Then a large bucket of boiling water was dumped on my head. That's when I woke up and found sweat running down the left side of my face."

"That's pretty odd."

"When I started to get out of bed I felt something sharp rubbing on my leg. I looked under the blanket and saw both of my yellow bangles shattered. That really bothered me since the yellow symbolized happiness."

Allison was about to respond when the pilot came on the loudspeaker and announced they were next for take-off. The engines roared as the plane started down the runway. Allison felt the lift of the aircraft and then the sound of the wheels pulling up.

"What an interesting story. I'm sure there's some explanation. By the way, I'm Allison." She extended her hand to the young girl.

The girl took Allison's hand and shook it. "In India, we place both of our hands together with our fingertips reaching our chin and then say Namaste. So, Namaste, Allison, very happy to meet you. I'm Kasi."

Chapter 3

LYNNE

LYNNE FOUND HER seat on the plane, put her carry-on in the overhead compartment, and sat down next to two girls. She smiled and nodded towards them when the one next to the window complained to her friend. "I don't know why we aren't in First Class. So mad—my dad should have upgraded my seat. I never sit in coach."

Lynne buckled her seatbelt and muttered under her breath, "Yeah, I can see you definitely have a problem."

"What's that mean?" the girl asked.

"Uh, you know, sitting in coach can be a problem."

The girl nodded in agreement.

"Uh, do you mind me asking what takes you to India?" Lynne asked.

"No, we are part of this kind of exchange program staying with families in their homes for a few weeks. I didn't want to do this. Actually, I hated the idea of doing this."

"Then why are you going?" Lynne asked.

"My dad said it would be good for me—something about appreciating what I have and not complaining about stuff that doesn't matter. I convinced Shelby here into going with me."

Lynne looked over at the friend who was fussing with the window shade.

"Hi, I'm Shelby. To be perfectly honest, I would rather

be going to the Keys with my family, but Kimberly here talked me into it."

"Are you college students?"

"Yeah, freshmen on break. So why are you going to India?" Kimberly asked.

Lynne proceeded to tell them about her assignment working with acid victims.

Kimberly and Shelby looked at each other.

"You're going to be doing that?" asked Shelby. "Aren't you grossed out about that?"

"No, not really. Actually, I find it not only challenging but a way of helping other women who have had a tough time of it."

It was like she was speaking a foreign language. Neither of these girls understood what she was driving at. Kimberly kept looking at her phone texting friends. Most likely, complaining about the hardships of being seated in coach. Shelby kept fussing with her hair. "I hope they won't make me wear those long dresses."

Lynne asked, "You mean saris? Actually, I think they're quite beautiful and functional. You might find this whole experience fun if you just go with it."

Kimberly looked up from her phone, "Huh?"

Lynne leaned back in her seat. "Never mind—just a thought I had. I hope the trip works out for both of you."

The flight attendant came over to speak to Kimberly. "I'm sorry, but you'll need to put your phone away."

"Why?" she asked in a sarcastic voice.

"Because we're taking off. All phones are to be turned off."

Lynne closed her eyes hoping the flight attendant didn't think she was traveling with these two idiots. It was going to be a long flight with them sitting next to her. She rested her head and listened to the roar of the engines as the plane raced along the runway. She felt the sensation as they lifted off the earth and heard the grinding noise from the aircraft as it pulled its wheels inside. A devilish grin appeared on her face as she envisioned these two spoiled debutantes settling into the Indian culture so different from anything they've ever experienced. Although she found the whole situation amusing, she couldn't help but feel sorry for their host families.

Chapter 4

ALLISON

SHE'S TRAVELED TO Asia twice now—Thailand as well as Viet Nam. You would think she would be a little accustomed to that long flight. Fifteen hours on a plane never was easy. She did a little work, read her book, watched three movies, and tried to sleep. Why do fifteen hours go by so quickly when in one's usual routine? Regardless, Allison was curious about the woman sitting next to her—the woman with the glass bangle bracelets. Kasi said her return to India was to attend a wedding. From all that she heard, weddings in India were five-day celebrations marked with food, music, dancing, and elaborate decorations.

It was nothing Allison could put her finger on, but she noted the sadness that showed in Kasi's eyes along with her words, *What happens, happens*. What did she mean by that? Was she worried about seeing her father for the first time since leaving India to get married in New York?

Allison stirred. Soon they would be touching ground so she asked Kasi if she would mind pulling up the window shade. When the girl did so, Allison saw the dark of night. They left in the dark and arrived in the dark. Daylight must have been sandwiched in the middle even though she never witnessed it. She raised her tray as the flight attendant made the routine announcements for the descent. Allison reminded herself to relax and stop analyzing everything. A journalist's mind can be quite problematic.

"Looks like we will be landing soon. I hope I didn't talk too much," Allison said.

"No," answered Kasi, "I enjoyed our conversation. It definitely made those fifteen hours of flight time pass by."

Allison reached into her purse and pulled out a business card. "If ever you want to get together for lunch when we're back in New York, give me a ring. We can swap stories about our time here in Delhi."

Kasi nodded. "I would love to." She looked at the card. "So you're a reporter?"

Allison laughed. "Yeah, I get that a lot but no worries. Lunch would be strictly social."

Getting through passport control and customs was tedious enough, but in India, it was incredibly laborious. Lines were long and visa acceptance needed to be stamped not once, but twice. You don't have that second stamp you are sent back to get it. One, two—done. Move onto baggage claim.

As Allison waited for her luggage, she watched some of the people on her flight as they maneuvered their baggage from the conveyor belt. She noticed Kasi having difficulty getting her piece from the quickly moving platform. Allison jumped in and assisted. Kasi looked up and smiled her thanks.

"I hope you have a pleasant time at your cousin's wedding," Allison said.

She nodded. "Thank you. It was very nice meeting you. I enjoyed our conversation. Hope to see you back in New York."

Allison watched her wheel her luggage out into the

Arrival Hall. Turning her attention back to the luggage, she saw the three girls who sat several rows behind her. One of them seemed confident, self-assured. The other two were totally disoriented. She wondered why they were traveling to India.

"Excuse me," the confident one asked. "Do you have the local time?"

Allison replied, "Yes, it's 9:00. Pretty dark out there. Do you have someone picking you up?"

"Yes, I've arranged for a driver to take me to a hotel tonight. Then tomorrow I'm off to Agra to begin my internship."

"Internship in Agra? That sounds exciting. What will you be doing there?"

"It's called the Mukta program—a café run by women who were victims of acid attacks. Have you heard of it?"

Allison quickly pulled out another card. "No, I haven't, but I would be interested in knowing more. I'm Allison Wagner, over here to do some research on women's issues. That sounds like something I would like to check out. Here's my card. Mind if I contact you to see how things are going?"

Lynne accepted the card and gave the reporter the address of where she would be staying. "Sure, right now I don't have a whole lot to tell you. I'll be there for twelve weeks—hope I can eventually help you out. By the way, I'm Lynne Fenton."

Allison pointed to the other two girls. "Your seatmates, are they with you?"

Lynne shrugged her shoulders. "Absolutely not. Two rich freshmen from the Hamptons—you want an interesting story? Check them out in a couple of days."

Laughing, Allison said, "Well, good luck with your project. I definitely will be in touch with you. Thanks."

Allison made her way out of the Arrival Hall. As she looked for a taxi, she spotted Kasi waiting for her ride. A silver hatchback pulled up to the curb, and a man got out and approached her. When Kasi spoke of her brother, Allison had imagined him to be much younger than this man. She didn't like the way he greeted her. Kasi hadn't been back to India for over two years. It seemed a warm welcome would be due instead of what she witnessed. Allison watched the pair as they appeared to be having a rather heavy conversation. Kasi kept looking around as though she was expecting someone else. Is this gruff-looking man her brother? The guy suddenly opened the trunk, picked up her luggage and threw it inside. From where Allison stood, it appeared Kasi wanted to open the trunk to get to her luggage. Allison began to feel uncomfortable about the scene that played out before her. Was Kasi resisting and if so, why? Allison started over towards them to inquire if everything was okay. As she tried making her way through the crowd, the man tugged Kasi's elbow and escorted her to the front of the car. More angry gestures and then the man opened the door and forced Kasi inside. Allison picked up the pace to reach them, but before she got there, the car sped off into the Delhi fog.

Early the following morning, Allison walked into the Delhi newsroom which had an affiliation with her New York office. It was difficult sleeping last night. Her thoughts were on over-drive as she found herself worrying about Kasi. Allison didn't have a good feeling over the situation she witnessed and wished she had reached out sooner. Then again, what would have been her approach and how crazy would it seem? Shaking off the guilt, she decided to stop looking too deeply into things that didn't concern her.

"Namaste, I'm Allison Wagner. I have an appointment with Mr. Arun."

"Yes, we've been expecting you," said the woman sitting at her well-kept desk.

Thoughts of her own disheveled workspace popped into her mind as she wondered how anyone could be so organized.

"I'm Abha. Could I get you some tea?" she asked.

"No, thanks, I'm good."

"Did you have a smooth flight?"

"I did. I've not even experienced jet lag."

"You're lucky."

"Travel is never a problem on the way out, but the return trip always leaves me exhausted," Allison said to the young girl whose beautiful face was framed by dark hair pulled back in a tie. On her forehead was a decorated mark that married women in India wore.

"I see you have a bindi. Are you married?"

"Actually, no, but you are right. Traditionally, only married women had a bindi as a protection for themselves, but today you'll find single women also wearing it. We say the bindi is a way to remember to look inside ourselves to find knowledge and peace."

"I like that. I heard it's like a third eye."

"Very much so. Are you sure I can't get you something to drink—maybe you prefer coffee?"

"Nahi, dhan-ya-vaad, I'm fine for now."

Allison secretly complimented herself for remembering the Hindi phrase for thank you.

Abha got up and tapped on the office door to announce Allison's arrival to the editor of the newspaper. "Mr. Arun, Ms. Wagner from New York is here."

Mr. Arun came out to greet Allison with a slight bow of the head and hands placed together in the Mudra position. She learned one hand represented the spiritual self while the other symbolized the worldly self. By putting both hands together indicated a show of respect and connection with the person you greet. Allison bowed and returned the honor.

"Come in. Is it fine with you if I call you Allison?"

"Of course, thank you for inviting me. Did Wesley fill you in on why I'm here?"

"Yes, I'm certain you arrived at a good time since in a couple of days there will be a women's march to protest the violence forced upon them by men."

"That's what I'm hearing. I know about the rape crisis over here, but more recently I've heard some things about acid attacks. Could you fill me in on that?"

"Unfortunately, these attacks have been on the increase. I would say close to 1000 acid attacks happened in India last year with many of them unreported. This is in spite of stricter laws and punishments."

"Why is that?"

"This crime is usually the result from passion mostly from family members or friends. The attacks need to stop, but this can only be done by raising the awareness of acid violence."

"My plan was to investigate women's issues as a whole, and then I met this young girl on the plane who told me about her involvement with this internship through her university. It's called the Mukta program. Do you know anything about it?"

"Sure, it's a café in Agra run by women who are acid

victims. From what I've heard, the program originated to help survivors get through potential depression and keep them from going into hiding because they are ashamed of their appearance. Most of these girls are young; many not older than twenty-five."

"How does the café operate?"

Mr. Arun reached into his file cabinet and pulled out a folder. "Here, take a look at this. It's a brochure on Mukta. Pretty much goes into how the café restarts a young woman's life. It's more than serving coffee but giving her the opportunity to become more socialized and unafraid to continue on with either her education or the life she had before she was harmed."

"Wow, I had no idea about any of this. I can see how the program would give these women a purpose and a way of earning money as they slowly return to their former life. How long has this café been operating?"

"Only a few years but they've accomplished so much in that short span of time. The name Mukta actually means liberated in Hindi. I found that rather interesting. Keep the brochure. There's an address on the front in case you want to pursue this. It's in Agra which is a distance from here but may be worth a visit. In the meantime, check out that women's march."

"I plan on participating. Do you have any info on it?"

Mr. Arun picked up yesterday's newspaper and handed it over to Allison. "Here you go. Everything you need to know is pretty much written in this article. It's referred to as the 'I Will Go Out' campaign. All of this resulted from a recent situation where several women were groped and assaulted by a mob in the city's business district on December 31. Things escalated after a government minister told TV networks that such things happen and blamed the women for dressing inappropriately and staying out late."

"Whew! Wrong thing to say."

"Yeah, he sure found that out."

Allison said, "I remember hearing about one rape case in Delhi that made world news. You know, the young girl assaulted by six men aboard a bus?"

"Yes, that was the catalyst giving women the courage to stand up against this violence."

Chapter 5

LYNNE

LYNNE PULLED OUT her journal and wrote the word brown. Everything outside the car window was just that—brown. There were patches of green here and there, but for the most part, she saw the color of dirt. Lynne passed small shops covered with corrugated metal roofs with large rocks sitting on top to keep the roofs from falling off. The roofs offered little protection to these unstable shacks that housed vendors selling all sorts of goods. The sidewalk that separated these shops from the road was made of loose dirt. Women, dressed in colorful saris, struggled to contain the dust by bending over small-handled cornhusk brooms sweeping the piles into the ditches nearby.

Before arriving in India, Lynne wondered if she would see a cow. After all, they were revered over here. As it turned out, cows were fairly easy to spot since they were everywhere—reclining under trees, walking alongside the shops, and laying in the middle of the road. Most rural Indian families have at least one dairy cow and consider it as a member of the family. In the city, a cow is not necessarily owned by anyone. It can essentially roam wherever it pleases searching for any scrubby grass it can find. She noted how people often fed these cows by leaving scraps of food and water in large containers sporadically placed throughout the city. No one disturbed these animals as they roamed the streets along with pigs and feral dogs. India protected the cow and to eat beef would be punishable by Hindu law. Just that morning Lynne overheard that the Delhi government defended in high court the law criminalizing the consumption of beef. Opponents argued the Cattle Preservation Act violated their rights to eat the food of their choice. Lynne quietly questioned the country's priorities to protect the cow while so many women lay victim to rape and disfigurement from acid attacks. So powerful and confusing were religious beliefs.

Travel time along the Taj Express Highway from Delhi to Agra took about three to four hours. It wasn't a boring trip. Lynne later emailed back home that looking outside her bus window felt like the unraveling of a fast-paced movie. This especially held true when they pulled over at a STOP sign and right next to her window stared the eyes of a camel. Lynne grabbed her camera and took a photo of this working animal attached to a wobbly cart carrying a load of rocks. On the cart's crudely made bench sat a man appearing much older than his years, most likely due to hard labor and India's unrelenting sun.

As the bus approached the entrance to the city of Agra, Lynne observed a canvas tent-like home with a kitchen set up in an open patio. Next to it were several corrugated roofs held up by thin wooden beams that didn't appear to have any function other than to act as both a sunbaked oven and a make-shift shelf to store large pancakes of cow dung left to dry and later sold as fuel. The ingenuity of taking a waste product and transforming it into something useful intrigued Lynne. Unlike other animal wastes, the dried dung did not have an odor or attract flies. She smiled as she spotted two cows in the middle of a muddy courtyard that supposedly supplied the raw material for this family business.

The deserted street led to a more crowded one as the bus forged itself amongst people who dodged cars, bikes, and motorcycles as they attempted to cross the road. She saw men dressed in western clothing with either sun-faded scarves or white turbans wrapped around their heads. Lynne found it curious that so many men but few women were out in the streets. Some of these men appeared to be busy, but she wondered about the many who hung out in groups as they drank a suspicious liquid from hardened clay cups. Were they employed?

The bus traveled a little further until it stopped in front of a bus station.

The bus driver motioned to Lynne. "This is where you get off. Do you have someone picking you up?"

"Yes, where should I wait?"

"Just sit on that outdoor bench over there." He helped her get her luggage from the belly of the bus and then took off.

Lynne felt sick to her stomach. She wasn't sure if it was her breakfast or anxiety. She smiled at a woman dressed in a red sari with a beige sash, and the woman smiled back as she held the hand of a small boy. For the first time; well, maybe fifth, Lynne questioned why she decided to come here. Before she allowed her fears to paralyze her, a small white Honda approached and a woman jumped out of the vehicle.

"Are you Lynne?"

"Yes, I am. Chandra?"

The woman pressed her hands together and bowed her head. "I am. Welcome to Agra."

Lynne stood up, returned the gesture of respect, and said, "I am so relieved to see you."

Chandra laughed. "Yes, India can be a little daunting to Westerners who are here for the first time. I promise that by the time you leave, everything will seem absolutely normal to you."

Lynne liked Chandra. She appeared different from the other women living in India—more of a blend of western and eastern elements. Her black hair was pulled tightly into a small bun, accentuating her sparkly eyes half-hidden behind a pair of glasses. Chandra didn't wear a sari but instead sported a colorfully fitted dress with a knitted burgundy scarf neatly draped around her neck.

"You have a British accent," said Lynne, getting into the car.

"My parents moved to London when I was a young child, so I was pretty much schooled in England," Chandra answered, her car working its way down the road dodging a pack of feral dogs.

Lynne studied her mentor's profile and saw a gentle but determined face. This was a woman who got things done. "So what brought you back to Agra?"

"Well, I came here to visit and ended up marrying an extraordinary man. It was a love marriage. You know about that?"

"I do but I thought that was discouraged with parents deciding who their children marry."

"Yes, but things are starting to change as young people venture off to other places. So, I was lucky to have my parents support my decision, even though they were not excited to have me leave England."

"It seems like you've adjusted."

"Yes, it wasn't always easy to get used to the poverty that surrounds us, but I am happy to be with my husband and the work I am doing at the Mukta Café. I am excited to have you here, Lynne. Right now I will take you to your residence and let you settle in. You will be living with an intern from Israel. Naomi arrived two weeks ago. She's a very nice person, and I sense you both will get on quite well."

"Will she be counseling as well?" Lynne asked.

"No, Naomi's background is in accounting. I have her modernizing the financial end of the café while teaching a couple of the women how to keep track of the books using an updated software program."

They turned the corner and ended up on a lovely street with only two concrete houses. Lynne gave a sigh of relief to see there were no cows, feral dogs, pigs or garbage in the ditches. The house had two levels with the second level being an open patio.

"I think you will find it quite comfortable here," Chandra said. "My husband is a builder, and he built this place. We live in the house next door."

Lynne pulled her luggage up the three steps and into the front door. The inside was immaculate and modern compared to India's standards. Lynne noticed that the furniture was sparse—a couch, two chairs, a dining table in the adjacent room and a small kitchen in the back. The floors were marble, walls concrete, and absolutely not one picture or plaque on the walls.

Chandra showed Lynne her bedroom. "The room next to you belongs to Naomi. She should be back in another two hours. I'll let you settle in and rest up after your long flight. Naomi will take you to the café tomorrow morning around eight so you can meet the ladies before we open at 9:00. If you don't have any questions, I will see you in the morning."

"Thank you, Chandra. Everything looks great. I think I'll be very comfortable here."

"Good—welcome to India, and I will see you tomorrow."

Chapter 6

KASI

"WHAT DO YOU want? Why is my brother not here?"

"Kasi, aren't you happy to see me?"

"No, I have no interest in seeing you. Why are you here? How did you know I was returning?"

The man smiled. "Will you give me a welcome hug? It has been so long since I've seen you."

"I have no desire to have anything more to do with you."

"Kasi, how can you say that when we were to be married? Our parents decided. You agreed and plans were made."

"I did not willingly agree. I was forced."

"No, you agreed. Wedding arrangements were being made, but then you suddenly disappeared. Later I heard you ran off to New York with some American."

"Hari, that was over two years ago. I didn't just run off. I met a very nice man at work. I told my family I wanted to marry him, not you."

"Kasi, do you know how humiliated I was when you left?"

"I didn't just leave. I tried to explain many times, but you wouldn't listen to me. I am sorry if I embarrassed you, Hari, but it was the only thing left for me to do. No one would listen to me. I have a husband now and have made a life for myself in America."

"No, Kasi, I think you returned because you are not

happy in America and want to come back. I think you know you made a mistake leaving me. Forget your American husband. He's not a good person. I will forgive you, and we will be married according to our country's law."

"Hari, I came back to go to Lina's wedding and for no other reason."

"Why are you here alone? Where is this American husband?"

"He stayed back in New York to finish a work project that had to be done. This is the first time I've returned, and he thought it would be nice if I spent the time alone with my family, especially since it was for Lina's wedding."

"No, I think he refused to return because he was a coward."

"What do you mean, a coward? Keith is not a coward. What is this foolish talk about?"

Hari picked up Kasi's luggage and threw it in the trunk of his car. "Yes, coward to face your family because he tricked you into going with him to America."

"Keith did not trick me. I married him because he was the one I wanted to marry and not you. Why did you put my luggage in your car? I'm waiting for my brother to come." She looked over Hari's shoulder to see if she could spot him. "By the way, how did you know I was returning to India? How did you know I would be arriving at this time?"

"Your brother told me. He had an emergency at the hospital, and everyone was busy with wedding plans. He asked me to pick you up."

"Why would he ask you? My family has no more connection with you."

"You don't know? I see your father often. He is not happy with what you've done to shame the family."

Hari opened the door with the pretense of helping Kasi

into the car, but she resisted. Catching her off-guard, he placed his hand under her elbow and pushed her into the front seat. Before she could react, Hari slammed the door, hurriedly jumped into the driver's seat, and sped off into the night.

Kasi looked at Hari in disbelief. She slid over to the door as far as she could go. "I do not want to go anywhere with you. Please let me out!"

"Stop causing a disturbance! I told Lalit I would pick you up at the airport and drive you home. This is good. It will give us a chance to talk."

"There is no reason for us to talk. What is done, is done."

"You say your husband didn't come because he needed to be at work. I think he had other reasons."

"What do you mean?" Kasi asked, staring at Hari's face. His eyes were deep black like the eyes of a tiger before it makes its kill. They frightened her.

"Your brother told me your American husband did not want to see your family."

"When did my brother say that?" Kasi questioned.

Hari laughed. "Many times and especially this morning when he called to ask me for the favor of picking you up. Lalit said your family was happy your husband wasn't coming. He, especially, had no interest in meeting him."

Kasi said nothing. Confused, she thought Hari could not have been in close contact with anyone in her family, particularly Lalit. When her brother was in New York three months ago for a medical conference, he met up with her and Keith for dinner at their apartment. Later that evening, he told Kasi that her parents grieved over her absence and wanted to reconnect. After a long conversation, Lalit dialed their number in Delhi and handed Kasi the phone. It was a tearful exchange but one of forgiveness and acceptance over what had transpired. It was during that conversation that her father suggested sending a plane ticket to come visit and attend Lani's wedding. What Hari is saying didn't make sense, and she began to worry. Kasi decided it was best not to antagonize Hari any further, uncertain of his emotional stability.

A black Honda drove up to the Passenger Arrival terminal at the Delhi airport, pulled over to the side and waited. After fifteen minutes the man inside anxiously checked his phone, shook his head and said to the woman sitting next to him, "Her plane arrived about one hour ago. I wonder where she is. We should have left the house earlier."

"Lalit, no worries. It takes time going through customs and picking up the luggage. She should be coming out soon."

"Kasi has been gone over two years, Rani. I just wanted to be here when she arrived."

"I know and we would have been if it wasn't for the two flat tires."

"I don't know when I drove over so many nails, Rani. The tires were fine when I drove the car home earlier this evening."

Lalit looked at his watch. "I'm going inside. She might be waiting in the terminal."

He went into the arrival hall where many people stood behind a rope holding signs addressing the person they were there to pick up. Looking at the monitor, Lalit saw that the flight from JFK had arrived as scheduled. He looked around but didn't see Kasi. Reaching for his phone, he put in a call to his father.

"No, she has not called here. Where could she be, Lalit?"

"I don't know. Call me if Kasi makes contact with you, Baba (father). Right now, do not worry ma about this. Maybe Kasi is having luggage problems and is trying to straighten it out. I'll get back with you once I have more information. Right now, I plan to check security here at the airport and have her paged."

An hour later Lalit returned to the car hoping that Kasi was there, but she wasn't.

"You've been gone so long, Lalit. You didn't find her?" Rani asked.

Lalit shook his head. "I don't know what else to do, Rani. I had her paged, but she never responded. Security checked baggage claim and said her luggage was picked up. Where could she be? She emailed that she was boarding the plane at JFK and the airline verified she was on the flight."

Rani said, "Main samjha nahin." (I don't understand).

Lalit got into the car and headed out onto the road. "The best thing right now is to return home. Perhaps she hired a taxi when she discovered we were not here."

Chapter 7

LYNNE

MORNING CAME AS Lynne struggled to leave the comfortable bed after the fifteen-hour flight from New York. At first, she was unaware of where she was but quickly remembered she was now in India and that Chandra drove her to her new residence in Agra.

Lynne put on her robe and quietly stepped outside to see if her new roommate, Naomi, was around. She recalled that Chandra mentioned Naomi would take her to the café that morning.

"Hi there, you must be Lynne."

Startled, Lynne turned around and saw a young girl with honey-blonde hair standing by the kitchen doorway. "Oh, sorry, I didn't see you there. Yes, I'm Lynne Fenton and you must be Naomi."

Naomi reached out to shake Lynne's hand. "I am. I guess we're going to be housemates for a few months. So glad to meet you. Chandra said I'm in charge of getting you orientated to India. Please don't expect too much as I've only been here two weeks."

Lynne laughed. She had a good feeling about this person. "Well, any advice you can share would certainly be welcomed. What I viewed from the bus window was crazy. I mean, a camel pulling a cart at a stop light? Who sees that in New York?"

"I know what you're saying. You'll get used to it."

"I don't know if I ever will, but that's also what Chandra said."

Naomi held up a pot of coffee. "Would you like some? I just made a pot."

"Yes."

Naomi poured a cup and handed it over to her. Both girls sat down at the small wooden table. "So you're from New York, I hear?"

Lynne nodded her head. "Upstate New York. Most people think New York State is only New York City when most of the state is made up of small towns."

Naomi nodded. "I sort of know about that. I used to live in the states until I was thirteen and then my family moved to Jerusalem."

"So you're American?"

"Yes, I have dual citizenship. I was born in Boston and lived there until my parents decided to return to Israel where both sets of grandparents lived. They never left the homeland and were starting to require some assistance. My parents tried to convince them to move to America but they refused."

"So instead you guys moved there?"

Naomi laughed. Pretty much that was how it went. At first, I didn't like the idea of moving but I adjusted to it."

"How long have you been in Israel?"

"It's going to be ten years. Since then both sets of grandparents passed away. It turned out to be the right decision because I got to know them before they died. You know, a two-week visit every few years doesn't do it."

"That's nice you went back to help out. So your parents are still over there?"

"Yeah, after my grandfather passed away, they moved

in with my mom's mother to take care of her, and that's where they still are."

"So your grandmother is now deceased?"

"Yep."

"Do you think they will move back to America?"

"No, they seemed to be pretty well settled in Israel. I thought perhaps someday I would return to the states. You know, to visit old friends I've kept in touch with."

"Chandra told me you're also here as an intern. Something about working in the office."

"I am. So far it's been an outstanding experience. You will find these women to be quite remarkable. The hardships they endured from men are unbelievable. I heard you'll be helping them deal with their issues?"

"Yes, I'm a university senior and have an internship to fulfill. I heard about this opportunity and decided to apply. I'm here for twelve weeks and then have another internship in the states to complete the remainder of my semester."

"Well, I'm sure you'll enjoy working with these women. I've found the Mukta Café to be a place of healing. There's so much more than coffee or tea served there. So, yeah, as soon as you're ready, I'll take you over."

Lynne looked at the clock. "Oh wow, I better get dressed. I don't want to be late the first day. What a bad impression that would make."

"We have about an hour before we need to leave." Naomi grabbed the two finished cups and carried them to the kitchen. "We have the weekends off. Are you the exploring type?"

"I am. Do you have any suggestions?"

"You know the Taj Mahal is not far from here. I've

already been but would love to go again since it was quite crowded when I was there last week. Are you in?"

"The Taj Mahal? Absolutely. By the way, how do we get to the café from here?"

"There's a bus stop only a block away—very convenient."

Chapter 8

ALLISON

ALLISON'S DESK AT the Delhi newspaper was crammed in the corner of the room while back in New York she had a relatively large office with a window overlooking 48th Street. Having put plans in place for the Women's March the following day, she felt quite organized and on top of things. As she walked across the room towards the copier, a photo of a woman on the newspaper's front page caught her eye. She quickly picked it up to see why it was in the paper but couldn't read the Hindi print. "Oh, wow! It's the woman with the bangle bracelets," she whispered under her breath.

"Did you say something, Allison?" asked Abha, sitting at an adjacent desk.

Allison brought the paper over to the receptionist. "Abha, I met this woman. I sat next to her on the plane. Could you tell me what the article is about?"

Abha turned away from her computer to scan the article. "Looks like she's missing."

"Missing?" questioned Allison. "Please, keep going. What else?"

"Well, it says here that she was to fly to Delhi to visit family, but when her brother arrived to pick her up at the airport, she wasn't there."

"I know about this. Yes, Kasi's brother was supposed to

pick her up. She was here for a family wedding—I think it was her cousin who was getting married."

"How do you know that?"

"She told me. We had a nice conversation on the plane. What a sweet girl. I hope nothing has happened to her."

"Allison, do you remember when you saw her last?"

"Yes, as a matter of fact, I remember feeling uneasy about it. Not sure why, just my intuition."

"Why is that?"

"I saw her get into a car with some man in front of the terminal."

"Allison, you might be the last person to have seen her. According to the paper, the family had notified her husband and he's arriving in India tomorrow."

"I need to speak to the police about this."

"Do you think you could identify the man or the car?" Abha asked.

"If I saw him, I think I could. He was several feet from me and there was a crowd of people between us. It was night but the terminal was lit up."

"What about the car?"

"Yeah, I remember the car being a silver hatchback. I think maybe a Toyota."

Pointing to the article, "Does the article say anymore?"

"Just that the family has been trying to find her. At first, they thought she might have taken a taxi, but there hasn't been any contact. She just disappeared."

"No, it wasn't a taxi. It was a man who was much older. I remember thinking they looked like they were in the middle of a disagreement."

"You definitely should report what you saw to the police. Don't do it by phone, go to the station."

"Where is it, Abha?"

"Not far from her—over on Mathura Road. It's that big whitish building across from the Apollo Hospital. Do you want me to go with you? We can go during our lunch."

"Would you? That would be fantastic. I may need your help especially if I run into a communication problem."

Two hours later, Abha and Allison walked inside the police station and up to the glass window where a fairly large man sat. "We need to speak to a detective or someone involved with the girl missing from the airport," Abha said.

The man nodded, picked up the phone, and after a quick conversation, motioned for the two of them to sit in the chairs by the wall. They waited only a short time before a middle-aged man dressed in matching khaki pants and shirt came over to greet them.

"I hear you have information on the missing woman."

Abha pointed to Allison. "She does, sir."

Allison stood up. "Hello, I'm Allison Wagner and I arrived from New York a couple of days ago. I saw an article in the newspaper this morning with a photo of a woman who happened to sit next to me on the plane. I'm a journalist from America and believe I might have some useful information."

"The detective looked from Allison to Abha, back to Allison again. "I'm Detective Mahor, come with me," he said, leading the two women to his office.

They sat across the desk from him. "Do you care if I put a recorder on?"

"No, not at all." Allison then described to the detective

what she knew about the missing girl as well as the awkward exchange she witnessed in front of the airport.

"So, you think this is the same person?"

"I know it is. Kasi told me her brother was picking her
up, but as I waited for a ride, the man who pulled up looked
much older than what I had imagined her brother to be."

"How do you know her brother wasn't older?"

"Kasi told me he went to medical school in America and
then returned to Delhi to practice five years ago. I figured
that would place him in his mid-thirties. This man was well
into his forties."

"I see. Do you have any other information?"

"I can't verify this 100% but from where I stood, I would
say a heated argument took place. I remember thinking how
strange that Kasi had been away from India for two years
and this is how she's greeted."

"I have your statement on the recorder but will need to
know how to get in touch with you if there is a need."

"Here's my card with all the information on it. I'm in
India for several weeks before I return to the states."

"I hope to be in touch with you before then. Thank you
for coming down to the station. Namaste."

Chapter 9

LYNNE

THE BUS STOPPED directly across from the Mukta Café. Lynne approached the café with some hesitation. For the first time, she questioned how she would react upon seeing these women severely scarred from acid. The café was very approachable with its bright blue banner stretched across the façade welcoming people in for a drink and a bite to eat. Cylindrical lanterns, hanging from the ceiling of the café's porch, were decorated with floral designs and strands of alternating tiny brass bells and beads extending from the lantern's base. Everything about the exterior of the café was joyful and alive. It was incredible that this place was operated by women with severe physical and emotional issues often thrust upon them by people they trusted. Lynne thought back to the irritating mornings when her hair didn't lay quite right, or perhaps a blemish popped out of nowhere. How superficial compared to what these women face each time they look in a mirror.

Naomi opened the door and greeted the women as they prepared for the opening of the shop. "Shubha Prabhat, ladies."

One woman near the door turned around and smiled. "Good morning to you, too, Naomi. Is this the girl from America?" she asked with a nod towards Lynne.

"Yes, it is, Parvati. Everyone, come around and meet Lynne."

"Hello, Lynne, I'm Parvati. Naomi likes to show off her newly learned Hindi. Most of us can speak English." Parvati extended her hand and smiled. Lynne noted that, like Maruti, she didn't seem to let any disfigurement hold her back. "I'm in charge of the front desk," she proudly noted.

Lynne smiled as she looked over at Naomi. "So glad you told me about the English, Parvati. Knowing no Hindu, I was getting a little worried."

Another young woman came forward with her hands together. "Namaste. Please, welcome to our café."

Lynne struggled as she tried to cover up the shock upon seeing this particular woman's face. She was in much worse condition than Parvati or Maruti. Scars from the acid spread all across her face affecting her partially closed left eye. Her skin had melted away.

"Thank you. I'm delighted to be here. What is your name?"

"Kiri, my name is Kiri. I have been here for two years. Naomi is helping me with managing the cash."

Naomi put her arm around Kiri and said, "She's a very fast learner. I'm afraid I will be out of a job if she learns any quicker."

Later, Chandra told Lynne that Kiri had undergone many skin transplants and that she is in much better shape than a year ago. "We had a hard time convincing her to leave her house. She had shades drawn and literally wouldn't come out. She didn't want anyone to see her."

"How did you get her to work at the café?" Lynne asked.

"Several of the women working here frequently visited her. After many days of conversation over tea, they reassured Kiri that working at the café was the best thing to do."

"That's amazing. Nothing helps more than talking to

someone who has been through the same thing as you. I hope I can be of help to these ladies."

Chandra smiled. "No worries, you and Naomi are like breaths of fresh air to them."

"Why is that?" Lynne asked.

"Well, it's important for them to feel valued as human beings not just from the women in this community, but also from other women having no disfigurements. The more they see that people such as yourself don't appear bothered by their scars, the more secure and confident they will become."

Lynne reflected on Chandra's words and thought back to Maruti, the woman who spoke to her university class. She accepted her scars and didn't let them keep her from intermingling with others and living her life.

As Lynne made her way around the room introducing herself to the women, she noticed a young girl sitting alone on a wooden bench in the corner of the room. She walked over and sat next to her. "Hello, do you speak English?"

The girl nodded her head. "My name is Jaya."

"How old are you, Jaya?"

"Seventeen," she said, pulling her scarf across her face.

"When did this happen to you?"

"Three months ago."

"Do you mind me asking who did this to you?"

Jaya shook her head. "No, it was my father. He was angry with me because I went to a party with my boyfriend. He didn't approve but I went anyway. When I returned home, he went into a rage and threw acid in my face, saying that no boy will like me now."

Jaya started to cry. Lynne pulled her up from the bench and led her to a small room.

"Let's go in here."

"Where is your father now, Jaya?"

"My mother had him arrested. He's in jail."

"Do you still live with your family?"

"I do, but sometimes I am afraid that my father will leave the jail and come back to find me. I know he is furious at my mother and me for having him arrested. I worry he will harm my mother as well."

"I certainly understand why you would feel that way. Was he always abusive?"

"Sometimes he was nice but when he was drinking, he would get angry. This last attack is the first time he used acid to punish me. Other times it was a beating with a hard stick."

"Do you have other siblings?"

"Siblings? What is that?"

Lynne smiled and said, "Let me ask it another way. Do you have brothers or sisters?"

"I do. I have two sisters. My father was angry about that as well. He wanted sons to help with work. He blamed my mother for only having daughters. He said we were useless, and it would cost him much to marry us off."

Lynne tried not to show any emotion. She couldn't imagine any father saying this to his children. She realized how fortunate she was to have a father who valued her.

"Jaya, would you care if I visited you at your home? It would be nice to get to know you better outside the café."

Jaya reached for Lynne's hand. "Yes, I would like that very much. You are a kind person."

"Thank you. Do you think it would be okay with your mother if I visited?"

"I will tell her about you. I know she will be happy to meet you."

"So, okay, it's a deal. Today is Wednesday. I have some

things to do to get settled but possibly check to see if Friday is good. If not, we can arrange another day."

Lynne squeezed Jaya's hand and the seventeen-year-old girl returned the gesture. They went back out into the café just as people started arriving for breakfast. Lynne noticed how the inside of the café mirrored the same energy as the outside. The bright blue walls had abstract shapes painted in watercolors positioned close to the ceiling around the perimeter of the room. Wooden tables and chairs occupied the space of the entire room. In the corner was a large bulletin board with photos of women who made up the staff. Announcements of upcoming events were posted alongside a newspaper article about the Mukta Café. In front of this board sat Kiri who checked in people as they arrived. Several other women, wearing white tee-shirts with the café's logo on it, waited on tables.

Lynne walked over to Chandra and said, "I hope I wasn't out of line."

Chandra looked at her. "Why do you say that?"

I just finished a conversation with Jaya. She's hurting and so I asked if I could come to her house to visit next week. I hope that's okay."

Chandra seemed surprised. "What was Jaya's reaction?"

"She appeared to be excited over that possibility. I felt she needed a friend. Was that okay?"

Chandra put the coffee pot down on the counter. "Yes, it's more than okay. We have been trying to get Jaya to open up about her situation. Her mother drops her off every morning, but she refuses to participate in the operation of the café. She sits in the corner and stares at the floor. For her to be excited about anything is a good sign. I have a positive feeling about you being here, Lynne. You will be good for Jaya as well as the other girls. Just do what you feel in your heart."

Chandra winked, picked up the pot, and worked her way around the room pouring coffee into the cups of her patrons.

Chapter 10

ALLISON

COUNTRIES THAT ARE several centuries old are often conflicted with keeping up with current trends while, at the same time, trying to maintain their distinct cultures. Allison noticed that Delhi was no different as she left her hotel in the newer part of the city where street performers provided entertainment amongst the monkeys that took up residency scampering along rooftops, across electrical wiring, and swinging their way back into trees. No one seemed to pay attention to any of these monkeys and their shenanigans. They were India's version of the American squirrel.

Young women in western clothing mingled on the streets amongst those practicing purdah—a more traditional style of clothes whereby a dupatta, or veil, is worn. Muslims initially introduced this more concealed dress, but it was later embraced by many Hindu women.

Allison had several hours before the start of the anticipated women's march. Upon Abha's suggestion, she decided to take a rickshaw ride through the Chandri Chowk (a covered bazaar). This area was a complete contrast to the more spacious and wide streets of New Delhi. Old Delhi was colorful but congested with green and yellow tut-tuts, motorbikes, large wheeled carts, and a variety of vehicles transporting any possible product. Pedestrians gave little regard to the road they shared. The drivers would figure out a method of dodging them as they blindly crossed the street.

The rickshaw, no longer physically pulled, was powered by a man peddling an attached bicycle. It was only a matter of time for an upgraded gas-powered version, similar to what she saw in Thailand, to hit the scene.

No one waited or slowed down—driver or pedestrian. Everyone rushed as they twisted in and out of lanes within an inch of possible death. Chaos pretty much described the scene. Horns continuously screamed at each other and vendors chased after Allison with merchandise in hand. It didn't matter if she rode in a tut-tut. They saw her as a Westerner and, thus, a potential customer.

"Cheap, you like? Do you want to buy? I give you a good price. Come inside; I show you." Ignoring them was the best way to handle the situation because the moment you showed a glimpse of interest, you were doomed.

After this unforgettable ride, Allison took a bus to Rajpath, a boulevard in New Delhi often used in ceremonies. Canals, park-like grass, and rows of trees were predominant, a stark contrast from the street scenes she viewed from the rickshaw.

Earlier that morning, Allison learned she missed the Republic Day parade by a few days. Republic Day was a national holiday having significant importance much like America's July 4th.

"You know, Allison, missing Republic Day is not necessarily a bad thing," Abha remarked, as Allison took off for the march. "It's quite hard getting around the city with all the people in town for the parade."

"Perhaps, but I would have enjoyed seeing it."

"Finding a place to view the parade is almost impossible. The best way to see it is on television."

"That's often true in the United States as well," Allison answered, leaving the office for the women's march.

Hundreds of women assembled in the park, many with signs demanding equal rights with men. Emotions revved up as a woman took to a podium with her bullhorn leading the protest with chants. Allison walked up to a group of women sitting on a blanket near the podium. She held up a microphone and said, "Namaste. I am a journalist with plans for publicizing your cause on mainstream news. Could you tell me what it is the women want?"

One girl stood up and said, "Yes, we are angry about the number of rapes and sexual assaults that occur in our city. Laws threaten death if a cow is hurt. But harm a woman? That does not have any importance."

"But isn't there a long-standing, religious belief protecting the cow?"

The girl nodded her head. "The Bharatiya Janata Party introduced the Cow Protection Bill which made harming a cow a crime punishable by death. We are not against that. We are protesting that there should be the same importance given to protecting women and their rights."

"So how do things currently stand?" Allison asked.

Anxious to give their opinions, two other girls got up to join their friend. "I am a university student. It is not safe to walk in the city after dark. Men have no problem being out after dark; but for us to be safe, we need to be inside before the sun sets. Is this right?"

The second girl nodded her head in agreement. "Yes, we demand safe places both night and day. They make laws but no one enforces them. A rapist and murderer get off easy, but if you eat beef? That can end in death. Is that morally right?"

Allison asked, "Has there been a surge in violence against women?"

The first girl repositioned herself to speak into the mike. "There are six rapes and twelve assaults against women reported every day in Delhi."

"Haan (yes), those are the ones reported. Many are not," said another woman.

Allison asked, "How can this be turned around?"

"Men can't treat women as objects," all three girls chanted.

The second girl added, "It's our culture that needs to change. As little girls, we were groomed to be only wives and have children so to preserve our Indian culture. Times are changing. We are becoming more educated. We want careers as well. Men need to accept this change and not be afraid of our assertiveness and equality in our society."

By now Allison was surrounded by women who recognized her as a journalist reporting on the Women's March. One such girl yelled into the recorder, "We march for our safety and the attention of laws made but not enforced."

"Haan (yes), instead what do we hear when we ask for safe space and equal rights? Our home minister says we try to copy western women in how we think and dress."

"Men say if we stay in our homes at night we won't be harmed. So you tell me why that is unfair and not a proper solution?"

Allison couldn't keep up with the women as they shouted into the microphone. Soon she found herself parading amongst them, arms pumped up and down, as they proceeded through the India Gate and onward toward Raj Ghat. She felt the passion through the chants that mirrored the signs they held.

"What do we want? Freedom! What do we want? Equal Rights!"

Traffic was at a standstill as the streets swelled with women—determined women who were not about to listen to a politician's rhetoric. The march ended at Raj Ghat, a beautiful park that housed a black marble platform where the cremation of Mahatma Gandhi took place after his assassination in 1948. Allison made note how symbolic that was. Gandhi, a wealthy lawyer from the Brahman caste, gave all that up to champion the injustices of the caste system and spoke out for the independence of India. What stood out was the way he went about it. Much like Martin Luther King, Gandhi promoted peaceful demonstrations without violence. He particularly grabbed the officials' attention by fasting from food, often within days of possible death.

Allison returned to her over-sized room at the hotel, spotless and beautifully decorated. From her window, she looked down upon the roofs of slum dwellings that were tucked away and not readily seen from the street. Allison grabbed her camera and returned to the window to photograph a woman gathering her dry wash from a clothesline strung up between two leaning poles. On another roof she noticed a woman, motionless on a mat, executing a yoga pose while the sun slowly dropped in the western sky.

The phone rang, startling Allison from her thoughts.

"Hi, Wes."

"Checking to see what you're up to, Allison."

Just returned from an emotionally motivated women's march."

"Is it late there?"

"Getting there—about ready to go to dinner. I was photographing some scenes from my hotel window. You know, there is so little land available, I find it quite functional how they use their flat rooftops for practical needs."

"How's that?" Wes asked.

"For instance, from where I am, I see clothes hung out to dry and another person is meditating on her roof. I even see gardens growing on some roofs. Much like what you see in New York."

"I had the same thought," Wes said. "Any smog or polluted smells?"

"I haven't noticed that so much during the day. Smog tends to be more pronounced in the early morning as well as in the evening. It doesn't seem to be problematic to people although from what I understand, it's much worse in the summer when the monsoons arrive. What is bad is the trash and litter on the streets and in the waterways. I wonder if these people are so accustomed to seeing this rubbish that they don't think much about it."

Wes said, "The struggle is getting people to think differently when, all their lives, this is all they knew."

"The TV news should soon be reporting about the march, Wes. How about if I give you a call back in a couple of days?"

Allison sat down in front of her laptop to summarize the day before any of the details escaped her. After the TV weather report, details of the Women's March came on. Allison stopped to watch. It never failed to amaze her how powerful a movement is when numbers gather. She hoped these women would continue the drive for their rights. How they've been treated was not right.

Chapter 11

LYNNE

THE HOUSE STOOD next to a vacant lot that held nothing but wild brush and a stack of hardened cow dung. At first sight, the house appeared to be under construction with a heap of bricks loosely thrown on top of the roof. Lynne thought perhaps the owner delayed completing the second floor as he waited for either time or money to become available. A wall of concrete made up the façade of the building as it faced a marsh partially filled with tall grasses and reeds. Lynne checked the directions given by Jaya as this couldn't be the place. It looked uninhabitable. She turned around ready to retrace her steps when the front door opened and Jaya ran out.

"Lynne, I'm here."

Lynne spun around to see the 17-year-old running towards her. Jaya wore what looked like a new red shirt with a black checkered scarf around her neck. In conversation, Chandra revealed that Jaya often used a scarf to cover her face whenever she felt uncomfortable.

"So there you are! I thought I had the wrong street. Can I come in?"

"Yes, of course. My mother wants to meet you. She made tea and jeera cookies for us to eat."

"Sounds awesome, Jaya, but what are jeera cookies?"

"You don't know? They are crunchy and taste very nice with tea. Come in, come in."

Lynne felt skeptical about eating or drinking anything but knew it would be rude if she refused. She stepped inside the drab exterior of the concrete house only to see walls of turquoise with a rare sighting of furniture. Everything was clean and tidy, and it puzzled her how anyone could keep the interior spotless while piles of rubble defaced the yard.

A woman, dressed in a pale blue sari, greeted her.

"You must be Jaya's mother. I'm Lynne."

"Namaste, welcome to our home. Jaya speaks kindly of you."

"Thank you."

"Come have a cup of tea."

Lynne sat down on the crude wooden bench. She looked around and could see a small kitchen and perhaps one bedroom. Everything was pretty functional with absolutely no decorative items. It did surprise her to see a TV in the corner of the room. "I see you have TV here."

Jaya smiled. It was a crooked smile since the acid ate away some of her muscle tissue. "Yes, it is new. My mother worked extra hard to save the money to buy it. She said it would cheer me up?"

"Has it?" Lynne asked.

"Sometimes it allows me to take my mind off my situation."

"That's always good, right? Have you returned to school?"

"No, I am nervous to do that."

"Jaya, are you afraid the kids will make fun of you?"

I don't know. Maybe, I am afraid of that and all the questions they will ask. I do have one friend who comes every day with my lessons. She is smart and shows me what to do. Then she takes my work to the teacher."

"I'm impressed that you do that, Jaya. You'll finish school in no time. Keep it up and soon you will graduate. Do you miss going to school?"

Jaya looked down at her hands. It was the same look she had when Lynne first saw her sitting alone in the corner of the café.

"What are you thinking about?" Lynne asked.

"I don't know."

"Yes, you do. Something is on your mind. Tell me."

"I sometimes wonder what I will do after I graduate. You know, who will hire me looking like this?"

"Don't think that way. To begin, you can work at the café and learn skills there. I can speak to Naomi and she will show you how to work the computer. If you feel uncomfortable in public, learning computer skills could be a consideration. Hey, something smells good. Is it cumin?"

"Yes, those are the tea biscuits mother prepared."

Jaya's mother brought in a tray of refreshments and set it on the table. She poured Lynne and Jaya a cup of tea. "So you both eat. I will be outside."

"You aren't joining us?" asked Lynne.

"No, no. You both visit. Go ahead and eat—talk."

After Jaya's mother left the room, Lynne asked, "Tell me how you are doing?"

Jaya slumped her shoulders. "Okay."

"I would like to make arrangements with a doctor to take a look and see if there is anything he can do to help you. Are you okay with that? Will you go?"

"I don't know. We have little money."

"I've spoken to someone in the government, and they will pay for most of it."

"They will? Why is that?"

"It has something to do with the law they passed. I'm surprised you never inquired about it."

"I've been depressed since the attack. There are times I don't feel like living anymore."

"Why?"

"I no longer feel like I have much of a future."

"But you do. From what Chandra told me, the café receives donations to help women in situations like yours. They will pick up the remainder of the bill. There's a rehab center that provides acid burn survivors with physical and occupational therapists who will work with you on building up the muscles around your neck and face. You know, make those muscles stronger so you can regain some of your facial expressions."

"I don't know. I'm embarrassed to have anyone see me."

"No, Jaya, you did nothing wrong. You are the victim, and that's why it's your father who is in prison and not you. Look at the bright side. You have a loving mother. Some of the girls don't have that. No matter how bad things look, remember some people have it worse."

"I know. One of the ladies at the café is completely blind, and she has a little girl to take care of."

"That's quite a responsibility. I don't believe I know who this person is. You'll have to introduce us."

"She's not always at the café, but I will the next time she's there."

Jaya took a cookie from the plate and slowly chewed it. She appeared to be rooted in thought, so Lynne decided to remain quiet and let her initiate the conversation.

"Lynne, where is this rehab center you talked about?"

"You have to go to a clinic here in Agra first, and then the doctor can write orders to send you to rehab. Once everything is set up, I will be happy to go with you. Are you okay with that?"

Jaya looked down at her folded hands that lay in her lap. After a moment of silence, she replied, "Yes, let's see what can happen."

Chapter 12

ALLISON

AFTER A LONG flight followed by a busy week of work, Allison looked forward to the weekend. She walked into the restaurant where she planned to meet up with Abha for lunch followed by a tour of Delhi.

Sitting at a table next to the door, Abha waved to her as she entered.

"Namaste, are you ready to see Delhi?"

"I sure am; that is, after a cup of coffee and some breakfast. Have you been here long?"

"No, I was afraid I would be late. I had some last minute adjustments to my dress. Did I mention that I'm getting married in a couple of weeks?"

"Abha, I had no idea that soon. And here I've asked you to show me around the city. You must have so much on your plate right now. We don't have to do the tour today."

"Everything is ready. I have little to do as we have a wedding planner taking care of all the details. Allison, I would love to have you come. Mr. Arun and his wife will be there. You can sit with them."

"I should still be in India and would love to come, but what about the guest list? Isn't it kind of late to include me?"

"No, everyone is invited. It will be at a hotel here in Delhi. Please come."

"Are you sure your family is okay with that?"

"I tell you, here in India we invite everyone we know."

"Is this a love or arranged marriage, Abha?"

Abha poured some tea into her cup, tasted it and replied, "Arranged, of course."

"Please don't take this wrong, but my curiosity about such things is getting to me right about now. How is it you don't mind marrying someone your parents choose?"

"Marriage is for spiritual growth. We believe that it is a way to learn about life through experience. It's the Hindu belief that marriages are arranged in heaven because it's not the meeting of two physical bodies, but the joining of two souls. Our parents decide who that person should be. They serve as the medium."

"Abha, have you met this man?"

"Yes, of course. After both of our parents agreed, they consulted our horoscopes to see if they matched. If they didn't, then there would be no marriage."

Interested, Allison asked, "Really, what determines that?"

"They considered the position of the stars at the time of our birth. Once that was approved, Jay and his family came to see me. Before that, we've seen only a picture of each other."

"Was that awkward?" asked Allison.

"For me, I was pretty nervous about it."

"So when you met, what did you do? I mean, did you have dinner or just sit and talk?"

Abha said, "The custom is for me to bring in a tray of sweets, tea, and coffee. That was when we got to see each other for the first time. We went into a room to talk and decide if we wanted to go ahead with the marriage. I was allowed to refuse, but decided my parents knew who was best suited for me. Then an auspicious day was set for the wedding."

"Really. How is that decided?"

"A priest consults an almanac and then gives the appointed date. I would like you to come and celebrate with us."

"I would be honored to come, Abha. Thank you for the invitation. Is there anything I should know before going? I know there are several ceremonies."

"Yes, the wedding takes place over several days with the first observance being the ring ceremony. This took place when I went to Jay's house with my family. Prayers were said and a contract was signed. Then rings were exchanged and we were considered betrothed. We need to observe several other ceremonies before the marriage is considered legal."

"That sounds a lot like what we call an engagement party."

"Next week is the Milani where all the women in my family will go to Jay's house and exchange gifts with his family. Then the Ghodi ceremony will take place at the Delhi Hotel." Abha reached into her purse and handed an envelope to Allison. "All the information for the actual wedding ceremony is on this invitation."

Allison opened the envelope and read the card. "This is exciting, Abha, and so unexpected. I'm pleased to be included. I do have a question for you. All of this makes me think of Kasi. You know, the missing girl who I sat next to on the plane coming over? She was betrothed but never went through with the marriage. Instead, she eloped and married someone she loved. He was an American. She's now living in New York with him."

"Whew, after the exchange of rings, the betrothal contract is considered irrevocable. There's a powerful feeling against breaking it. That must have been a bad scene."

"Kasi mentioned that no one was happy about what she did. It took a while for her father to accept her American husband but eventually, he did. I've been so busy that I have no idea if anyone located her."

Abha shrugged her shoulders. "The news from this morning says they're still looking for her."

"That doesn't sound good. I know Kasi was here to attend a wedding. I wonder how all of that will work out for the family."

Abha picked up the check and motioned to the waitress. "Not a good scene for sure. Okay, let's go see Delhi."

Chapter 13

LYNNE

SHE DIDN'T NOTICE it right away as she went through the Seedi Gate entrance; then only a glimpse, a peek, an alluring hint of what was to come. She walked through the Main Gate and there it was—all dressed in white and set along the Yamuna River. Such a familiar landmark that she thought she had been here before—the ornamental pool, the bench, the double rows of cypress trees, the elevated lotus pool that mirrored all of its grandeur complete with the octagonal center chamber topped by an onion-shaped dome. If ever a building could take on a feminine air it would be this one, the Taj Mahal.

From a distance it resembled a substantial marble palace; but as she approached, it became apparent that it was more than that. The façade had intricate carvings that resembled lace. Along the border were colorful mosaics showing green stems that gracefully bent while emphasizing the weight of its enameled red petals. Lynne stopped to take several photos.

"This is beautiful, Naomi. I can't believe I'm standing here looking at this."

"Yeah, it's the real deal. What surprised me was to learn that the interior is just one open area. With it being so large, wouldn't you think there would be rooms inside?"

"Yeah, it looks like a palace, but it's a mausoleum," said Lynne. "So who is buried here?"

Naomi opened her book on India and read, "Says here that the Taj was built by Emperor Shah Jahan to place his wife's body after she died."

Lynne said, "Never knew that about this place."

Both girls walked the extended set of stairs behind the white marble wall into the mausoleum. Inside a latticed gate, they saw the tombs of both the Empress and the Emperor. Above their remains, a lighted lamp hung from the three-storied ceiling.

Naomi said, "The actual graves are underneath these two tombs. I guess back in the 1600's, it was customary to build two identical tombs. One would be over the actual one so that no one could walk over them."

"Hmm . . . that's interesting. Look, there's a back door that leads to a courtyard overlooking the river." They walked out onto the marble enclosure where they saw the Yamuna River. It wasn't a wide river, but it wound along a bend until its end was no longer within sight. On the other side of the river stood an unfinished black building.

"What does your book say about that?"

Naomi skimmed through the pages until she found a matching illustration. "Okay, it's called the Black Taj Mahal. It says the Shah wanted to build a black marble mausoleum for himself with a bridge connecting the two, but the real story is that these were white stones that turned black."

"Why did he never finish it?" asked Lynne.

"There seems to be some question about that. Some say it's a myth while others believe the Shah got into a war with his son, Aurangzeb, who stopped it from being completed because he felt his father was spending too much money. According to this theory, Aurangzeb imprisoned his father in the corner room of their palace for seven years."

As they left the grounds of the Taj Mahal, Lynne stopped to take one last look. "I don't think I've ever seen anything so beautiful."

On the grounds just outside of the Taj were several women, dressed in saris, squatting on the grass digging out weeds.

"At first I wondered why they are using primitive hand tools to do the weeding as it takes twice the time using twice the people," Naomi said. "Then I thought perhaps it wasn't a bad thing because it's giving these women a job. Do you want to stop and get a bite to eat? I know of a great restaurant near the Western Gate that serves traditional Indian food. Are you hungry?"

"I'm always hungry," laughed Lynne.

They walked around the entrance to the Taj until they came to a small restaurant with long tables and red plastic chairs. "Nothing fancy here," said Naomi, "but the food is good." They sat down and looked at the menu.

"What do you recommend?" asked Lynne.

"I like the rogan josh. It's a lamb dish. Do you like curry?"

"Yes, which is probably a good thing since I'm in India for quite some time."

After they ordered, Lynne told Naomi about her visit to Jaya's house. "I feel it went pretty well. Her mom is very supportive, but I worry over what will happen to them once her father is out of prison. He seems like an angry person who wouldn't hesitate to retaliate."

"Do you think Jaya will come around? Right now she refuses to interact with any of the women at the café. She sits in her corner and stares at the floor."

"You know, I didn't see any of that when I was there. Jaya was very open and ready to talk once she felt comfortable around me. I mentioned I was going to find a doctor to take a further look into her condition to see if she could benefit from any more procedures."

"Well, you'll have your work cut out for you. I've heard she's already had several operations," Naomi said, digging into the meal placed in front of her.

"I need to find a good plastic surgeon."

Naomi shook her head. "You might want to try the hospital near the Delhi Gate. I heard they do cosmetic surgery. Parvati had plastic surgery there."

"Maybe I'll run over after we get through with lunch."

"Hey, you might want to slow down a little."

Lynne looked puzzled. "What do you mean?"

"This is your day off. Be sure to take it or you'll burn out."

"Okay, I'll wait until tomorrow."

Chapter 14

KASI

BRUISED AND BEATEN, Kasi laid on the bed and stared at the window as the sun's early morning rays seeped through the closed window shade. Her eyes, now wide open, focused on the environment around her. The room, with its faded yellow walls, housed only the bed and a nearby chair. She tried to move, but the chains that attached her right arm and left leg to the bedposts left her immobile. She no longer tried to wiggle out of their confines due to sores that abscessed and blistered. Instead, she surrendered to her existing destiny.

She had no idea how long she had been in this situation. After Hari forced her into his car at the airport, he never drove to her parents' home as he said he would. Instead, he brought her to this unoccupied house. His planning was evident with adequate food and other provisions readily available. Where was she? Why is this happening to her? The last few days were brutal, but she bravely absorbed any of the abuses he readily handed out to her. She felt his anger—a fury that collectively worsened each day. He showed no love, no compassion, and no willingness to let her go. She feared the present but was petrified of the future.

Kasi worried over her mother. Lalit mentioned her mother's fraility, and the pain caused by her absence. This trip was to be joyous and one she looked forward to. Why was her brother not there to pick her up? How did Hari know she would be in front of the airport waiting for a ride? So many questions bubbled up in her mind. Whenever she asked, the response was always the same. "Your brother told me."

Hari was a tall man—taller than most men in this part of India. She saw his hugeness back when they were engaged; after she left, he grew heavier. His arrogance revealed itself as he positioned his immense body on top of hers. She shrieked but he didn't care. He stuffed a rag in her mouth and continued. Several times each day; many times during the night. There was no rest. Time had been lost; he needed to make up for it and he did.

But today was different. This morning after he brought in food for her to eat, he unlocked the chain on her right wrist. He told her that was her reward for being a good wife. There would be more rewards if she continued to cooperate. She obeyed. She no longer struggled. She closed her eyes, her mind, her soul, and did what he said.

She could hear his footsteps in the outer room. They were heavy but few. She thought his stride had to be long since it seemed to take little time for him to walk from one end of the room to the other. He could quickly over-power her. She laid there, breakfast untouched, and quietly cried to herself—never loudly because that would anger him.

A clock had to be nearby since she heard the ticks. She occupied her mind by counting the tick-tocks—60 would make a minute; 3600 would be an hour. The activity was pointless but it kept her from losing control. She knew she needed to keep it together. Protesting would not work. Cooperation was the answer. Even though it sickened her, she knew she had to cooperate.

He returned and looked at the untouched breakfast. "You haven't eaten anything?"

Kasi shook her head. "I'm not hungry."

"You didn't eat anything yesterday or the day before that."

Kasi grew silent and stared through him.

He grew angry and slapped the side of her face leaving a red handprint. "You must eat or you will die. Do you want to die?"

She wanted to say she did but feared that would warrant another fist to the head. Instead, she shook her head and replied, "No."

"Then eat," he yelled, stuffing the cold rice down her throat. She put her freed hand to her mouth and promised she would, and she did. He left the room satisfied.

She heard the sound of a door shutting. Nothing but stillness—no heavy footsteps, no sounds of dishes rattling, quiet. Did he leave? He must have. He left her with only one leg chained to the post. She struggled to remove it, but couldn't. She left the bed attempting to reach the window but it was too far away.

The front door opened—she heard the squeaks of the hinges. Quickly she jumped back on the bed and pretended to be asleep. He didn't come in as he had before. Instead, the silence was interrupted by the ripped sounds of a box opening. Curious, she couldn't make out what the sounds were until she heard voices. Not voices from people in the next room, but TV voices.

A Bollywood style show had ended and then the news came on. A report of a Women's March with what sounded like chanting in the background was then followed by an update of a missing woman. Kasi froze. She heard her brother's voice as he was interviewed.

"I arrived at the airport to pick up my sister but she never showed up. We have no idea where she is or what has happened to her. There was a report that she may have been kidnapped."

"How do you know this?" the reporter asked.

"A woman who sat next to my sister on the plane said she saw her get into a car driven by a heavy-set man."

Kasi quietly mumbled under her breath. "Oh, that was Allison. I remember looking back and seeing her coming towards us as we drove off. She did see me."

The reporter continued. "Did she give any indication of the kind of car your sister drove off in?"

"Yes, she said it was a silver hatchback. Kasi, if you are listening, let us know where you are."

"I would if I could, Lalit," Kasi sobbed in her pillow.

The reporter asked, "Did your sister travel alone?"

"Yes, her husband stayed back in New York. We expect him to be here soon."

"He's not here?" asked the reporter.

"No, he had some work matters to tie up. We expect him to arrive tomorrow evening."

A comforting feeling came over her once she realized her family was aware of her disappearance. Not fully understanding why Keith wasn't there, she was reassured to hear he was on his way. Recently, work had been a struggle for him in New York resulting in long work days. He told her stories of how his manager held him accountable for so many responsibilities and that living in New York City was expensive. She looked for employment but was unable to find any. The job she had with the export company in India was not available in New York. Much of Keith's salary was based on commission, and he felt the pressure of having to make his quota. With him always preoccupied, she never brought up the subject. She admired his work ethic and wanted to be a supportive wife. Certainly, he'll be here as soon as possible.

Chapter 15

ALLISON

"DELHI IS ONE of India's three largest cities including Mumbai and Bangalore. It's also the capital city of our country," said Abha, as she maneuvered her car around the crowded streets. "Oh boy, I had a feeling we should have started earlier. Parking is tough around this part of the city."

"So are we in Old Delhi or New Delhi?" asked Allison.

"Are you ready to be confused?" Abha laughed. "There are eight Delhi's. Where we are heading is the Red Fort which was constructed by the Mughal emperor, Shah Jahan in the 17th Century and is part of the 7th Delhi."

"When was the 8th established?"

"In 1911 by the British."

"Ah, so that's when the British got onto the scene?"

"Well, I won't bore you with all of the ugly details. Just keep thinking of this city as Delhi and Old Delhi; but to answer your question, we are in Old Delhi. Here's a spot to park. Let's grab it—this is our lucky day."

The girls parked the car and started the three block walk to the Red Fort. "What is the Red Fort all about, Abha?"

"Soon you'll see why it's called the Red Fort—it's constructed of red sandstone. We refer to it as Lal Qila. For over 200 years it was the main residence of the Mughal Dynasty. Now it pretty much houses several museums."

It was not an easy task getting through the streets of

Old Delhi. So much confusion resulted from the narrow streets packed with tuk-tuks, motorbikes, cars, people, and cows. Allison looked up and saw knotted telephone and electrical cords twisted into messed-up balls of black lines that sagged from the corner of one building to the roof of another.

"I find it intriguing how the city hung your electrical wiring with what appears to be little planning, Abha. What happens when there is an outage? How can they ever find and repair the problem?"

"It's a mystery to me, as well. Okay, now we go inside this arcade called the Chatta Chowk. The arcade leads into the Naubat Khana where musicians once played for the Emperor. You have to go through a major fiasco to get inside, so prepare yourself for the besiege of good deals, Allison."

"Thanks for the warning. I already experienced a little of that when I was on my rickshaw ride through the Chandni Chowk."

"Here's an interesting tidbit about the Chandni Chowk. Back when we were under British rule, I think it was around 1912, a bomb was thrown at Viceroy Lord Hardinge as he rode his elephant through the bazaar."

"After having experienced the insanity of the Chandni Chowk, I wouldn't be surprised by anything. That place was wild."

"Seeing you already had your first experience in a bazaar, hold your breath and get ready for another."

The narrow lanes of the bazaar were chucked full of stuff including kiosks displaying crafts, elephant statues, jewelry, dolls, silks—things you might think you needed, but mostly merchandise and souvenirs that were of little use. It was tempting to stop and take it all in. The sheer abundance of it all so neatly stacked, folded or hung— a real feast for the eyes.

"I know what you are thinking, Allison, but don't be tempted to look because that would be the end of seeing Delhi for the day. These vendors possess hard-sell skills and will pounce like a tiger upon their victim, not giving up until they set their teeth deep in your wallet."

"I love the way you describe this, Abha. I'll certainly take your advice, but it's hard not to take a glance."

"You glance and you'll be sucked in!"

"I do feel a little vulnerable walking through. Somehow being wheeled in a rickshaw gave me a false sense of security."

Eventually, the madness of the bazaar was behind them as they reached the courtyard behind the Naubat Khana. Once inside, there was this relieved notion that things had returned to order and peace.

Abha pointed to the sandstone wall and said, "These walls you see here were built to keep out invaders."

Allison snickered and added, "And now they keep out the noise and confusion of the street."

"Perfect description."

Part of the morning was spent walking from one hall to another with the formal Charbagh gardens, complete with its fountains and pavilions, connecting all of these buildings. Birds were everywhere. Some flying overhead, but most perched upon roofs as they patiently readied themselves for combat over a discarded crumb.

"Are you okay with leaving this place and driving by some of the more famous monuments scattered throughout the city?

"Sure, let's do it."

The girls returned to the car and waited for a painted elephant to pass by so they could ease back into traffic.

"Abha, I don't think I will ever grow used to sharing the road with elephants and camels. This whole scene is so foreign to me."

Abha laughed. "What? No camels in New York City?"

"I've seen lots of crazy things in New York but never a camel."

"Okay, right now we're passing the Jama Masjid—very impressive, don't you agree? It's the largest mosque in India and can house up to 20,000 people at one time. I think it's a good plan to drive around and see some of the important monuments of the city. Then if there is anything you want to spend more time at, you'll know where to find it."

"Great idea."

"Look to your left. Soon you will see a tower that I feel is striking. Let me pull over to the side of the road."

"Wow! What is that?"

"It's called the Qutub Minar. It's made up of sandstone and marble and claims to be the highest stone tower in India. Notice how it has five sections or floors."

"Looks like there's a balcony around each of the sections. Can you go inside?"

"No, unfortunately, not anymore. I wasn't born yet, but my mother told me that in 1981 there was a freak accident inside where forty-five people died due to a stampede."

"That's horrible!"

"Yes, how frightening to be trapped inside with no place to escape. There's also damage to the structure caused by earthquakes and lightning. The tower is continuously monitored and in constant repair."

Allison bent her head down so she could see the whole monument. "Is it an optical illusion or is the tower tilted to one side?"

"No, you see a tilt. Does it remind you of the tower in Pisa?"

"Yeah. What do you know about this tower, Abha?"

"Only a little, I'm afraid. I know slaves were involved with its construction which started at the end of the 12th Century. Slaves built lots of World Heritage sites."

"It's beautiful. I love how Delhi sets it off from the traffic by using grass and shrubbery along with stretching tall palms around the perimeter. Very impressive."

Abha looked at her watch. "Okay, your hotel is not far from here. I'm going to drop you off since I do have a few errands to run before the end of the afternoon. How's that for you?"

"Perfect, Abha. Thanks so much for spending your free day showing me around your city, especially since your wedding is not far off."

"I enjoyed your company, Allison. As I mentioned earlier, everything for the wedding has been taken care of, and this diversion allowed me to take my mind off it."

"I know. I pushed Kasi to the back of my mind for at least a few hours. I don't understand why no one has heard from her. I spent only 15 hours on a flight sitting next to the girl. During that time she shared so much about her life and culture, I left feeling like I knew her. I'm pretty worried about her being missing. I mean, that can't be a good thing."

"I would think not. Well, get rested and I'll see you at the office in the morning."

"No, I'm meeting with Kasi's brother at the police station in the morning. He wants to talk to me. I told the detective

I'd be glad to meet up with him, although I don't know what else I can tell him."

"Hope things work out well for this girl, Allison. Namaste."

Chapter 16

LYNNE

THE VISIT TO the Taj Mahal was the highlight of the weekend. Lynne emailed her family about the world famous mausoleum but had difficulty articulating its incredible beauty. She later learned how lucky she was that it was a gorgeous, blue-sky day with absolutely no smog ensuing in disappointment. Not too many months before, the Taj was undergoing maintenance which meant scaffolding hid much of its beauty. Lynne could not have asked for better luck; her photos were proof. She particularly loved the picture Naomi captured of her standing in the foreground with her arm raised making her fingers appear as though they were touching the tip of the Taj.

The white brilliance of the monument, improved by months of sandblasting, might have captivated Lynne, but what intrigued her was its attached trivia.

"Listen to this, Naomi," Lynne said reading from her guidebook. "The Taj was built by 20,000 workers over a period of 22 years for the interment of Emperor Shah Jahan's wife, Mumtaz Mahal. So that this building would not be replicated, all of the workers' thumbs were cut off."

"Really? That's crazy. I've always found that the story behind the story is what's really interesting."

The girls spent part of Sunday shopping for groceries and getting things organized for the busy week ahead. Lynne promised Jaya she would look into the possibility of plastic surgery to help diminish the physical effects of the acid attack. She planned to speak to some of the girls at the café about their surgical procedures.

"Naomi, you know the girls better than me. Do you think you could ask Parvati and Kiri if they would share the procedures they had to go through to get to where they are now?"

"Sure, the ladies are very open. The beauty of the café is that it has given the girls the confidence needed to talk about their assault. Let me open the conversation, and then I'll let you take over."

"Thanks, that would be great. I want to help Jaya. She has so much potential but shies away due to her lack of confidence. I can't say I would be any different."

Both girls stepped off the bus that left them only a few steps from the café. Most everyone had already arrived and were busy getting the restaurant ready for their first set of customers. Naomi went over to the small office space set up at the side of the room to talk to Kiri and Parvati. After a few minutes of conversation, she waved Lynne over. "They agreed to answer any questions you may have to help Jaya."

Lynne motioned for them to sit on the couch at the far end of the room. "Thanks, girls. Can you tell me what happened to you and why?"

"Sure, I'll be glad to go first," said Kiri. "I had an abusive husband and decided not to take it anymore. I took my son and we went back to live with my family. I had just gotten hired as a make-up artist at a studio. I remember feeling on top of the world, thinking about how much better my life was since I had made that move. On my way to work, I sensed someone following me. I turned around and it was my husband, Deepak. He wanted me to return but I refused.

I told him that our marriage was over and I wanted him to leave me alone."

"How did he accept that?"

"Not well. I could see the veins in Deepak's neck become more . . . how you say, big?"

Lynne nodded her head. "I'm sure that was the result of his frustration that he no longer had control over you."

"He wanted to see Kumar, our son, but I didn't want him anywhere near him. I feared what he would do to Kumar to spite me. Before I knew it, he pulled out this small jar. As he started to open it, I turned to run away."

"Did you know what it was?"

"I had a strong suspicion. Deepak soon caught up to me and threw it in my face. I could barely breathe. All I could see was black and my skin felt like it was on fire."

Lynne put her arm around Kiri. "You don't need to continue if this is too painful."

"No, I can. It is good to talk about it. Otherwise, I push it further down into my mind where it can hurt me even more. You know how water sits on your skin?"

"Yeah."

"Well, acid doesn't sit. It quickly seeps into your skin. My face was disfigured burning off my eyebrows and melting my nose which quickly closed up my nostrils. I was lucky that it didn't completely destroy my eyesight. Can you imagine saying that after an acid attack? You know . . . that I was lucky?"

"What happened to Deepak?"

"He's in prison now but could be free in five years. I worry about that."

"Naomi told me you've had many surgical operations?"

"Yes, this doctor transplanted hair from the back of

my skull to my face to take the place of my disintegrated eyebrows."

"That can be done? Does the hair grow?"

"It does. It takes around six months, but it will grow back as normal since it was transplanted. See?" Kiri turned her face so that Lynne could see the results.

"That is amazing, Kiri."

"Yes, I've been through a lot. As for my nose, it was scarred and swollen to twice its original size. It has taken over twenty procedures to repair it. Still, it doesn't look right, but I am satisfied because my nose was in much worse shape. You see, it wasn't just a cosmetic thing. The doctor needed to restore the nose's function."

"How has the café helped you?"

"The café has been everything to me. I had to give up my job. I mean, who was going to be comfortable having someone with a heavily scarred face and a melted nose put make-up on them? I ended up staying inside my house, refusing to get involved with anyone who was not part of my family. I wouldn't go anywhere. I cried. It was Chandra who insisted I come to the café. I found companionship with girls looking like me. That allowed me to feel more comfortable—not so much like a freak. Getting used to customers was difficult, but everyone who comes here is so pleasant and supportive. It made a difference. Eventually, Chandra promoted me from waiting on tables to taking care of the books. Naomi has only been here a few weeks, but she's taught me so much."

"Parvati, is your story similar to Kiri's?"

Parvati was quiet as she listened to Kiri describe what happened to her, but her situation was not the same. "No, with me it was different. Two girls attacked me because of jealousy."

"Girls? Now that surprises me."

"Yeah, it's normally men but these girls were mean. Before the attack, I had the potential of a successful modeling career. I signed a contract with an agency and was to start right after I graduated from school."

"Were these girls jealous?" asked Lynne.

"Yes, they kept telling me I acted like I was better than them when that wasn't true. I rarely spoke of my modeling prospects, but you know how word gets around. Anyway, these two girls had been a problem for several years. They constantly bullied me, but I shrugged it off."

"What happened?'

"Just before graduation, they came up to me pretending to be my friend. One of the girls asked me if I wanted to go to her home after school. I couldn't believe how friendly these girls were. I felt happy to think I was accepted. I look back at it all now and think how stupid I was."

"I don't think stupid is a good word, Parvati. Perhaps a little naïve?"

"Yes, that, too. So I went with them to the one girl's house. No one was home. They invited me into the kitchen. We sat down at the table and then both of them started to laugh. I sensed there was an inside joke between the two of them. I started to become uncomfortable because the laughing was meant to be mean. One of the girls went to the cupboard and brought out a small pitcher. I thought we were going to have a snack; but instead, she threw the contents at me. I screamed and they laughed. I could feel my eyelids and lips burn off. Like Kiri, my nose melted and my ears shriveled. Some of the acid splashed onto my neck and burned my skin."

"What did you do?"

"I remember running to the sink trying to get water on it, but that seemed to make everything worse. I ran out of the house and into the street screaming until someone came over and called the police. They took me for treatment at the hospital."

"What about the girls?"

"They said I lied and that I was about to throw the acid at them when I tripped and fell. Instead, it spilt on me. I don't think the police believed those girls, but it was their word against mine."

"So nothing was done?"

Kunta shook her head and said, "Absolutely nothing."

Kiri said, "Kunta has had over twenty-five procedures, and she probably needs thirty more to repair the damage."

Kunta said, "It's expensive. The government gave me $4500 towards the operations, but that was hardly enough. Each procedure cost from $3000 to $6000."

"How have you both been able to pay for these operations?"

Kiri said, "We've applied for funds from organizations that help with victim costs."

"And there's a surgeon in Delhi who offers up his services to acid attack victims," added Kunta. "He comes to Agra for a week every couple of months. We have been very fortunate to receive his help. He's a very caring person."

"Do you know the next time he will be here?" asked Lynne.

"Sure, he's scheduled to be in Agra sometime this week," said Kiri.

"Can you give me his name and number?"

"Yes, let me check my purse for his card," said Kiri.

"Do you plan on talking to him about Jaya?" asked Parvati.

"Yes, I know he must have a full schedule, but maybe he would agree to evaluate her."

Shortly, Kiri returned with his card. "Dr. Lalit Joshi will be in Agra in two days."

Chapter 17

ALLISON

ALLISON HAD ALREADY been awake when the alarm went off that morning. She dressed, made a quick cup of coffee, and sat down to read the newspaper pushed under her door at the hotel. Allison had a nine o'clock appointment at the Delhi police station to meet with Detective Mahor and Kasi's brother. From what she knew, there were no further leads. They wanted to have her look at some photos of possible people who may have picked Kasi up at the airport.

She always found it interesting to read newspapers from other countries. That morning a particular article grabbed her attention. It was the story of a 5-year-old girl who lived in an area close to a tea plantation. She had been missing for close to a week when a search party discovered her body not far from where she lived. The news article went on to say that the child was unmercifully raped, beaten and decapitated by a machete. Two men, laborers on the tea plantation, were arrested and now imprisoned.

Allison put her coffee cup down and shook her head in disgust. She wondered how anyone could be so sick to do that to another human being—especially an innocent child. What happened along the way to make a person become that disturbed and twisted? It also bothered her to know these men were at the same jail that she was scheduled to be visiting in another hour.

Allison took a taxi to the station. By now she knew where it was located having been there only a week ago. Allison volunteered her testimony and had hoped it would help in finding that sweet girl who sat next to her on the plane from New York. Kasi was so excited to be returning home after being away for over two years. There she was opening her bag and showing Allison her gift of several bangles to the bride whose wedding she was eager to attend. Allison wondered if the marriage would still go on. Undoubtedly, her cousin would postpone it. How tragic for the whole family. To not know had to be agonizing.

Allison thought about the child who was kidnapped and killed. This tragedy was now that family's reality. Hopefully, Kasi's family will have a happier ending. Allison prayed for that but was not hopeful.

The taxi stopped in front of the police headquarters which was a relatively modern building with a glass façade. Allison nervously got out of the cab and headed towards the overhang that extended above the walkway leading to the front door. About ten men sat upon a scattering of benches, presumably waiting for their bus. The intensity of their eyes bore into her, watching her every move. The poise she attempted to project gave rise to a major case of anxiety. Men of this sort knew that. They enjoyed making women feel awkward and uncomfortable. She wasn't going to give them that satisfaction, so she raised her head and marched along with contrived confidence.

As she passed them, she thought of the TV journalist who reported on a woman who rode a rickshaw through the Chandni Chowk—the very same neighborhood Allison rode through only a week ago. While Allison endured the hassling from vendors, this women suffered jeers, whistles and endless name calling. At first, she tried ignoring them, but several kept following her and getting in her face until she got out of the rickshaw, threw one of the main abusers down to the ground, and dragged him to the police station around the corner. The woman had years of Martial Arts training. Allison considered that might not be such a bad idea and quickly resolved to check it out when she returned home.

Once inside the station, the receptionist let Detective Mahor know she had arrived, and he quickly came out to greet her. "Namaste, Ms. Wagner."

Allison put her hands together, bowed her head, and echoed the greeting.

"Please come inside my office. Dr. Joshi is already here."

Allison followed him into the office and saw Kasi's brother. He stood up and bowed, "Namaste. Thank you for coming today. I have to leave for Agra tomorrow, and I did want to speak to you before going."

"Of course. Anything I can do to help." She took a chair across from him. "Have you heard anything about your sister's whereabouts?"

"Unfortunately, no we haven't, but we have some ideas. We would like to pass them by you to see if anything rings a bell."

"I'll try, but I'm not sure how helpful I can be."

"I understand you sat next to Kasi on the airplane coming over from New York."

"Yes, we spent several hours talking about things. Kasi's quite friendly and you might say we clicked. We even decided we would look each other up for lunch when we both returned to New York."

"Was that the last time you talked with her?" asked the detective.

"Yes, if you don't count baggage claim. Kasi had a little difficulty pulling her luggage off the moving belt, so I helped her with that. We exchanged goodbyes, and I told her I hope she has fun at her cousin's wedding. That was pretty much it." Allison turned away from the detective and looked at Kasi's brother. "What's happening with your cousin's wedding?"

Lalit shrugged his shoulders and said, "My family is distraught over this. After much consideration, Lina decided to postpone the wedding for now. She was able to move the date to a later time. Many of the wedding guests live in Delhi so that won't be too inconvenient for most of them."

"I understand. Hard to celebrate under these circumstances."

Detective Mahor pulled out a folder and laid several photos down on the table.

"Here are examples of cars. Can you think back to the car that Kasi entered? Any here that look similar?"

Allison looked at each photo before pulling several out of the pile. "None of these, for sure. Let me take a closer look at the others." She went through the remaining pictures and pulled out two that were hatchbacks. "Okay, this is the one. It was a silver hatchback."

Lalit looked at the car and said, "Was it a Toyota?"

"Not sure of the make but if this is a Toyota, then I would say that was a strong possibility."

The detective asked, "Anyone you know with a silver Toyota hatchback?"

Lalit shook his head. "Can't think of anyone."

The detective turned back to Allison. "Did you get the feeling that this man was perhaps a stranger? You know, someone who happened along and tricked her into the car?"

Trying to remember what she saw, she said, "No, I got the impression they were involved in an upsetting conversation. At first, she appeared to be caught off-guard, but then things seemed to escalate. I guess the best way to describe her behavior would be agitated."

"So you think she knew the man?" asked Lalit.

"I can't say for sure, you know. Not only were there too many people between us, but there was a considerable amount of smog that evening. If I had to bet on it, I would say she knew him."

Detective Mahor turned to Lalit. "Can you think of anyone who would have issues with your sister?"

"No, Kasi got along with everyone. There wasn't anyone who didn't like her."

Allison said, "Obviously, I don't know her well at all, but the little time we spent together, I found her to be a lovely person."

The detective put the car photos back in the folder except for the Toyota hatchback that Allison had chosen.

"Did your sister work while she lived here?" the detective asked Lalit.

"Yes, she was an administrative assistant at a small firm that dealt with importing and exporting. Matter of fact, that's where she met Keith."

Detective Mahor asked, "Keith is her husband?"

"Yes."

"Is he here?"

"He arrived last night."

"Why did it take him so long to come?" the detective asked.

"Well, at first he didn't realize there was much of a problem. Then when we called him back several days later to tell him Kasi still could not be found, he decided to make the trip back."

Allison listened to the exchange between the detective and Kasi's brother. She understood the detective's concerns. She also wondered why he didn't come right away.

Allison said, "You know, I just now thought of something else. Lalit, what do you know about broken bangles?"

"Broken bangles? Well, there's this superstition that when a bride gets married, she is given bangles by her mother-in-law. Each one is of a different color symbolizing some trait. We say it's not good if any break."

"That was also my understanding," said Allison. "With the upcoming wedding of your cousin, your sister and I got talking about bangles. She explained what the different colors meant. I noticed she didn't have any yellow ones. Kasi told me they broke while she slept."

"What are you getting at?" asked the detective.

"Yellow stands for happiness, and it was the yellow ones that broke. I questioned why she didn't replace them and she said, 'What happens, happens.' At the time I thought that was a rather odd answer. I guess I still do."

The detective asked, "Did your sister give any indication of how her marriage was going?"

"No, everything seemed fine. Kasi always talked about what they were doing and seemed okay whenever we skyped with her."

"What about her husband? Do you like him?"

"We don't know him well. Kasi worked with Keith in Delhi—that's how they met.

The detective shuffled through some papers in his folder. "Were things good between your father and Kasi when she left for America?"

Lalit said, "Not at first but my father is okay with everything now."

The detective then turned to Allison. "We have a chart with a variety of facial parts—noses, mouths, eyebrows, chins. I want you to study this chart and see if you can match any with the man who picked up Kasi." He then called in a man who entered holding a drawing pad.

Allison studied the features. "I believe this nose fits. Maybe these eyes, not sure about the mouth. That was hard to see from where I was standing." She pointed to hair parted on the left. "This might be it. A week has gone by and I can still see his face, but I'm having a hard time picking out specific features."

The police artist used the chosen features and started drawing as Allison assisted by giving further details. After 15 minutes, the artist came up with a pencil drawing. Allison looked at it and said, "No, you need to make the face fuller. He was rather on the heavier side. Not fat, just sort of—you know, bulky."

The artist made the changes and Allison seemed satisfied. He held the photo up for Lalit to see.

"Does this person look familiar?"

Lalit stared at it. "You know, it looks a lot like Hari."

"Who is Hari?" asked the detective.

Allison looked at Lalit. "Wasn't he the guy Kasi was supposed to marry?"

The detective stood up from his chair. "Tell me more about this Hari.

Lalit rubbed his chin several times. "Hari Chubney was the man my parents had arranged for Kasi to marry, but weeks before the wedding she flatly refused creating tension between the two families. Not only were all the arrangements made; but out of the blue, she announced she's marrying this American man. We had never met him, didn't know she was even dating him. My parents were not happy. No one was happy, but Kasi didn't care. She found love and was following through with it."

Detective Mahor paced back and forth behind Lalit. "Hadn't you thought this might be something of importance to mention?"

Lalit said, "That happened over two years ago. I didn't think it could have any bearing on what's going on now."

"You know, let me be the determinant of that. Now, is there anything else? Have you seen this guy, Hari, recently?"

"No, after my sister left he just faded from the scene. I haven't seen him since. I didn't know him. His parents knew my parents. They wanted to marry off their son, felt he was getting too old and needed to be married. My father was happy to see he owned his own business and home which would mean Kasi would be well taken care of. That is all I know."

"Was this kind of behavior typical of your sister?"

"No, not at all. She was always a very compliant daughter."

Allison asked, "What kind of business does this Hari own?"

"I don't know a whole lot about him. I only met him once. I have to say I didn't like him."

"Why's that?" Detective Mahor asked.

"I didn't think he would fit in well with my family. You know, he looked moody, sullen—more on the dark side."

"That doesn't sound like a good match," Allison said. But then Allison grew silent as she remembered her own experience in Thailand. Things didn't work out well for her either. She came close to making the same mistake as Kasi.

Lalit hit his fist on the table. "I just remembered. Hari owns a small car dealership."

The detective asked, "Where?"

"That I don't know, but I believe it's a Toyota.

Chapter 18

LYNNE

"I DON'T FEEL comfortable doing this, Lynne."

"You'll do just fine, Jaya. I called the clinic yesterday and explained the situation, and they said to come in today at noon. Dr. Joshi said he would cut his lunch short and see you then. So, you see, we can't be a no-show if he's willing to do that, right?"

The two girls walked into the clinic and reported to the reception desk. After a 10-minute wait, a woman came out and invited them into the examining room. They sat and waited a few minutes more until a young doctor entered the room and greeted them with a soft smile.

"Sorry to keep you waiting. I grabbed a quick bite to eat. I need to keep my energy up for the rest of the day."

"We hadn't waited long at all," said Lynne.

"So Jaya, I understand you are seeking treatment?"

Jaya instinctively pulled her scarf up around her face. She said nothing.

"Yes, she is. I brought Jaya to the clinic in hopes you could help her out."

The doctor sat across from Jaya and asked, "May I take a look?"

Jaya nodded and slowly removed the scarf. It wasn't easy exposing herself to any scrutiny—especially to a man.

Lynne said, "She's had a tough time of it since the attack.

We heard that you've helped others heal from the damage caused by acid."

"Yes, to some extent. You see, I pretty much specialize in congenital disabilities but lately have become involved with restoration procedures from acid attacks. Unfortunately, there is too much of that in India. Let me take a look to see what's going on here."

Dr. Joshi gently turned Jaya's head to examine the damage done to several of her facial features as well as the outer layer of her skin. "I can see your situation requires more than cosmetic procedures. I can graft skin from another part of your body to recreate your left ear. It's important to restore functionality and prevent any infection. We can tattoo eyebrows to cover up the lack of brows. I have an assistant who specializes in that sort of thing. We'll need to get the swelling down before we can do anything with your nose."

Jaya asked, "How long will all of that take?"

Doctor Joshi looked towards the ceiling as though he were calculating the time. "Most likely a couple of years. You see, we can't do it all at once but need to space it out allowing for the tissues to heal. How did this happen to you, Jaya?"

"My father was mad that I disobeyed him. I went to a school dance after he told me I couldn't go."

"Was his offensive behavior isolated to this one time or was your father abusive at other times as well?"

"He continuously scolded me and tried to control all my decisions. Often he said I should have been born a boy because girls are worthless to the family. Sometimes I would be locked in my room or he'd slap me, but never used acid until that day."

"What makes men do such horrible things, Doctor?" Lynne asked.

Dr. Joshi sighed. "Attackers rarely want to kill the person but instead desire to kill the victim's potential. They may inflict this type of permanent damage to separate the person from society. You know, to keep her from getting a job or even from getting married."

"Sounds like a need to establish dominance and control."

Dr. Joshi said, "Very much so. Often the offender wants to punish the victim because he believes she defied his will or needs to answer for causing dishonor to him or the family. Do you know what kind of acid he used, Jaya?"

"I was told sulfuric."

The doctor nodded. "Sulfuric acid can be quite corrosive, and the effects are almost instant. Did you rinse your face with water?"

Jaya said, "Yes, I had to because I felt like my face was burning up."

The doctor turned to Lynne and said, "Immediately you feel a hot sensation, and then this is followed by agonizing pain as the skin swells and shrivels. That I see is what happened here."

Lynne asked, "So, it's not a good idea to apply water?"

"Certainly not small amounts. When Jaya did that, she further heated the acid and it caused more damage."

Jaya started to cry. "I didn't know what to do. I panicked. All I remember is I wanted the burning to stop."

The doctor placed his hand on her shoulder. "Of course you didn't know. Splashing water on the burn is instinctive. By the way, using water isn't a bad thing if you apply an abundant amount for ten to twelve hours in order to wash the acid away."

"What do you suggest for Jaya, Doctor?" asked Lynne.

"Well, we need to fix her left ear and reconstruct this area around the eye. Fortunately, her eyesight was not damaged. Scar tissue has formed on her face due to severe burns. I suggest excisional surgery for that."

Lynne and Jaya looked at each other. "What's that?" asked Jaya.

"After carefully removing the damaged layers of the dermis, I'd make an incision through the dead skin and shave off layers of the damaged tissue. This procedure prepares the area for new skin. Then we graft layers of skin from your buttock to this affected area. The trick is to do a little at a time, not all at once. It's a process and has to be performed months apart giving the tissue time to heal."

"How does the grafting work?" asked Lynne.

"The new skin is placed on the wound and secured with dressing and stitches. Recovery takes up to six weeks each time."

Lynne turned to Jaya and asked, "Are you up for this?"

Jaya nodded her head. "I'll do anything to make this better."

Dr. Joshi smiled. "It's a partnership and we'll work together as a team. I do want you to know that the results won't be perfect. You'll look as though the grafted skin is pasted on your face."

"I understand," said Jaya. "I've seen the results on the other girls at the café, but it's still an improvement over how I look now."

Dr. Joshi explained that new technology is taking place and that lasers have been known to help cover scars and improve the coloration of the skin."

"What are lasers?" asked Jaya.

"It's an intense, high energy light—stronger and more concentrated than normal light from, let's say, a flashlight. I am hoping to find a way to obtain a laser for the clinic here."

"You don't have lasers?" asked Lynne.

"No, a good one that is effective in scar removal can cost between $150,000- $200,000. I did manage to obtain one at the clinic in Delhi. The other problem is it requires a great deal of training to use it effectively and safely."

Lynne asked, "Are you trained?"

Dr. Joshi answered, "Actually, I am. I've traveled to New York on several occasions to become certified. We need to get the equipment. I do need to caution you, Jaya. Treatment isn't as effective on dark color skin. Bleaching techniques will also be necessary."

"When can we start all of this, Doctor?" asked Lynne.

Jaya quickly inserted, "How much does it cost? My mother and I don't have much money."

Dr. Joshi answered, "We use whatever the government gives you as compensation plus any charitable contributions you might be able to garner for help with the clinic expenses. As for my services, I donate one week of my time every couple of months."

"Can Jaya be accepted into the program?"

Dr. Joshi said, "Yes, I'll see what I can do. We'll get her first treatment started, and then she'll need to follow an after-care program before the second treatment is applied."

"That is wonderful. Are you able to fit her in while you're here this week?" asked Lynne.

"We'll start this process tomorrow. Can you come in tomorrow afternoon, Jaya?"

Lynne enthusiastically answered, "Yes, she can. Isn't that right, Jaya?"

Jaya nodded. "Sure, it's worth a try."

"Good. I'll need to start tomorrow to make sure no infection sets in over the following days. Due to a family emergency, my visit this time will only be five days instead of my normal seven."

Lynne stood up and shook his hand. "Thank you so much for your time and for your willingness to help women like Jaya who can't afford to take on the expense."

Dr. Joshi sighed. "You know, a person never knows what will be handed down to him. If anyone can be of help in time, skill or money, that is a way of giving thanks for being spared such hardships. By the way, are you an American?"

"Yes, I am. I've only been here a short time."

"Is Jaya a personal friend of yours?"

Lynne looked over at Jaya and smiled. Yes, Jaya's become one. I'm here doing an internship with Mukta's Café which is how Jaya and I met."

"I'm quite familiar with that place. I've done work on several of the ladies who work there."

"Yes, they recommended you. I'm so grateful you're taking Jaya on as a patient."

"That's why I'm here. So Jaya, you'll need to sign several papers, make an appointment with my receptionist for tomorrow, and we'll get this thing started."

Chapter 19

KASI

UNSURE OF HOW long she had been locked up in this room, she decided to play along. Kasi disliked this man when they were theoretically engaged, but she detested him now. Everything about him repulsed her. The way he chewed his food, the gulping noises he made when he drank his beer, the odor of his body from never bathing—all of it sickened her. Each day followed the same pattern. He would come into the room with a disgusting breakfast that he forced her to eat. Then he spent several hours watching TV only to leave for a while. She never knew where he went. At first, she thought he went to work but eventually learned that he surrendered the dealership he once owned due to poor management and lack of finances. Eviction from his house followed, resulting in moving into this uninhabitable structure that someone he supposedly knew owned. He said the owner was a friend and had permitted him to use it. Kasi doubted that. She wondered how he got the money to buy food but eventually came to the realization that it was either stolen or donated by the soup kitchen. Hari's luck and good fortune had slipped away, and he blamed it all on her. After all, it was she who caused him to drink. If she hadn't left, none of this would have happened.

Kasi knew she needed a plan if she were to escape this hell hole. So a week into her abduction she decided to play along. She engaged in conversation, sympathized with his misfortunes, apologized for her misbehavior, and warmed up to his advances. Twice a night he came onto her, left and drank several beers, and returned in a stupor to continue where he left off. Like a prostitute, she allowed her mind to become detached from her body. If she hadn't, none of this could be tolerable.

She convinced him that he no longer needed to chain her to the bed. Instead, he cut her free and quietly locked the door whenever he left the building. After all, things were quite nice for him. She came to her senses and realized how much she wanted to be with him and not with that American.

Kasi permitted her mind to drift to a better time. A more pleasant time—days when she and Keith enjoyed simple moments. The past year had not been good. She left India feeling happy and fortunate. It took less than a year for all of that to change. Being in a strange country, away from family and friends, no work attachments—all of that culminated in depression. Keith was rarely at home. Was Hari right? Maybe she did make a mistake. Maybe Hari figured it out, long before Kasi did. He told her she returned to India because she realized she made a mistake marrying Keith. Did she? If so, how could Hari know that? Was Lina's wedding an excuse to get away from the loneliness she experienced in such a big city as New York?

Kasi reacted enthusiastically upon meeting Allison on the plane. Never had she shared so much with a stranger as she did that evening flying to India. She thirsted for a friend. Allison expressed an interest in getting together for lunch once they returned from India. She was ready for that. Having Allison as a friend would have been a positive thing. That is if Keith didn't squash the idea by telling her she shouldn't recklessly spend money they didn't have. Yes, Keith changed and so had she.

Kasi thought about Keith. She worried about what her family was going through with the continuous reports of her being missing. She convinced Hari to permit her to listen to the news about her disappearance. The press called it a kidnapping.

Hari laughed. "They say some person kidnapped you, Kasi. Were you kidnapped?"

Kasi smiled and forced herself to appear amused. "Of course not, Hari. You know how much I've grown to care for you these past two weeks."

"Look, you are famous," said Hari, pointing to the photo of her on the TV. Next, a news reporter came on as well as her husband, Keith.

"It's Keith!" Kasi wouldn't allow herself to exhale for fear she would miss a word of what he had to say.

He gave the simple account of how his wife left New York to return to India for a family wedding. "No one has heard from her. Kasi, if you are listening, please contact your family or me."

"You think he cares about you, Kasi? Ha! No one but me cares about you," Hari insisted, rubbing her arm. Although Kasi cringed at his touch, she managed a smile.

"That Keith is not such a fine person," he added, taking a swallow of his cheap beer.

Kasi stared at him. "You say that often, Hari. Tell me, what do you mean by that? You don't know him. Why do you keep telling me this?"

Hari leaned over and kissed her neck. "Never mind, know he's not a good person. Besides, you're my wife now and so it doesn't matter."

"Hari, when do you think I could call my mother to tell her I'm all right? You heard how worried my family is."

Hari stiffened. "Why do you want to do that? You are my family now."

"Yes, of course. But my mother is anxious about me. I know she's having a bad time, probably not eating or sleeping. I worry how all of this is affecting her. I've seen her on TV and she doesn't look well. Surely, you understand how that affects me, right?"

Kasi leaned in and kissed his hand—his ugly, fat hand that smelled of beer.

"Wouldn't it be better if I called and told everyone I'm okay . . . you know, that I made a mistake and decided to return to you? Then all of this attention in the news will be gone."

Hari took another swig of his beer and pulled her over to him. "No, not yet. Someday maybe, but not now. First, I need to work out this plan."

"What kind of plan?"

"A good plan—one that will give us lots of money."

Kasi pulled away and looked at him. "Hari, what is going on? Are you blackmailing my family?"

"No, no blackmail."

"Then let me speak to them. I need to do that."

"If I do that, they will trace the call to where we are. I can't let that happen—too soon."

Kasi thought about the conversation they just had. She speculated over what he meant about a plan. What plan could bring him money? She thought perhaps she was being held as ransom but never had that been mentioned in any of the news reports. It worried her that the reporting seemed to be turning from a missing person to a potential murder. She wanted to scream through the television to give up looking in the barren fields occupied by feral dogs, pigs, and garbage. All of that was a waste of time. There she was in this rat-infested building. But where? She had no idea. Determination and patience continuously oppose each other, and she needed both to get through this ordeal.

Chapter 20

ALLISON

THIS MORNING IN Delhi couldn't have been more delightful. Temps were in the 70's, absolutely no smog, blue sky—all ingredients that would tempt anyone to play hookey. Being the true professional, Allison took a deep breath and opened the door to the Delhi Newspaper office.

"Oh, there you are. I've been worried about you."

"Why's that, Abha? I mentioned yesterday I would be late. I needed to go to the police station to meet up with Kasi's brother. Let me tell you; it was quite an interesting morning."

Abha pointed to the TV hanging on the wall. A reporter was standing in front of the station with a frenzied mob behind him.

"What's going on? Is that in front of the police station?"

Abha turned down the volume and said, "You know that little girl that was recently found brutally murdered?"

"Yeah, yesterday I heard they captured the two men who did it. I guess they were laborers from the tea plantation near her home."

"Well, it appears a mob, estimated to be around 800 men, stormed the police station demanding for the release of the two prisoners into their custody."

"Are you kidding? 800 men? Abha, absolutely nothing was going on when I left that place only two hours ago."

"Looks like you got out of there just in time. I knew you were scheduled to be at the station and terrified you were caught up in that mess."

"You know, when I entered the building, about ten men were sitting on the benches outside. I didn't feel good about them. I don't know. It was something about how their eyes looked—very dark and sullen. They frightened me as I walked by. I told myself it would probably be a good idea if I took a martial arts class when I returned to New York. At the time, I assumed they were waiting for the bus but maybe not, huh?"

Abha added, "Yeah, could be they were waiting for the rest of the crowd to show up. You know, the other 790 men. Good thing you got out of there."

"Turn up the volume, Abha. I want to hear what the reporter is saying."

"The police refused to hand over the two men," the reporter said, "so the mob overpowered the police and ran inside, broke open the two cells, and dragged the men out of the building. Right now, we have no idea where they took them. It was like a swarm of locusts that surrounded the area and rapidly disappeared down the road."

"That doesn't sound good. Does mob mentality happen a lot here?"

Abha said, "At times, yes. This little girl was missing for over a week. Sentiments were high as it was. When the police found her body yesterday, they reported she was brutally beaten, raped and decapitated before being thrown in a ravine."

Allison put her hand over her mouth and shook her head. "That poor child—how awful. Violence, it just never seems to end. Hold on . . . looks like . . . something new is being reported."

"I'm here to update the latest on the death of the small child. After the mob dragged the two accused men out of their cells, they brought them down here to the center of the market area." The reporter pointed to the huge crowd assembled across the street. "You can see the crowd of people is starting to thin out as the police head over towards them with tear gas. From what I'm learning, many in the crowd used wooden clubs to beat the suspects to death. The accused were believed to be laborers at the tea plantation not far from where the child lived."

"You are so lucky to have gotten out of there when you did."

"Have any police been harmed? I'm wondering about the detective I spoke with as well as Kasi's brother."

"No word on any casualties other than the two suspects. Once the mob showed up and learned of the denial of their requests, they stormed the building and grabbed the two prisoners. By the way, speaking of meetings, how did yours go?"

"It went pretty well. The detective had me pick out some facial features that resembled the man I saw picking up Kasi. It proved to be a little confusing; after the selection started, it got a little easier. You know, I'm not used to being on the side of giving the answers. It was a new experience for me."

"I can imagine," said Abha, pouring Allison a cup of coffee. "Here, I think we could both use a cup of coffee."

"Then this artist entered the room and he started sketching faces. One of them was pretty close to what I remember as being the man."

"Really?"

"It gets even crazier. When the artist finished, he held

the sketch up, and Lalit immediately identified him as being Hari. You know, the man I told you about."

Abha said, "You're kidding? The man Kasi was engaged to marry?"

"The one and only—so now the police have something more to go on. That is until this mob activity broke out."

"Does Lalit know where this guy lives?"

Allison said, "No, but he did mention that he owns a small Toyota dealership. What's pretty weird is that the car that drove up to the airport was a Toyota hatchback."

"Yeah, more than a strange coincidence. I'm sure when you took off for India you had no idea you would be the central witness in a disappearance case."

"You know, every time I step out of the United States, I seem to become involved with some crime. In Nepal, it was human trafficking. When I went to Thailand, I was involved with the theft of a valuable pin."

"Not sure if I want to travel with you," Abha said.

"I certainly don't blame you. Hey, how are your nerves over your upcoming wedding?"

Abha smiled. "Oh, a little frazzled."

Allison laughed. "I'd be nervous, too, especially if I was about to marry someone I had just met."

"Allison, it's a cultural thing. By the way, have you purchased your sari for the wedding?"

"I never thought of that. Should I be dressed in a sari?"

"Yes, unless you want to stand out in the crowd as the only woman in Western clothing."

"You mean, I'll have to go inside one of those crazy chowks again?"

Abha smiled. "It won't be so bad. Think of all the personal attention you'll receive."

Chapter 21

LYNNE

ALL NIGHT THE rain pelted the roof of the house. It sounded like an overhead train as its force hit the metal covering that protected her from the wet. Lynne didn't look forward to the challenges the adverse weather would generate as she made her way to the clinic to pick up Jaya.

"The first procedure went as best as could be expected," reported Dr. Joshi after the operation the previous day. "I started the reconstruction of her damaged ear and managed to shave off the outer layer of dead skin that covered the left side of her face. We need to keep her here overnight to make sure there are no complications, especially with infection. So, you can pick her up in the morning."

Lynne sat alone on the half-empty bus knowing that soon she would be dropped off a block from the clinic's front door. From the window, she observed a couple wading through knee-deep water as they shared one umbrella. She wondered what was so urgent that they needed to fight these flooded conditions. Although the rain continued, that didn't stop another man from pulling his cart over to the side of the road while attempting to sell naan from under his small umbrella. She shook her head as she quietly thought about those two girls from Long Island who bemoaned their fate in having to sit in the coach section of the plane flying to Delhi. "I wonder how that situation is going," she quietly mused. Then there were the rickshaw drivers, draped in cheap plastic ponchos, cycling their carriages through the flooded streets. Many of the rickshaws were empty except for one or two carrying a passenger tucked inside a plastic shell-like cocoon.

The news reported that this monsoon-type rain was not typical at this time of the year. It was good that the temperature remained in the low 70's instead of reaching over 100 degrees as it will two months later. Lynne wondered how that would look. Certainly, the combination of high humidity and scorching temps would bring out all the negative sides of India—dust turning to mud, garbage floating in undrained rainwater, mosquitoes breeding, and unsightly huts now drenched both inside as well as out.

Lynne was absorbed in thought as the bus made an abrupt stop. It couldn't go any further which meant she needed to brave the elements and walk the remaining four blocks to the clinic. She worried over how she would get Jaya back to her house.

An ambulance blocked the entrance of the hospital as the medical personnel quickly removed a body of a child who died after the tin roof of his three-room house collapsed. The sobbing of the grief-stricken mother resonated throughout the corridor. Lynne stood in the shadows of the small reception room not wanting to interfere with the tragedy taking place in front of her. Lynne's heart quickened once she realized that the cries of the anguished mother came from Kiri, the girl working with Naomi at Mukta's Café.

"You must stay back," the nurse warned.

"No, you don't understand. I'm a therapist working with burned victims at the Mukta Café. I know the mother. I need to see her."

Kiri saw Lynne trying to get inside the room. She cried

out to her, "Lynne, Lynne, my son died." She ran out into the corridor and fell into Lynne's arms.

"Please, can I take her somewhere?"

The nurse relented and directed the two women into a private room behind the reception desk.

Lynne held onto Kiri as she eased her onto a couch in the corner of the room. "Kiri, what happened?"

"My son, Kumar, was asleep in his bed. He had difficulty sleeping because the rain frightened him. I stayed with him until he fell asleep. Then I went to my room. The whole night it rained, but Kumar slept through it. Then I heard this loud crash coming from Kumar's room. I jumped out of bed and ran to his room seeing the collapse of everything on that side of our house. Lynne, Kumar was under all of that rubble. I tried to find him but couldn't. I ran outside and screamed for people to help me. Someone called the police and an ambulance. We searched for nearly an hour, sifting through debris and concrete until someone found him."

"Oh, Kiri, I am so sorry," said Lynne, knowing that no words at this time could bring relief and comfort. Instead, she hugged Kiri as hard as she could. Kiri sobbed until exhausted. Her wet tears drenched the shoulder of Lynne's rain jacket until nothing remained inside except the awareness that this nightmare would not go away.

"Kumar was a kind boy. He always wanted to help others."

"How old was he, Kiri?"

"Eleven—only eleven-years-old. Kumar was all that I had. His father accused me of being unfaithful, but I wasn't. I spent my days looking after my family. Nothing more. Then that night when my husband threw acid in my face, everything changed for us. Everything. One moment of anger changes your whole life. After the court put Deepak in prison, I refused to have anything to do with him. All I had left was my son, Kumar. That was all I needed."

Kiri broke down once more and cried so hard that her body convulsed. Lynne continued to hold her releasing any little strength she had in her body to Kiri.

One of the doctors came into the room and spoke to Kiri. "I'm very sorry about your son. Can you tell me what happened?"

Kiri repeated the story she told Lynne. "I feel terrible that I couldn't provide a sturdier house for us because I needed money for medical procedures. That was all I could afford."

The doctor said, "Do not take what happened as your fault. It wasn't. What happened to Kumar was a freak accident."

"Can I see my boy?"

The doctor agreed. Upon Kiri's request that Lynne accompanied her, the two women held hands as they entered the room. Kumar's frail body lay on the table. Kiri caressed him and took part of her sari to wipe the caked blood from his cheek. No other visible bruises showed. The doctor said that death was caused by internal injuries from the crush of the roof as it buckled and collapsed upon him.

Lynne watched as Kiri began the tradition of chanting the death mantra into her son's right ear. A Hindu priest arrived with sandal paste and applied it to the boy's forehead. The priest readied the body for removal by placing drops of holy water in his mouth.

The immediate problem of where to send Kumar's body became an issue.

"I have an idea," said Lynne, "let me make a phone call and I'll be back with you on this."

Lynne quietly excused herself and called Chandra at the

café. After explaining the situation, Chandra agreed to close the café and have Kiri's son brought there for the first stage of burial. Lynne returned to the room and reassured Kiri that her son had a temporary resting place. Then she left the room allowing Kiri further privacy to grieve.

"Where is she?" Naomi asked, rushing into the clinic.

Lynne, who now sat on a bench outside the room, pointed to the closed door.

"How is she doing?" asked Naomi.

"Not good. Kiri is having difficulty processing all of this. As if things couldn't be bad enough, but now she's forced to make immediate funeral arrangements. Do the ladies at the café know about the accident?"

"Yes, Chandra informed everyone about Kumar's accident and the loss of Kiri's house. She also told us of the closing of the café for Kumar's viewing. Oh, one more thing. Parvati is offering Kiri a place to stay until she can get things under control."

"Those ladies are truly a blessing," said Lynne.

"I don't know how they cope," said Naomi. "I guess adversity toughens them."

Chapter 22

KASI

KASI WOKE UP to the sound of heavy rain. June was the month the rains came. Rarely would they show up in January. Then again, nothing was ordinary anymore. She closed her eyes and listened to the patter that surrounded her. It brought back happy memories of being a child, running outside and dancing from puddle to puddle. How simple things were back then. How free she was. Will she ever know that kind of freedom again?

Soon Hari would return to the room for payback. That's what he called the sex he forced upon her. Payback for canceling the wedding and leaving him. Payback for humiliating him in front of his family, friends, and employees. Payback for turning to alcohol as a way to cope, all resulting in the loss of his home, his business, and his friends. Kasi owed him a debt that he was determined to collect and he did.

This morning was different. Hari didn't come to Kasi's bed and throw himself on top of her slight body. Instead, she heard only his voice—a one-sided, angry voice that appeared to be in a heated conversation with someone on the phone. Kasi strained to listen to the conversation, but it was difficult with the pounding of the rain upon the roof. She sat up in bed thinking it would be easier to understand.

Hari argued, "That was not what we agreed to. You are changing things, and I'm not going along with this new idea of yours. Hey, we stick to the plan. Besides, haha, I'm having too good of a time, if you know what I mean. By the way, I have to thank you for such a nice wedding present. . . . Oh, you don't know? She's consented to our relationship and we are now married. By the way, it didn't take a lot to convince her either. Haha! . . . Sure, I need money but I'm not getting it that way. So why are you changing things now? . . . What do I have to say to get you to understand it's what we agreed upon or nothing? . . . Hey, you're in no position to threaten me. I'll drag you down. Am I making myself understood?"

It was difficult piecing together the one-sided conversation. Who was on the phone with Hari? What was the other person demanding that Hari no longer wanted to do? Why was she so important to the plan?

Kasi heard the call come to an abrupt end, so she quickly laid down pretending to be asleep. After a trip to the kitchen, Hari opened the bedroom door and walked over to her holding the daily breakfast that she hated almost as much as she hated him. He woke her, "Here you go. Time to eat. You need to keep up your strength so I can get my payback."

Kasi turned over to her other side.

"You're not going back to playing stupid, are you?" he asked.

Kasi said, "Who were you talking to just now?"

Hari said, "A friend."

"It didn't sound like a friend. What kind of plan were you discussing?"

Hari put the breakfast down on the floor. "So, now you're listening in on my conversations, huh?"

"It wasn't hard. You were yelling into your phone. I'm not deaf, you know. What is the plan and why am I a part of it?"

"Look, you keep yourself out of my business."

"What did you mean when you said that was not what you agreed to? Who were you talking to?"

Hari stood up and started pacing back and forth. "I thought things were good between us—you know, you and me."

Kasi saw the veins starting to bulge on his neck and knew she overstepped her boundary. She needed to retreat and not push so hard if she were to get out of this mess. Feigning love and co-operation is what would keep her alive, and that was the primary goal right now—staying alive.

Softening the tone of her voice, she said, "Of course, Hari. I thought you knew I've grown fond of you. I'm just confused as to what you meant when you referred to me as part of the plan. Come over here and hug me."

Hari grinned. "Now that's much better. That's what I like to hear. Tell me, are you happier with me than with that guy who stole you from me?"

Kasi said, "Oh sure, I told you. I made a mistake."

"Yes, and now we have to do more payback, right?"

"Of course, I'm always ready to make it up to you." Kasi wanted to throw up. Instead, she mentally chanted the mantra that allowed her to stomach his kiss, his touch, his smelly breath—need to stay alive, stay alive, stay alive.

Chapter 23

ALLISON

"HELLO, WES? HOW'RE things in New York?"

"Other than the snow that keeps falling, we're doing well. Most likely no snow in Delhi, huh?"

"No snow, but we did have a couple of days of abnormal rainfall throughout most of Northern India."

"I'll take rain over the snow," said Wesley Gerhart, Allison's editor at the New York office.

"No fooling. It wasn't good. Lots of street flooding in some lower lying areas, but the sun is out now and things are starting to return to normal."

"Hope you're getting some good stuff for me."

Allison laughed. She wondered what it was with editors always questioning the process until they see the final result. "Stay with me on this, Wes. From my other work, I've found it better to stick with the more personal story. One kind of fell in my lap coming over on the plane."

"You mean that missing girl you sat next to?"

"The same," Allison said.

"Has she been found?"

"No, but something interesting happened. I was called back in to speak to the detective that's on the case. Kasi's brother was also there. I had to work with an artist to come up with a sketch of the man I saw pick her up at the airport."

"And?"

"Well, her brother said it looked a lot like the guy she originally planned to marry before breaking it off to marry someone else."

"Now that sounds like a good lead."

"Very much so. Also, I'm getting the scoop on women's rights. It's becoming harder for men in India to disregard the atrocities handed to women. One thing we don't hear so much about in the United States are acid attacks. It's time the world knows what is happening, and I hope to shine light on the problem. I plan to contact this gal who is doing an internship in Agra at a café run by acid attack victims."

"Who is it, Allison?"

"She's a college student I met on the plane."

"Allison, why did I send you to India? I should just have you hang out at JFK."

"Haha, the key is to network which is what I'm doing."

"So what's on the agenda for today?"

"Well, I heard there's this free soup kitchen in the city that serves something like 100,000 people every day by using hundreds of volunteers as staff. I have an appointment with this guy named Arpan who's going to show me around and give a briefing on how the operation works. The office here is letting me bring along a cameraman to document."

"That sounds interesting," Wes said.

"I thought so. The Sikh religion runs this food kitchen. It bases its beliefs on equality amongst people with no compliance towards the caste system. Arpan's name came up when I further investigated women's rights. With the Sikh, they regard women on the same level as men. In India, Wes, that is huge. The birth of a daughter is not considered a bad thing. I wanted to find out how they were able to establish this philosophy in a setting that is so gendered biased."

Wes said, "I think the Sikh religion has been around for some time."

"Yeah, over 500 years."

"Okay, let me know how all that works out."

"Wes, I can draw material from so many different areas. It's hard to decide. So I'm going with the unusual. Talk to you later."

"Okay, try not to get into any trouble."

"Who me? I'll try not."

Allison passed by the hotel concierge to get directions to the free kitchen, grabbed a taxi and headed over with the cameraman.

Arpan, dressed in white pants, a long white tunic, and topped with a white turban, met her at the door with a big smile.

"Namaste, Allison Wagner."

"Namaste. You must be Arpan?"

"Yes, I am happy to tell you whatever you would like to know about Sikhism and the free kitchen."

"This place is massive—did not expect this."

"We feed over 100,000 people a day, so it is big to accommodate not just the people but also the preparation and storage of food."

"Do you mind if my assistant takes photos?"

"Yes, please. Photos are permitted."

"I understand the people of the Sikh religion run this kitchen."

"Yes, part of our belief is service to others. Most of the people you'll see here are all volunteers."

"I need to ask a more personal question, Arpan. Whenever

I see a man dressed in a turban such as yours, does that distinguish him as being a Sikh follower?"

"Yes, we stick to a code—pants or shorts, a turban, a steel bracelet, and sword. The sword is to defend righteousness and this steel bracelet, the Kara, reminds us to have high moral character."

"Often I see gentlemen in America wearing these turbans. I guess they are Sikh followers?"

Arpan nodded his head. "Under my turban, my hair is tied up in a knot over the top of my head. To be a true follower, we are not allowed to cut or trim our hair."

"I've heard that," said Allison.

"We believe all people are equal. There are no classes and women are equal to men."

"One of the reasons I'm over here is to report on women's rights and their current standing in the Indian culture."

"Sikh women are considered equal inhabitants. The religion was intended to end the caste system. In India, you can tell the caste the person is in by the last name. In Sikh society, all men have Singh in their names and all women have Kaur. This way women establish an identity separate from their father or husband."

"You aren't born into this?"

"Not necessarily. Men or women of any nationality, race or social status can be baptized into the Sikh family as long as they hold true to the traditions and rules. No consumption of alcohol, tobacco, eating meat, adultery—all considered sins. We are an optimistic group because, with optimism, there is hope."

"Fascinating and quite basic in leading a good life."

Arpan nodded his head. "Come, let's go inside and see the operation."

Close to the rear entrance was a tiled room stacked ceiling high with sacks of wheat flour which was used to make the dough for rotis, a flat Indian bread.

"Until recently, we made the rotis by hand," Arpan said, "but now we have an electric machine. Come and see."

A machine with a sizeable paddle-looking gadget pulled the dough until it formed a large ball. Allison followed the ball to another apparatus with large rollers that transformed the ball to the flat rotis. Once baked in the oven, volunteers dropped them into large vats.

Arpan explained, "We prepare over 200,000 rotis every day."

"I see people doing this by hand as well," Allison said, pointing to a row of women sitting on the floor rolling the dough on flat boards.

"No, they are rolling out the dough for chapatis. Then the chapatis are cooked on that large griddle over there."

Allison looked to where Arpan pointed. Both men and women used long, thin wooden spatulas to flip the flatbread. Once ready, someone gently placed them in plastic baskets.

After watching the people flip the flatbread without any breakage, Allison moved on to the rear of the kitchen. Here she saw an elevated area with large iron pots sitting above a fire pit fueled by a wood fire.

"What's inside the pots?"

"Lentil soup in these larger iron kettles, and rice in the smaller stainless pots over there," he said.

"The men you see standing next to the kettles are stirring the lentil soup with long stainless poles."

"That pole is taller than the man. How do you fund all of this equipment and food?"

Arpan explained, "Donations pay for everything. People

in our religion are required to donate ten percent of their earnings to people who have needs. Local communities and outlying farms donate the food."

Walking into a separate room off the kitchen, volunteers sat on the floor behind piles of potatoes, quietly chatting as they peeled. In front of them were other workers who chopped the vegetables eventually served with the lentil soup.

As Allison continued the journey around the kitchen, she noticed a large hall with a marble floor. "What happens in there, Arpan?"

"Right now the men have finished cleaning the floor with the yellow machines you see in the corner. Soon long strips of carpet will be laid down in rows. The doors will open, and the people will file into that large room. Volunteers pass out the food between the rows of people."

"They sit on the floor to eat?"

"Yes, everyone does the same. We treat all people as equals. We teach the etiquette of sitting and eating—like a family or community."

In another part of this vast area, stainless dishes piled up waiting to be washed by other volunteers.

"These are from the last meal," Arpan said. "We serve three meals a day. Each dish is washed, but the utensils have three rounds of washing to be sure everything is clean."

"This whole operation is amazing." Looking through a large glass window, Allison could see the people waiting to enter.

The doors opened and a massive line of people quietly filed in, barefooted, with no one racing ahead. For such a large number, there was little noise. As soon as the people filled up a row, they sat down waiting for the volunteers to come along and fill up their plates with rice, lentil soup, and vegetables. Although far from being gourmet or colorful to look at, the meal was hot, tasty and filled their stomachs.

Allison watched the volunteers as they walked up the rows with large pots filling each dish—organized, orderly, and without any disruption. After a short prayer delivered by a man with a megaphone, they were able to eat. Having learned about the operation of the soup kitchen, Allison thanked Arpan for the tour.

Just as Allison turned to leave, she saw him. Frozen in one spot, she could barely move. She took out her phone and pointed it at him as he sat there, cross-legged, and dipping the roti into his lentil soup. Thanking the cameraman for his help, she dismissed him by saying she had something else to do before returning to the office.

"Tell Abha I'll be a little late."

Unaware of being photographed, he ate and she watched. Then she dialed the number the detective gave her.

"Hello, sir. Allison Wagner is calling. I want to tell you that I stumbled upon Hari at the soup kitchen that's run by the Sikh. He's here now but not sure how much longer."

"Allison, I'll send someone right over, but he may not get there in time. Will you be able to follow him without calling attention to yourself?"

"I'll try. Even though Hari won't recognize me, I'll try not to be too conspicuous. I took several photos and will send them to you."

"Thanks, please be careful. Hari may be dangerous. We're not sure what kinds of things he's capable of."

"Okay, I think he's getting ready to leave. I better hang up."

Allison hurriedly walked over to where the exit door

was and hid behind a post. Soon everyone started filing out. She waited and waited until finally there he was, heading towards the same car she saw drive up to the airport. Quickly finding a cab, she directed the driver to shadow the Toyota.

They traveled only a couple of miles when the car stopped in front of a run-down house overcome by weeds and undergrowth. The house appeared to be uninhabitable and in disrepair with the windows boarded with plywood. She asked the driver to pull over to the side of the road so she could watch as the man headed towards the door. He pulled out a key and attempted to open a large padlock attached to the door. He strained to push the door open and stepped inside. Just as he started to close it, he looked up and saw a parked car with two people watching him. Allison rapidly ducked behind the driver's seat.

"Do you think he saw us?" she asked the driver.

The driver turned around and observed his passenger crouched on the floor. "Yes, I believe he did. Okay, lady, what's this all about?"

"Nothing, go. Take me to the police station now!"

Chapter 24

LYNNE

SUNSHINE FOLLOWED THE several days of rain, but there was little happiness at the Mukta Café as the women prepared the site for Kumar's last rites. It's always sad to accept death, but so much harder when the life of the deceased had barely begun.

The women removed the tables in the café and set up chairs at the side of the room. Kumar's body was transported from the hospital and laid at rest on a mat positioned on the floor so that his head pointed towards the south.

"This is the direction of the dead," Chandra explained. Then she lit an oil lamp and placed it near his young body. "The purpose of this lamp is to shed light onto the soul as it leaves the body."

"What is the red string for?" asked Lynne.

"We call this the Molli," answered Chandra. "After cleansing the body, we will tie the string around Kumar's big toes. This process will help the soul leave the body."

Parvati brought over a jar of purified water. The two women bathed the boy's body to remove all impurities and dressed the child in a white garment. They smeared sandalwood paste on his forehead and dribbled several drops of water from the Ganges River onto his tongue.

"Is this all part of liberating the soul?" asked Lynne.

"Yes, all of this is to help the soul leave the body."

Kiri, consumed with grief, insisted on helping as she placed a few basil leaves at Kumar's right side and then sprinkled turmeric around his body.

"What Kiri is doing is forming a protective boundary to keep negative energies from damaging the soul," Chandra pointed out.

Several men placed Kumar's body on an Arthi made of bamboo and hay. They wrapped a garland of marigolds around his neck and positioned his hands in prayer. Parvati, whose job was to greet customers as they entered the café, now greeted mourners as they arrived to view and pray over the body. Several people read hymns and prayers from the Vedas, a book of sacred Hindu scriptures written in Sanskrit. The priest then led the small group of mourners with the recitation of various mantras to ensure a peaceful change-over for Kumar as he crossed over to his next life.

"We do not touch the body at this time, Lynne," cautioned Chandra, covering Kumar's body with more marigolds. "We consider the body to be impure."

Kiri's oldest brother presided over the funeral rites. "We refer to his role as the Karta," said Chandra.

"Do the men shave their heads for this?" asked Lynne. "None of them have hair."

"Yes, it's protocol. I hired a barber to be in attendance to assist with this ritual."

Barefooted, the men were now ready to parade the stretcher over to the crematory while the women remained back at the café.

Lynne walked over to Naomi and whispered, "Why is it the women don't attend?"

"Ya got me. Maybe it's a superstition," said Naomi. "Do you know what they do once they reach the crematory?"

"I think Kiri's brother is the one who lights the fire," said Lynne, "at least that's what I've heard. Here comes Parvati. Let's ask her."

"Parvati, what happens once the men reach the crematory?"

"Kumar's body will be placed upon a pyre. Then Kiri's brother will encircle the boy three times in a counter-clock-wise direction, sprinkling water on him."

"Is it Kiri's brother who lights the fire?" asked Naomi.

"Yes, he's the Karta. He'll set the pyre on fire with a torch."

"That would be hard for me to watch," said Lynne.

Parvati smiled. "Yes, and think how difficult that would be for Kiri to witness which is why we have the men go to the crematory."

Lynne nodded her head. "That answers the other question we had."

"After the cremation, they will go to their homes to bathe and change into clean clothes," Parvati continued. "Tonight they'll return for a meal which we'll prepare."

Two days later, Kiri's brother went to Parvati's house where Kiri was staying until she could find more permanent living arrangements. Lynne and Naomi happened to be there to help her as she progressed through this challenging period of mourning. Her brother, carefully holding onto a package, handed it over to his sister. "Here is the urn with Kumar's ashes."

Kiri broke into deep sobs as she held the urn close to her chest. Lynne walked over and sat down next to her on the couch. She held onto Kiri as she had done a few days before at the hospital. So much change for Kiri in only a week's time.

"What about the ashes?" Lynne asked Kiri's brother. "I've heard they eventually have to be placed in a river, is that right?"

Kiri looked up at Lynne. "I want to go to Varanasi to drop Kumar's ashes in the Ganges River."

"Varanasi? Where's that?" asked Lynne.

"Kiri, that's such a distance," cautioned Parvati.

"I know, but that's what I need to do. I can go by bus."

Kiri's brother said, "That's about a 24-hour trip."

"How long is it by car?" asked Lynne.

"Eight hours," said Naomi. "You know, Varanasi is a city I planned to travel to while I was here. Do you think Chandra would lend us her car?"

Kiri's face brightened. "Will you two go with me?"

"I don't know. We would need to get permission from Chandra to not only use her car but to get a couple of days off from the café," said Naomi.

"We could go over the weekend and just take Monday off," suggested Lynne.

Kiri's brother listened carefully to the conversation. "Okay, you can use my car." Naomi and Lynne looked at each other.

Lynne said, "Well, there is one small problem. Who will drive? Not me."

"Me, neither," said Naomi, "not on roads shared with camels, elephants, and cows. Plus driving on the opposite side of the road with the steering wheel on the right side of the car. That's a disaster waiting to happen."

"Not a problem," said Kiri, "I can drive."

"You can? Okay, if we can get Monday off and you drive your brother's car, we're in."

Chapter 25

KASI

"I DIDN'T TELL anyone where I was! Why don't you believe me?" Kasi cried out to Hari as he looked through a crack in one of the boards covering the front window.

"I tell you a car with two people inside followed me here. When I pulled over, so did they. I wasn't sure at first, but as I was shutting the door, I looked over and saw them watching me. Some man was driving, and the lady in the back ducked behind the seat. Someone knows where we are. I didn't tell anyone, so it must have been you." He reached over and grabbed Kasi's hair.

"Ow! Stop it! I know nothing about this."

"I'm going to ask one more time. Who did you tell?"

"Who could I tell? You have me locked up in a room all day. I haven't left this place for . . . I don't know how long. So, you tell me, how could I tell anyone?"

Hari shoved Kasi into the bedroom and locked the door. He reached for the phone and punched in some numbers.

"Hey, it's me. Someone is casing the house. I'm pretty sure of it. A car with two people inside followed me and pulled over to the side of the road. I noticed them as I started to close the door. I've got to get out of here, and that's going to take some money."

Kasi pressed her ear to the door trying desperately to hear what was said, but it was difficult following the one-sided conversation. She knew there had to be someone else involved. It no longer made sense that revenge was the motive. There had to be another reason, but what was it? It was difficult following the one-sided conversation.

"Look, I'm sick of this whole thing. You made it sound like such an easy way to earn some cash. The deal we decided on is not the deal you're asking for now . . . Hey, I was supposed to grab and hide her. That was the deal. Now that I have done that, you want me to go a step further and do away with her? I've done stuff before but never killed anyone. Besides, we've grown fond of each other, ya know? . . . Hey, you need to fork over some cash. I'm totally out of money . . . Oh no, if you want her dead, then you do it yourself. I agreed to the hiding stuff—never that. . . . You never mentioned anything about killing her . . . You better hand over some cash tonight. Things are getting desperate. Look, I'll meet you at the Nizammuddin Railway Station just southeast of India Gate tonight at 10:00. You better be there with money."

What Hari said baffled her. Who was on the other side of the phone conversation? Who wanted her dead? She heard Hari's heavy footsteps, so she rushed back to the bed. He opened the door and barked his orders, "Come on, we gotta get out of here."

"Where are you taking me? I need to know what's going on."

Hari grabbed her wrist, yanked her off the bed, and attempted to drag her out of the room. Upon doing so, two of Kasi's glass bangles broke apart and smashed to the floor. She looked behind her as she saw the shattered pieces strewn across the room.

"Please, stop pulling my arm. I'll come. You're hurting me."

Hari looked out the door and saw no one, so he hurried Kasi over to the car and shoved her onto the floor of the backseat. He instructed not to get off the floor and she obeyed. Her wrists were sore with the left one bloodied from the cuts of the broken glass as it ripped from her arm. She felt her strength slowly leave her body. Broken and unable to function, she wasn't surprised that the two smashed bangles were silver. Silver symbolized strength. Hers was gone.

They drove for an hour before Hari came to a stop.

"Don't move, you hear me?" he yelled.

She heard the car door open and then slam shut. Worried as to where he took her and concerned about the phone conversation she overheard, she knew she needed to be on the alert for a way out. As she laid on the floor, it dawned on her that the air seemed different. Not fresher—just different. She no longer smelled the carbon gases of the city. With trepidation, she raised her body from its fetal position on the floor to look out the window. There were no buildings, no traffic, and no signs of human life in a city of over 18 million. They had to be in a remote area. Something as simple as the absence of car horns gave that away. All she saw were fields of dirt. Little growth, no trees—everything looked wasted and dried out.

Dusk approached and that frightened her. As a young child, she required a light when she slept. The dark stimulated her imagination, and she woke up screaming. Years later, she outgrew that need, but some circumstances triggered those concerns. This situation was one of them.

She looked towards the direction she believed Hari disappeared. Although difficult to tell with the night quickly descending, she thought she could see the outline of a shack behind a hedge of scrubby bushes. She ducked behind the seat when she realized he was heading back to the car. Opening the door, he dragged her out of the car and pushed her towards the shack. Once inside, he grabbed the restraints he hadn't used in several days and bound her to an iron bed set up in the far corner of the room. With not a word spoken, he left.

Kasi sat on the floor trying to adjust her eyes to the dark. The room was musty with the mixed smells of rotten wood and urine. She jumped upon feeling something furry run across her leg. She hoped it was a mouse, but knew otherwise. How did her life take such a terrible turn? All she wanted right now was to see her family. A few weeks ago, she excitedly packed to return for a family wedding. Kasi had been lonely living in New York, unable to work and with little opportunity to meet friends. She worried over how this nightmare would end.

Hari pulled up to the Nizammuddin Railway Station, turned off his lights and waited. He looked at his phone but there were no messages. Unsure of the kind of car the guy he was meeting drove, he held his breath each time the headlights of a vehicle approached. Checking the time—it was 10:15. He was late. Would he show? He better show. Hari desperately needed the money.

He rechecked the time—10:45. Just as he started to leave, a black Honda appeared.

Although Hari had never met this guy, he certainly could identify his voice. His heartbeat quickened as he spotted a rather tall, well-dressed fellow step out of the car and approach his vehicle.

"Hari, is that you?"

Hari got out of his car to meet up with him. "Yes, over here. Did you bring the cash?"

"Not all of it, but enough to get by until you fulfill your end of the deal."

Hari surveyed the guy who stood before him. He laughed.

"What's funny?" the guy asked.

"You, with all your respectability, your fine clothes, your gentlemanly manners. You are pure evil and you want to know why?"

"Not really. I don't have time for all this crap."

"I'm telling ya anyways. You deceive, trick and mislead. You pretend to be what you aren't. Now that I see you, I realize just how wicked you are."

"Shut up! Where is she?"

"Oh, well hidden. She's beginning to be a crank around my neck. Not sure why I wanted to marry her."

The guy laughed and handed him an envelope containing a hundred dollars' worth of rupees. "This is what you'll get for now. Sort of like a down payment, you know? I thought this would all be over by now. You're screwing things up. Get the damn job done. All of Delhi is looking for her."

"Hey, what about the rest of the money, and what am I supposed to do with her?"

"You know what to do. I'm not wasting my time spelling it out anymore," he said, heading towards his car.

Hari threw the envelope on the ground, spat on it, and watched the car speed off into the night.

Chapter 26

ALLISON

"THAT'S THE HOUSE," said Allison, pointing across the road.

"Are you certain?" asked the detective.

"Positive . . . I saw him go inside. Looks like no one lives there, but that could make it a good hide-away, don't you think?"

"Possibly." The detective got on his phone and sent a message to the station informing them of their location. He turned to Allison and said, "Okay, you stay in the car while we check it out."

Detective Mahor and Yash went up to the front door while a second officer walked to the back to case the place out. "No back door," he reported, "and all the windows are boarded up. Looks like the only way out is the front door."

They knocked and when no one answered, Yash checked the door and found it unlocked. The detective carefully went through each of the three rooms but found no one there.

One of the officers said, "It definitely looks like someone was here not that long ago. I see some clothing and traces of fairly fresh food."

After ten minutes of sitting in the car, Allison grew impatient and walked up to the house. She peeked around the open door to see what was going on but saw no one other than the police officers and detective.

"Find anything?" she asked in a hushed voice.

"Well, there were people here, for sure. Looks like they left rather suddenly. Do you think he saw you?"

"I don't believe so. We tried to be discreet but you never know."

"Well, people hiding tend to be hypersensitive and alert to their surroundings. Look around and see if anything familiar pops out at you."

Allison went from room to room and saw little until she headed into the bedroom.

On the floor she saw what appeared to be a couple of bangles that were smashed and scattered by the side of the bed.

"Guys, come here." She pointed to the broken pieces of glass. "I'm pretty sure these were part of a set of bangles Kasi wore on her wrist. Many of the bangles I've seen over here are made out of lacquer wood. Hers were made of glass very similar to these silver ones. Matter of fact, these could be hers. I remember she wore silver bangles as well as numerous other colors."

The detective took several photos. Then he bent down and swept the pieces into an envelope, secured and marked it as *bedroom*. While they were discussing the possibilities of how they ended up broken on the floor, the other two officers tested for fingerprints and took photos throughout the three rooms.

"Kasi seemed to be really invested in the bangles," said Allison. "I remember feeling her joy and enthusiasm as she expounded upon the symbolism of each color."

"These are silver. What do you know about silver?" he asked.

"Let me see," she said, pulling her notebook out of her

purse. "I remember jotting that down because I thought it sounded rather interesting. Here it is, silver stands for strength. Oh boy, I hope that doesn't mean anything."

Like what?"

"You know, from the loss of the silver bangles, she also lost her strength," explained Allison.

Just then, one of the officers called them into the kitchen. "Come see what I found." Yash pointed to a scrap of paper with a scribbled phone number on it. "Looks like our friend left a bag behind. Not much of value inside except for this piece of paper."

He handed the paper over to the detective. "Interesting, it appears to be a phone number." Looking at it more closely, he continued, "Definitely a number not found in India."

Allison glanced over his shoulder. "Huh, that's strange."

"What? Do you recognize it?"

"I sure do. It has a Manhattan area code. This number has to be a New York listing."

"Isn't Kasi living in New York?" the detective asked.

"Yes, she is. If it's hers, why would it be in his bag?"

Detective Mahor slipped the paper into a folder and marked it as evidence. "I'm taking a look outside to see if there is anything of interest."

Having committed the phone number to memory, Allison waited until the detective left the house and then wrote it down in her notebook.

Chapter 27

LYNNE

THE TRIP WAS long, the roads were not always smooth, and the sights from the car were unforgettable. No matter what Lynne and Naomi experienced in Agra, nothing could compare to the city of Varanasi. The city was considered to be one of the world's oldest inhabited cities in the world. The Hindu people believe the Hindu god, Lord Shiva, founded it. Located on the banks of the Ganges River, the Hindu people regarded it as the holy river. As the three girls traveled the eight hours, Kiri explained why it was essential to place her son's ashes in this body of water.

"You see, we believe that after death, there is another life."

"Reincarnation?" asked Naomi.

"Yes, how well we live now and the good deeds we do in this life will determine what will happen later."

"Isn't that called karma?" asked Lynne.

"Exactly. Think of all of this as a reflection. When you look in a mirror or the still water, what do you see? You see your reflection, right? How good you look depends on how much work you put into having a righteous life. This philosophy holds true whether it's preparing a meal, sowing seeds, or showing kindness to others."

Naomi said, "Someone once told me that reincarnation is like changing your clothes except your soul is changing its body."

Kiri thought about that and then nodded her head. "Interesting thought, Naomi. We feel if you are lazy or if you live a life of negativity that will affect your next life. Did I explain this okay?"

Lynne said, "Yes, of course. Please, Kiri, keep going. I find this pretty interesting."

"We believe that it takes about 52 million births and rebirths to be born a human."

"Fifty-two million?" asked Naomi.

"Yes, so we say if you are a human, be a good human or you will go backward, and in your next life you'll be born an animal."

"So what is nirvana?" asked Lynne.

"Nirvana is the state we reach when we no longer are reborn. We call it moksha. The purpose of the Hindu people is to reach moksha. But then there is the world of wealth, jealousy, temptations—all of that can interfere with living a good life."

"Probably our ego as well?" asked Lynne.

"Yes, our ego gets in the way, for sure. It is always a fight to control the ego."

"So tell us, Kiri, why is the Ganges River so important in all of this? I mean, not everyone who is a Hindu can have their ashes distributed in that river. What happens to them?" asked Naomi.

"See that sign?" Kiri asked. "It tells me to turn here to go to Varanasi. If I don't go on that road, I might not reach my destination. That doesn't mean I will never arrive. I might have to turn around or look for another way, but all of that will take a longer time, right?"

Both girls nodded.

We believe where we scatter a person's ashes is very

important. The holier the place, the better chance you will achieve moksha. Think of it as a direct road."

Lynne thought about what Kiri said. Not knowing much about eastern religions, it took a while to process. "Okay, so the Ganges River is considered a very holy place. Are you saying that you have a better chance of escaping the cycle of rebirth by having your ashes thrown in that river?"

"Yes, rivers are long, huh? The locations of many cities are on that river, but the part of the Ganges that runs by the banks of Varanasi is especially holy. If we lay a deceased person's ashes in the river, the transport of the soul to Nirvana will be swift."

Lynne added, "Which we call heaven."

Kiri replied, "Yes, heaven. Otherwise, there is a good chance you might return to Earth as a cow or a bird."

"Or an insect," laughed Naomi.

"See, all this conversation is good because we are now approaching the city. I have to tell you, don't be worried. This place is extraordinary, very holy. It is not an easy place to visit, but I believe you will leave feeling different about your life."

"What do you mean?" asked Naomi.

"You will see. Just be open to the experience. I reserved each of us a room at one of the ashrams. There are hotels in the city, but an ashram is the best place to be for this experience."

"What's an ashram?" asked Naomi.

"It's a hostel along the river bank—very reasonable cost. Many people prefer to stay there if they come for cremation or meditation and yoga.

It hadn't taken long to catch onto the uniqueness of this city. The evening approached and from a distance, Lynne could see the black sky highlighted with red and bright orange embers. Dust coated the streets resulting in dense air.

"Is that where the cremations are taking place?" Naomi asked.

"Yes," said Kiri. "It never stops. It goes on every day, all day. There is something like 200 bodies burned every day."

Naomi and Lynne looked at each other. No need to respond. They knew what the other was thinking. So did Kiri.

"Are you wondering if someone throws the ashes of those 200 bodies in the river?"

Naomi said, "Yes, how can the river handle that?"

"Varanasi is called the City of the Dead. So many people come here at the end of their life waiting to die and be cremated. Many people are hired to work at the crematories. Even the air smells of fire and smoke."

By now they had reached the ashram where they would stay for the night.

"Tomorrow will be an early start," said Kiri. "We need to be at the ghats to see the sunrise—very special to see that."

Lynne asked, "I don't mean to have so many questions, but what is a ghat?"

Kiri smiled. "No, please ask. I welcome questions. How else will you understand? The ghats are the steps leading from the street level down to the river. There are 88 sets of ghats along the river in Varanasi. Different ghats have different purposes. Some are for prayer services, some for bathing and others for the release of ashes and remains. If you look further downstream, that's where you see the orange sky from the fires. Those are the ghats where the cremations take place."

"So they cremate the bodies outside?"

Kiri sadly nodded her head. "Much like with my Kumar."

Chapter 28

ALLISON

"WHAT A BEAUTIFUL evening for a wedding!" Allison said, greeting Mr. Arun and his wife at the hotel.

"Have you ever attended an Indian wedding ceremony?" asked Mrs. Arun.

"No, I'm excited to be here," said Allison, looking at all the ladies wearing their colorful saris. "I even purchased one."

"Very nice," said Mr. Arun. "You fit right in."

"I had to have the housekeeper at my hotel help me put it on. There's a trick to all of this."

Mrs. Arun smiled, "Yes, but it does become easier."

Small white lights, clustered inside the trees and hedgerows, decorated the exterior of the hotel. The front canopy received the same treatment with strung lights stretched from one side to the other. Next to the massive front door, long strands of marigolds intertwined with lights dangled from the roof to the ground.

"This setting is breath-taking," said Allison. "It looks like a fairy tale."

"Have you seen the garden behind the hotel?" Mrs. Arun asked.

Allison shook her head. "Not yet. I just got here."

Mrs. Arun smiled and said, "Well, wait until you see the garden. It's spectacular."

The medley of drums and cymbals alerted the guests of the approaching band.

"What's that coming?" asked Allison.

"The Barat procession announcing the arrival of the groom," answered Mrs. Arun. "He will be sitting on a white horse surrounded by many men beating on drums and clanging cymbals. Much patience is needed because it will take him quite some time to walk the short block to us."

"Why so long?"

"It's part of the ceremony. Friends of his will walk beside him and encircle the horse as they dance and wave their arms to the constant beat of the drums."

Allison looked around at the crowd in attendance. "So many guests including children."

"Yes, in India, everyone is invited."

As Mrs. Arun predicted, the guests waited for over two hours for the groom to reach the hotel. The beat of the drums amplified as its distance narrowed. Finally, the groom arrived sitting on a horse decorated with red and gold embroidered livery. He wore an achkan or long white coat, white pants, and a white turban.

"He looks nervous," whispered Allison.

"Getting married can be an anxious experience. Are you married, Allison?" asked Mrs. Arun.

"I was but no longer. We ended up having different goals, and it just didn't work out."

"Oh, so sorry to hear that."

"No, it's okay. We married too young. Both of us didn't know what we wanted at the time. Who does when you're in college?"

Mrs. Arun shrugged her shoulders. "In India, many girls are married at a young age. Abha is an older bride."

"Older bride—at 26? That's amazing."

"We believe marriage is more of a sacrament than a contract. It's a means of spiritual growth."

"Abha told me that weddings span several days. She's been away from the office all week."

"Yes, we call this special part of the ceremony the Ghodi. You see the groom? How fine he's dressed? Much like a king. Soon you will see him strike a wooden plate, the Toran, with a sword."

The groom dismounted the horse and the men in the wedding party escorted him to a private room where he exchanged garlands with Abha. As this Varmala ceremony took place, hotel personnel directed the guests to the gardens located behind the hotel. Mrs. Arun was correct. As beautifully decorated the front of the hotel was, it didn't compare to what Allison saw in the gardens. The first thing she spotted was a large tree, heavy with leaves. From its branches hung colorful tea kettles. She wasn't sure what the symbolism of that was, but it didn't matter. It was different, memorable, and whimsical.

A short distance from the tree stood a long, four-foot barrier covered with white pleated fabric. Behind it was an elegant white love seat positioned on an elevated platform with a draped screen separating it from the night.

Everywhere she looked she saw a variety of unique groupings—round tables surrounded by linen cushioned chairs; draperies hung from metal frames above upholstered couches and settees; stations of food elegantly displayed; and over-sized, mushroomed-shaped fixtures positioned in strategic places to shed light.

Suddenly, Abha appeared in a red sari walking beside Jay, her groom.

"Oh, she's beautiful! In our country the bride wears white."

Mrs. Arun said, "Here we wear red. Do you see the decorative art covering her hands?"

"I think that's called henna," said Allison. It showed a long, curvy vine connecting delicate flowers that stretched from her hand onto several fingers.

"Yes, it's only a temporary tattoo and will fade away in a few days," said Mrs. Arun.

"Abha came into work earlier this week for only a few minutes after having her tattoo done. Has the tradition of henna been around for a while?"

"Over 5000 years. We say the darker the henna, the more your partner loves you."

"I find all this overwhelming," said Allison, "your country is so much older than mine."

Overhearing the conversation, Mr. Arun reached over and tapped Allison's hand.

"Most countries are." All three laughed.

The dancing, eating and partying continued throughout the night and early morning. It wasn't until dawn that Allison fell into bed.

Chapter 29

LYNNE

LYNNE WOKE UP the following morning with an intense headache. The smell of burnt embers permeated the walls of her room in the ashram that overlooked the Ganges. She forced herself out of bed, walked over to the window and saw the fires still burning. Below was the river. She thought back to the time when she was at the beach with her friends, Abby, Sara and Trina. Such close friends but not once had she corresponded with them. She reminded herself to do that.

What she saw below was no beach. The Ganges River was brown, polluted with garbage and human ash. The earliest part of a January morning was traditionally cool and crisp in India, but not here in Varanasi. Lynne figured it had less to do with the positioning of the earth and more with the constant bonfires that raged from the funeral pyres.

Soon the sun would make its grand entrance. The designated time to meet up with Kiri and Naomi was 5 AM to be at the ghats to view the sunrise. Below, wooden boats suddenly appeared out of the darkness. Boats that carried stacks of wood—wood piled higher than she thought possible without having the boats topple over into the river. Lynne wondered about that wood. How much lumber did the country go through to keep those pyres burning? From where did they get the wood? Were unprotected forests being stripped?

She hadn't seen too many wooded areas while traveling through the country.

All three women met in the downstairs lobby. They arrived at the ashram late at night and didn't have too much of a chance to look around. Lynne stepped outside and took a photo with her phone thinking she would send this to her parents as well as her friends back in New York. She wondered what they would think when they saw it. The ashram was larger than she had imagined—four floors with the top floor being an outdoor patio. The second and third floors housed rooms, each having a narrow balcony.

The building was bright red with blue shuttered windows. Black Sanskrit letters written on large signs hung on the façade that faced the river. She had no idea what they said and thought perhaps they were either advertisements or graffiti. The inside was spacious with high ceilings and tacky furnishings. This place was, after all, a hostel. A place where people stayed to meditate by the holy river and further pursue their yoga skills. Pilgrims and students never saw the site as gaudy. Her room was neat—not much more than a bed and a chair, but it was clean. She decided that her expectations needed to be adjusted. After all, this was Varanasi, India.

Kiri clutched a small clay vessel that held the remains of her son. Lynne knew this had to be an emotional day for her. The conversation in the car yesterday provided a brief reprieve as they drove to the city. It was an opportunity for Kiri to focus on something else—a distraction. This morning was different as reality sunk in.

Kiri, still sensitive to the burn scars on her face, partially covered herself with her scarf. At the café she was amongst her friends, other burned victims. The customers that came in knew her. She could pretend to be the Kiri she once was, open and bubbly. Here, in an unknown city, she felt self-conscious.

Lynne's instincts were correct, so she was thankful she decided to accompany her. Having Naomi along was also a positive thing. Kiri had grown close to Naomi as the two worked together on administrative affairs. Hoping to build her confidence, Naomi and Lynne decided to take a back-seat and let Kiri take charge. She would lead the way. This ended up being an excellent plan because now that they were in Varanasi, neither of the two girls knew where they were going.

They followed Kiri from the ashram to the street level.

"Couldn't you scatter your son's ashes in the water in front of our place?" asked Naomi.

"No, we have to go further downstream. There are boats we can rent that will take us further out into the river. I think that would be best, so none of Kumar's ashes get caught up close to the bathers."

"That makes sense," said Lynne.

Lynne found this city fascinating as she watched hordes of people going about their day at 5:30 in the morning. There was something different about these people from the ones in Agra. They smiled less, appeared to be needier, and many looked sickly.

"First we make a stop at the money changers," Kiri said. "What we do is change a few rupees into smaller coins to give to the beggars as we approach the ghats."

The girls followed Kiri's lead, not entirely understanding what would confront them. The money changer's kiosk contained a multiple of items—clay vessels, large water containers, CDs, brass bells, scarves, the usual hodge-podge of stuff. With their coins in hand, they approached the ghats by the river. Here the smells were the strongest—a blend of cooked food and burnt residue.

People of all ages, each on their own step, sat with blankets draped around their shoulders. Frail knees bent to chins, walking sticks propped against their bodies, and hands stretched out. It was automatic; a response practiced daily. No words spoken. No harassment. Just the open palm of a hand as two dark eyes bore into the giver's soul. Each step Lynne took meant a coin left her hand and went into theirs. It hardly seemed enough. She should have changed more. There was no utterance of appreciation or plea for more. Lynne wondered if there was life inside the bodies that lined each step leading down to the holy river.

On several of the ghats there appeared to be somewhat of a community with small groups of three or four gathered together cooking their morning meal over a small Bunsen burner.

Naomi gestured to a lone man walking barefoot, wearing a ragged white shawl and holding a long make-shift walking stick. His dreadlocks were tied up into a knotted ball partially hidden by a red scarf wrapped around his head.

Kiri said, "That's a sadhu, a holy man. They are people who gave up on everything material. They've left behind homes, families, jobs, and money. They support themselves by accepting donations from people on the street. If you take their photo, expect to give them a rupee."

"Do they have mental or emotional issues?" asked Lynne.

"I don't know," said Kiri. "You know that karma we talked about on the drive up here? They pretty much have none. Some sadhus have renounced the world and are devoted to Vishnu, a Hindu god. We have many of them in India and Nepal, and they pretty much roam from place to place. That man is from a specific sect called Vaishanava. I know this because he has three vertical red lines on his forehead."

"So there are other sects?" asked Naomi.

"I say maybe five. I've found the strangest are the Nagas and Aghori Sadhus. The Nagas cover their body with ashes to remind them of the end. They tend to live in caves specifically found in the mountains. The Aghori Sadhus live with ghosts and pretty much hang out in cemeteries."

"You have cemeteries? Why would you need cemeteries if you cremate the deceased?" asked Naomi.

"Oh, some people are never cremated—the sadhus being one. It's the belief that these holy men do not have any attachment to their body and have already given up their karma, so they are buried sitting in the lotus position."

"Really?" asked Lynne, approaching the steps leading to the water. "Who else doesn't get cremated?"

"Children under five. They're innocent at that age, so there's no bad karma."

"I see, no need to quicken the release of their soul from their body to start their next rebirth?" said Lynne.

"Yes, you are learning fast, Lynne. Okay, now that we are on the steps leading into the water, let's stop and take this scene in."

"Is there a reason these men are swimming?" asked Naomi.

"No, not swimming. They are bathing in the holy waters."

"I've seen this on TV," said Naomi. "I can't believe I'm here where it all happens. Amazing."

"They come here to bathe to rid themselves of their sins. The Ganges River heals," said Kiri. "Stay here while I talk to that man about his boat."

As Kiri walked over to negotiate a price with one of the boat owners, Naomi and Lynne stood mesmerized. The drone of constant chatter, bells, people purchasing food, laughter, cries of babies—all of this provided sensory overload.

"Lynne, look over at the horizon. The sun is coming up."

"It's such a brilliant color of orange," said Lynne.

"Its light is crafting quite a mystical setting with the fog hanging over the water. I've never experienced anything like this before," said Naomi.

Taking a quick photo, Lynne said, "This moment needs to be preserved."

Kiri came up to them and announced, "We have a boat. Let's go. It's nothing fancy; a little rickety but not expensive."

The man rowed the boat up to the dock for the girls to climb in. "So this is safe?" Naomi asked.

"Yes, this is good. No worries." Kiri climbed in and made her way to the far end as she held her precious clay vessel. Naomi and Lynne each took a seat at the side of the boat, anxious to view all the activity they passed on the shoreline.

The view of the ghats taken from the river was rather interesting. As they rowed closer to the crematories, they could see bare-chested men stoking the pyres with long poles. Some wore scarves around their mouth and nose to keep from breathing the full effects of the smoke. The girls could hear the crackle noise of the flames as the fires spewed cinders that coated the ground. Amongst the piles of rubbish roamed strayed goats looking for their next meal and feral dogs searched for scraps to fill their empty stomachs.

Lynne pulled the scarf from around her neck up to her eyes to protect them from the sting of smoke. Seeing vast piles of wood stacked as high as a three-story building, she remembered the questions she had. Lynne looked over at the man rowing the boat and asked, "How much wood is burnt every year?"

"Wood? Ah, yes. About 50 million trees every year."

"Fifty million trees?" repeated Lynne.

"Yes, much wood, right? For one corpse alone, it takes 600 pounds of wood. That is what my friend told me. He works at the crematory."

"Where does the wood come from?"

"I don't know. I see it stacked on boats coming down the river." He turned his attention from this girl with so many annoying questions.

Kiri continued to hold her precious Kumar's remains to her heart as she quietly meditated and stared at the water splashing against the side of the boat.

"We are away from the pyres," the rower said. "This would be a good time for you to scatter your ashes."

Kiri held onto the vessel not wanting to release it even though she knew she must. Quietly, Lynne and Naomi sat as Kiri prayed, opened the clay vessel and slowly lowered it into the river. The water swept up the ashes and carried them away. Kiri continued to watch as the boat returned to the departure ghat. No longer seeing any trace of Kumar's remains, she pulled out a garland of flowers and offered it to the holy river.

Approaching the dock, Lynne spotted a monkey positioned on a wall with a baby clung to her body. The monkey understood Kiri's loss and grieved for her.

Chapter 30

KASI

"I BOUGHT A burner, a cast iron frying pan, a large pot, and vegetables to make soup," Hari said, putting everything down on the table."

"I thought you had no money," said Kasi.

"A friend paid me money owed for doing a job."

"Job? What kind of job?"

"Why do you need to know what I do, huh? Make the soup." Hari filled the kettle with water and placed it on the burner. He pulled Kasi out of the bedroom and pointed to the vegetables. "Now, you cook."

Hari's breath smelled of alcohol. "Did you use some of that money to buy liquor?" Kasi asked.

"No more talk from you," he barked. "Cook . . . make the soup!"

Kasi walked over to the bag of groceries and pulled out onions, potatoes, carrots, and tomatoes. "I need a knife."

Hari surveyed the food laid out on the table. "Why do you need a knife? No knife."

"How do I cut the vegetables—with my teeth?"

"Oh," Hari reached in his pocket and pulled out a pocket knife, "here . . . now shut up."

Hari stumbled out of the make-shift kitchen area to the bedroom. He counted the money left in the envelope. "Shit, 1200 rupees. All this trouble and only 1200 rupees left." He looked over at the crumpled blanket on the stained mattress and laughed. "At least I get payback. That's worth something. Hey, Kasi, come here. Payback time."

Kasi closed her eyes and pretended not to hear.

"Hey, woman, payback time."

She knew just how far she could push and when he drank, it wasn't far. Shaking her head, she yelled, "Not now, Hari, I'm making you the soup. Later, okay?"

Slowly, she diced the onions, peeled the potatoes, and cut the carrots. She felt it essential to drag out this whole process of making soup. It gave her the time needed to plot how she would escape from this hell-hole situation. Not much time passed when Hari's snoring vibrated throughout the shack. How she hated that snoring. How she hated him.

She peeked inside the bedroom and saw he was in a deep sleep. On the floor next to where he doze, she spotted his phone and the key to the front door. Cautiously, she tiptoed into the room and picked up both items. Her heart pounded so hard she thought for sure it would awaken him. For the first time, she felt there was hope and knew she needed both of those items to get away. As she turned to leave, she saw Hari's phone showed a missed call. Out of curiosity, she opened it only to realize the number was familiar. It was Keith's cell number. Why would he be calling Hari?

Hari stopped snoring and turned over on his side. She carefully placed the phone back on the floor and left the room with only the key. With no time to lose, she struggled to figure out how to unlock the door. After years of neglect, the rusted lock did not properly work. She turned the key and pulled on the door. It was stuck. Just as it started to give, a hand reached over her shoulder and slammed it shut.

"Where do you think you're going, huh?"

Kasi, frozen in her tracks, attempted to move but her feet would not function. Hari's big arm wrapped around her neck and pulled her away from the door. She struggled, but his grip tightened until he lifted her up and threw her across the room. Her body hit the stove and fell to the floor dumping the hot soup over the left side of her body. Hari pulled her up off the floor and slapped her across the face. Kasi struggled, grabbed a cast iron pan and swung it against the side of Hari's head. Realizing she knocked him unconscious, she knew this wasn't the time to surrender to the excruciating pain that tore at every nerve in her body. She headed towards the half-opened door and onto the overgrown path leading to freedom.

Kasi wore no shoes, making it difficult running on the stony path. She refused to rest or even turn around for fear he would be right behind her. If he was, she didn't want to know. After what seemed like an endless amount of time, her body begged to slow down. Out of breath and with bloody feet, her body screamed of pain. She pulled at her soaked blouse that now clung to blistered skin. The adrenaline that gave her the strength to move, no longer existed. Ahead, she spotted two women carrying burlap sacks of dried grass on their heads.

"Help me, krip-yaah (please)?" she screamed.

The two women turned and saw a woman with a blackened eye and a swollen lip stumbling towards them. Her soaked blouse was torn down to her waist. One of the women pulled her bundle of grass off her head and reached out towards her.

"What happened to you? Where did you come from?"

Kasi fell into her arms crying. "I've been abducted and raped by this awful man, Hari Chubney. I got away by knocking him out with a pan. He had me locked up in a shack a mile or so down the road."

One of the women said, "Oh, the Sumer farm's shed. Is he still there?"

"Haan (yes), I think so but he may be coming after me. I don't know. Krip-yaah, help me."

"Come with us. We'll take you to our house." They unloaded their bundles onto the ground and supported her as she walked over the uneven path.

Hari opened his eyes and saw double. He put his hand on the back of his head and felt blood. At first, he was unsure of what happened or how he ended up on the floor with his head thrashed in pain. The room started to move. He looked around and saw the spilled soup on the floor lying near the iron frying pan. Slowly, his vision returned, and he mentally focused on the events leading up to the struggle that took place between him and Kasi. Hari stood up and stumbled towards the open door. Once outside, he was uncertain which direction she went. Looking around the surrounding area, Hari saw no trace of anyone. Hari reached for the opened bottle of liquor he left on the porch. He swallowed a mouthful, sat down on the porch step and held his head. How could all of this get so screwed up? Returning to the cabin to get his phone and car keys, he realized he better leave. They would be searching for him.

Chapter 31

ALLISON

"MS. WAGNER, THIS is Detective Mahor. I have some good news for you."

"Good news? Is it about Kasi?"

"Yes, she was found late last night."

"Is she okay?"

"She's in the hospital right now. She has first degree burns on one side of her body due to a pot of soup that tipped over on her. So that's being addressed as well as serious bruising on her face, neck and torso—some in different stages of healing."

"So she'll be okay?"

"Physically, she'll recover. Right now the concern is centered on her emotional health. She's endured some pretty scary stuff the past couple of weeks."

"Can she have any visitors?"

"From what I've heard, not at this time. She's exhausted and is in great need of rest. Plus her assailant is still loose. We secured her room, and only family and medical personnel can visit."

"I understand, Detective Mahor."

"Anyway, you've been of great help to her family and me. I wanted you to hear the news from me instead of reading about it in the paper. News should break sometime today. We have photos of this Hari Chubney that we will be posting both in tomorrow's paper and on TV hoping someone knows of his whereabouts."

"Could you let me know when it would be okay to visit?"

"Yes, we'll let you know. Namaste."

Allison turned back to the notes she had on Abha's wedding. She planned a section of her documentary to address arranged marriages. It was not an easy topic to cover because the line that separated centuries of cultural practices and women's rights was blurred.

Today Abha and Jay left for their wedding trip to Sawai Madhopur in Rajasthan. Abha mentioned they plan to spend several days on a safari in Ranthambore National Park. Abha showed Allison a brochure of the hotel that looked more like a palace.

"Everything is marble," Abha said. "There are several courtyards with rooms along the perimeter. Each room is huge with an equally large bath. The best part is the pool. Think of a large Olympic size pool surrounded by marble lions."

Allison thought it's probably good to go on a trip where the wedding couple can start bonding through shared experiences. The safari activity they signed onto sounded like fun. Besides seeing deer, monkeys and other forest type animals, the search will be for the tiger. Abha told her they would be fortunate if they spotted a tiger.

Allison wanted to tell Abha that Kasi had been found and is now recuperating in the hospital but knew not to impose. It was an unrelenting urge that forced her to pick up her phone and text the message, "They found Kasi. She's in the hospital and will be okay. Still looking for Hari." She pressed SEND. *There, I let her know without imposing. If she wants to know more, she'll get in touch.*

"That was a good solution," she said aloud.

"What was a good solution?" asked Mr. Arun, walking into the office.

"Oh, good morning. Great wedding over the weekend, right?"

"Yes, it was. The weddings over here can be over the top."

"I'll say. There must have been something like 400 guests. That had to be expensive paying for the dinners, drinks, decorations—everything."

"The bride's parents pick up the cost of rooms and transportation for out-of-town guests as well."

"Really? I can't wrap my head around that."

"Makes me thankful I have two sons," Mr. Arun said, laughing. "Getting back to my question. What is a good solution?"

"Oh, haha. You know the missing girl? They found her. I don't know too much about it, but Detective Mahor called me just now to let me know. I wanted to let Abha know but didn't want to butt in on their honeymoon. I thought Jay might not appreciate that, so I text her. That way she'll know."

"That's fantastic news! Are you going to the hospital later in the day?"

"No, Detective Mahor said it was too soon. Right now her room is guarded because Hari is still at large."

Just then her phone vibrated. Allison looked and sure enough recognized Abha's cell number.

"Received a reply from Abha." Allison looked at her phone and laughed. "She said, 'That's achchha! Looking forward to hearing about the details when I get back.'

Hmm . . . must be things are going well. By the way, what does *achchha* mean?"

Mr. Arun picked up a file and headed toward his inner office. "It means good news."

Chapter 32

LYNNE

"YEAH, VARANASI WAS hard to describe. You know how you sometimes decide to do something for someone, but then get much more back in return?" asked Lynne.

Chandra smiled. "Happens a lot."

"I mean, I would never have traveled to that place. I never heard of it. I thought it would be, you know, just another city like Delhi and Agra. Seeing the ghats, the fires from the crematories and the activity alongside the Ganges River was surreal."

"That was kind of you and Naomi to accompany Kiri. How did she handle everything?"

"In the beginning, I'd say she did okay. We had a lot of questions for her which took her mind off her problems, but the next morning when the time came to release Kumar's ashes, that was quite rough on her."

Just then the door swung open and Naomi stepped into the café. "Are you telling Chandra about our visit to Varanasi?"

Lynne nodded her head. "I said that I would have never gone to Varanasi if it wasn't for Kiri wanting us to join her."

Naomi nodded. "I knew of Varanasi and hoped that I could figure out how to get there. I feel terrible that it was under such terrible circumstances. Chandra, did Lynne tell you about the monkey?"

"I didn't," said Lynne, "go ahead and tell her."

"Well, we were on this boat that took us out on the river so that Kiri could release Kumar's remains. She was having a difficult time with that until finally, she opened the lid and dipped the vessel into the water letting the ashes disperse. On our way back to the ghat, we saw this monkey sitting on a wall watching us. I mean, no fooling, she had us in her vision the whole time."

"Plus she was nursing her baby," added Lynne, "don't forget that part."

"Yeah, that made it even more dramatic. So we get to the shoreline, and I swear the mother monkey was crying."

Chandra asked, "Do you think she understood what was happening?"

"Yes," said Naomi, "no doubt in my mind. She knew Kiri lost her child and felt compassion for her. I never thought much about animals displaying compassion."

Chandra asked, "Ever have a pet dog? They know when their owner is sad or frightened. Animals can feel that."

Naomi said, "I never had a pet so experiencing that was never a possibility."

"Monkeys are sensitive animals. That's an incredible story," said Chandra.

Lynne said, "Yeah, a perfect closure to all that happened."

"Hey, Lynne, not meaning to change the subject, but how is Jaya?"

"Right now she's recuperating from her first procedure. I received a phone call from Dr. Joshi's office in Delhi. I guess he had some family problems and had to leave before the end of his week here. He asked if she could travel to Delhi for another procedure next week. He feels enough time will have passed for the swelling to go down and wants to finish the grafting around her ear. I didn't pass it by her but told the office we could make the trip by bus. Is that okay with you, Chandra?"

"When it comes to these girls and their mental stability, you are in charge. I'm not interfering with that. Why are you smiling, Lynne?"

"What you said makes me feel good inside. I appreciate the trust you have in me. Thank you for that. It sure boosts my confidence."

"If I thought you were making wrong decisions, I would step in. So far you are doing a great job. Keep it going. Plus the ladies like you, Lynne. That's important."

"Speaking of the ladies, I have this idea I want to swing by you," said Lynne. "Dr. Joshi had mentioned there was this laser machine that does an amazing job minimalizing scar tissue with very little evasive cutting. I guess it costs around $150,000 to $200,000. He said there was one at the Delhi Hospital, but the clinic here doesn't have this equipment. I got to thinking maybe we could help raise money for one— you know, have fund-raisers and telethons. It might take a few years, but if we set up the fund-raisers as annual events, maybe the money to buy the machine could be raised."

"What's your take on that, Naomi?" asked Chandra.

"I like that idea, but what will happen after we leave? We'll be gone in a couple of months."

"Perhaps we could get a few things started. You know, set the groundwork. We can form committees so that each of the ladies would have a turn working at their special fund-raiser. Then after we leave, the precedent will have been set."

"What kind of fundraiser do you have in mind?" asked Chandra.

"What about our first one being a fashion show?"

"A fashion show?" questioned Naomi.

"Yeah, why not? Fashion shows have beautiful models, right? What better way for the ladies to feel lovely than to dress them up in beautiful outfits and walk the runway."

Chandra said, "I think you're onto something here, but we'll need to present it to the ladies. I don't want anyone feeling uncomfortable."

Lynne said, "Okay after the café closes tonight, can we hold a short staff meeting? I'll explain everything to them."

"You'll need to let them know that this is something they don't have to do if they feel uncomfortable," warned Chandra.

Naomi laughed. "No worries, Chandra, by the time Lynne gets through explaining all of this, they'll all be fighting to be models."

"Now, what do you mean by that, Naomi?" laughed Lynne.

"It's all good. You have this persuasive way about you, that's all."

"Yeah, I heard that a lot from my mother."

Later that day, Lynne waited until everyone finished their shift work. She made a pot of tea and went out to get the makings of sandwiches. While they were busy closing the shop, she and Naomi busily put chicken sandwiches together. They passed out the snacks; as the girls ate, Lynne described the laser machine and how helpful it would be for them as well as anyone else who was a victim to acid attacks or other severe burns.

Naomi said, "You know, the idea of a craft fair for a fundraiser could be fun. All we would need to do is set things up, and the vendors would rent spaces for the kiosks."

Lynne said, "Doesn't seem complicated. I also like that idea of a fashion show. What do you girls think about doing that?" Both Lynne and Naomi could feel the nervous energy as they discussed that event.

Lynne said, "The mission of the café is to let the public know that because something terrible has happened to your exterior, doesn't mean that you aren't the same person on the inside. What better way to show this than having a fashion show."

By the end of the talk, every girl signed up to be models. Everyone except Jaya and Kiri. It was too soon for them. Lynne let up on Jaya. She didn't want to put any pressure on her or make her feel uneasy in front of the rest of the girls. After the meeting, all the ladies excitedly talked about where they could inquire about donations of clothing to be used for the fashion show.

"I think we should model the latest in saris. The Sari Shop, several blocks away, might be the perfect solution. We could model their merchandise, and maybe the ladies attending would be interested enough to buy one or two," Parvati said.

"Now this surprises me," whispered Chandra. "The girls are excited about this."

"Naomi laughed. "Told you that would happen. Lynne here should give up her plans of becoming a counselor and go into being a carnival barker."

Lynne playfully punched her in the arm and then turned her attention to Jaya. "Hey, Jaya, how about walking me out to the bus stop?"

The two girls said their goodbyes and walked out into the evening air. "I don't want to be in the show, Lynne."

"You don't have to be if you don't want to, Jaya, but there are other ways you could help. For example, I need someone who is good at art. I think you are, right?"

"Yeah, why?"

"We'll need to put together tickets for the event. Plus posters advertising the fashion show will need to be made and tacked up around town. Then there's the job of setting up chairs and selling the tickets. Do you think you could do any of that?"

"Yes, all of it."

"Alright, let's meet tomorrow after the café closes and plan this out. Okay?"

"Yeah, that sounds good. And Lynne? Thanks."

Chapter 33

KASI

SHE STIRRED AND slowly opened her eyes. Above her was a tube dripping a clear solution into her vein. On the side table sat an apparatus hooked up to some other tube inserted in her nose. Her face felt funny and when she tried to touch it, all she felt were bandages wrapped around her head. The left side of her body felt numb. Bandages covered her shoulder and stretched down the side of her ribcage. She could only lift her head a few inches from the pillow, and when she did, a bright light shone in her eyes. It was the sun. A woman walked into the room, smiled, and wished her a good morning. She walked over to the window and closed the drape to keep the sun from irritating her eyes.

"Where am I?" the girl asked.

"You're in the Delhi Hospital."

"How did I get here?"

The nurse sat in the chair next to the bed. Some women coming from the field saw you running up to them. They believed you were running away from something or someone."

"Why am I in so much pain?"

"Do you remember anything? The left side of your body has been burned. We found you with your blouse soaked in scalding water."

The girl listened. "Yes, I do now. Where's Hari? Is he here?"

"No one by the name of Hari is around. Did you want to see him?"

"No . . . No! I never want to see him!"

"Then you won't," said the nurse. "Do you know your name?"

The girl said, "Yes, Kasi. My name is Kasi Beckham . . . er . . . Joshi—Kasi Joshi."

"So, Kasi, your family is here, and they're very anxious to see you. Would you like me to send them in?"

Kasi nodded her head. "I want to see my mother first. Is she here?"

"She is," said the nurse, "as well as your father, brother and husband."

Kasi flinched. "My husband is here? He's supposed to be in New York."

"Well, you've been missing a few weeks. Everyone has been searching for you, did you know that?"

Kasi said, "This wretched man grabbed me. I wanted to get away but couldn't."

"Don't worry; you're safe now. I'll go find your mother."

Shortly after, the door slowly opened and Kasi saw her mother. She looked much older than the last time Kasi saw her more than two-years-ago.

'Maa," Kasi cried.

Her mother rushed over and gently held her, mindful that her body was burned and bruised.

"Kasi, I was so worried. We didn't know what happened to you."

"Maa, I'm so sorry. I waited for Lalit in front of the airport, but then Hari showed up. He said Lalit had an emergency and asked him to go pick me up. That confused me. I couldn't understand why anyone would send Hari. Then he pushed me into his car and took me to this horrible house that was filthy."

"The police found that house. Were you there the whole time?"

"Pretty much until Hari became nervous thinking he was spotted. We then moved to this cabin far from the city. That place was even worse. Rats were running around. I think we were there for only a day or two. I had trouble keeping track of the time. It seemed like this nightmare went on forever."

"How were you burned?" asked her mother.

"Hari came back to the cabin acting drunk. He came into some money so bought a few vegetables as well as liquor. Hari always grew nasty when he drank. After demanding I make soup out of the vegetables, he went into the bedroom and fell asleep. I snuck into the room and grabbed his keys. As I struggled to unlock the door, he woke up. Hari was so angry, Maa. I was scared he would kill me."

Kasi's mother gently held her. "You don't have to say anymore if you don't want to."

"He threw me across the room, and I bumped the pot of soup off the burner. It tipped over and spilled all over me."

Kasi remembered what happened next. "Oh no, I now remember picking up one of those iron frying pans and hitting Hari on the head. I knocked him out which is how I got out of there. Do you know if he's dead?"

Kasi's mother shook her head. "No, the police are looking for him."

Kasi's heart almost stopped. "Maa, he's probably trying to find me."

"Detective Mahor assigned two officers to sit by your door for the next two days."

After a few minutes, Kasi's father and brother came in. They had an emotional reunion with Kasi's father apologizing for being so hard on her when she didn't want to marry Hari. "I didn't know he was such a bad person, Kasi."

"Nobody knew, Baap (father), nobody knew. I didn't like him."

Lalit expressed his regrets for showing up to the airport so late. "If I had only been at the airport on time, none of this would have happened."

Baap (*Father*) said, "Lalit, I always thought it very strange that both rear tires were flat. Why not the front tires? How did they get so many nails in them?"

Lalit agreed. "Never understood it. I now believe Hari had something to do with it, you know, to make me late."

Kasi spoke not a word. Instead, she listened to the dialogue taking place amongst her family members.

Maa said, "Kasi told me she was able to escape when Hari fell asleep, and she found his keys laying on the floor next to him."

"You were lucky, Kasi," said Baap.

Kasi nodded her head while fuming thoughts occupied her mind. *Was I lucky? You have no idea the abuse that man put me through. I would never call that luck!*

Her eyes scanned the room focusing first on her mother and then her father. When her eyes met up with Lalit's, his expression told her that he understood. No one needed to explain to him what kind of abuse she experienced. He knew.

Lalit put his arm around his mother's shoulder and said, "Okay Maa and Baap, we need to go and let Keith come in. Kasi, we'll let you rest and will come back later today, okay?"

Suddenly, the image of Hari's phone lying next to his keys popped into Kasi's mind. She wanted to tell her family she was frightened to see Keith, but they would think she was crazy. After all, Keith was in New York. He didn't know Hari. Why would he want Hari to harm her? Kasi recalled the moment she spotted his number as a missed call on Hari's phone. That was strange. Was he involved in all of this? She told herself there had to be an explanation. Maybe Hari contacted him for ransom money, and Keith tried to return the call. There had to be a simple explanation.

The door opened and in walked Keith. "Hello, sweetheart, so glad we found you."

Sweetheart? He's never called me sweetheart.

He continued talking, explaining in great detail all he went through in trying to locate her. Kasi listened but had trouble believing a word. It was always about him. This performance of concern and compassion was not what Kasi was accustomed to seeing.

He immediately started quizzing her about her abductor. What did she know about him? Did she know where he was now? She tried to remain calm, but inside she wanted to scream. *Were you the one who Hari talked to on the phone about a plan he didn't want to carry out? Were you the person who gave him money—the same money that kept him in liquor? What was that plan? Was it to kill me?* Instead, she remained silent.

She had nothing but a gut feeling and a missed call message on the phone. She needed to know more but realized she wouldn't be able to get any additional information if Keith thought she suspected his involvement.

Kasi closed her eyes hoping that would send a signal for Keith to leave the room. Instead, he stayed, watching her as she pretended to sleep. Through her partially closed eyes she saw him inspecting the apparatus hooked up to a breathing tube. *What is he doing?*

The door opened and Lalit walked in with another doctor. "Keith, this is Doctor Kallawat, my partner. He's agreed to take Kasi as a patient."

Keith grew agitated. "Shouldn't I be consulted as to the care Kasi receives? She is my wife."

Lalit stepped back, a little surprised. "Of course, but we are here in Delhi, and I thought you would appreciate the help I could offer my sister. Dr. Kallawat is very experienced in the care of burn victims. Kasi does have first degree burns along the left side of her face, shoulders, and chest."

Keith nodded. "You're right. I'm just a little anxious right now."

Lalit said, "No worries, Keith. We all are pretty tired."

Kasi tried to alert Lalit with her eyes, but she wasn't getting through to him. When he and Dr. Kallawat started to leave, she desperately asked her brother to stay. She did not want to be alone with Keith. How could she tell her brother this? What logic could support those fears?

Dr. Kallawat left the room leaving Lalit and Keith sitting next to her bed. She closed her eyes pretending to be asleep. No one spoke. Ten minutes later, Keith received a text message so he excused himself from the room. Kasi opened her eyes and motioned for her brother to come close.

"Lalit, I have a very strong suspicion that Keith hired Hari to kill me."

"What? Kasi, that's crazy."

"No, it's not."

"Why would he want to do that?"

Kasi took a deep breath. "The past year, things hadn't

been going well with us. He's always agitated and complaining there's never enough money. I wanted to help out by getting a job, but he would not allow that. Instead, he constantly complained that I didn't budget the money well. It always seemed to be my fault."

"What does that have to do with killing you, Kasi?"

"I heard Hari tell someone on the phone that all he agreed to was to hide me, not to kill me. He kept wanting to know when he would get his money."

"What makes you think Hari was talking to Keith?"

"Remember when I told you that I grabbed Hari's keys as he slept? I also grabbed his phone and saw Keith's number listed as a missed call. Why would Keith be calling Hari? How did he even know Hari's number?"

Lalit stood up and walked over to the window. They were on the third floor facing an alley. The view wasn't the best—piles of trash with goats rummaging, looking for something to eat. A small boy, riding a rusted bike with a missing seat, raced through a wet mud puddle left over from the previous night's rain.

Lalit returned to Kasi's bedside. You know, I've been puzzled over how anyone knew the date and time of your flight's arrival. When I discovered it was Hari who picked you up, I wondered who told him. The only people who knew the details of your arrival were Maa, Baap, Rani and me."

Kasi struggled to speak. "What about Keith? He knew." Her breathing became labored. Struggling to sit up, she couldn't. Lalit examined her breathing tube and noticed someone had played around with the apparatus.

"I need to speak to the floor nurse. The oxygen flow going into your breathing tube is not correct."

Kasi said, "I fell asleep for a short time, and when I opened my eyes, I saw Keith looking at my breathing apparatus. You see, he's trying to kill me."

Lalit said, "Do you know if he took out a life insurance policy on you?"

Kasi shook her head. "I'm not aware of one, but I don't know much about that kind of thing."

"Okay, I'm going to see this through, Kasi, don't worry."

"I am worried. I don't want to be alone with him, Lalit."

Chapter 34

ALLISON

RELIEVED TO BE back in her room after a long week at work, Allison kicked off her shoes and flopped onto the bed. Weekends were for rest and catching up on personal matters, but none of that happened last weekend. Abha's wedding, however, was not anything she would have wanted to miss. Tables of food and drink were set up throughout the garden while small tea lights that hung in the trees gave the setting a magical appearance. But it took hours for Jay to arrive at the hotel on his white horse and to have all the guests at the wedding seated to witness the various ceremonies. Famished, it had been well into the night before she had anything to eat.

Allison felt fortunate to have been invited to Abha and Jay's wedding. Abha had explained the difference between love and arranged marriages and how functional it was for their parents to arrange their meeting. It was coincidental that this subject came up twice in the short time Allison was in India. Not only did she get a first-hand account from Abha, but Kasi had described her experience going against tradition and marrying for love.

Kasi? Allison felt relieved she was safe but troubled over where her abductor was and what he would do once his options ran out. Suddenly, she remembered the slip of paper with the phone number scribbled on it. She walked over to her purse and pulled it out. It had fallen to the bottom of her bag and was now crumpled and a little torn. She smoothed it out on the desk and took a good look at it.

"Yes, this is a Manhattan area code," she said aloud as though someone was in the room to hear. She reached for her phone and dialed the number. There was no immediate answer, and it soon went into voice mail.

"Hello, you've reached Keith. Leave a message, and I'll get back to you."

Allison hung up and stared at the phone. Keith? Kasi's Keith? Why was his phone number in Hari's bag?

She thought back to their conversation on the plane and her puzzlement over Kasi's answer when asked why she didn't replace the broken yellow bangles—the color symbolizing happiness in a marriage. *What happens, happens.* Allison had thought that was a strange response back then but even more so now. Kasi had explained that it was bad luck if any of the bridal glass broke. Just how controlling was that superstition?

Why didn't Keith come to India and accompany her to the wedding? Wouldn't he want to meet her family after two years of marriage? Could it be money, time or discomfort over the situation? Allison recalled Kasi's long silence when she asked if her husband traveled with her. She went from being a talkative girl, sharing and eager for conversation, to sudden shutdown with only a simple reply that her husband didn't come. Had a nerve been struck? Allison grabbed her jacket and decided she needed to share this information with the detective.

The bus trip to the station had become familiar. When Allison stepped off the bus, she felt relief to see the group of men who previously sat on benches and along the wall were no longer there. Once inside, the detective welcomed her into his office. He went into a general explanation of how these women discovered Kasi and the condition she was in both physically and emotionally.

"As of now, only family members are allowed to see her."

"Is her husband here?"

"Yes, he arrived after hearing she went missing."

"What's he like?" Allison asked.

"He seems to be attentive and concerned. Why?"

Allison pulled out the slip of paper. "When the officers were checking the house he had Kasi hidden in, one of them found a slip of paper with this phone number on it."

"What number is that?" the detective asked.

Allison seemed surprised that the detective didn't recall finding this.

"Oh, remember? They found it in a duffle bag that was left behind at the house. I happened to notice it had a Manhattan area code. I memorized the number and quickly jotted it down before I forgot. Never thought about it until today."

"Oh yeah, do you know whose number it is?"

"I called and it switched to Kasi's husband's voice mail. At least the voice on the recording identified himself as Keith."

"Do you have the number on you?"

"I do . . . here."

She handed it over to him. The detective gave it a quick scan. "This is Manhattan's area code?"

Allison nodded her head. He dialed it, but this time Keith answered.

"Hello, Keith here."

Caught off-guard, the detective replied, "Yes, this is

Detective Mahor. Uh . . . yeah, I'm calling to see how every-thing is with your wife."

"Oh, she's doing much better physically, but she doesn't want to talk about what happened to her."

"You might have to give her some time. She's probably in shock."

"Yeah, you may be right. By the way, how did you get my number?"

"Ah, one of the officers gave it to me. Not sure where he got it from, probably from someone in the family."

An awkward silence between the two took on a life of its own until Detective Mahor said, "Okay, we'll be talking."

The detective looked at Allison, nodded his head and said, "I believe we've found the answer to the question of how Hari knew the time of Kasi's arrival in India. Not posi-tive, hunches don't hold up in court, but the edginess of that conversation I had with her husband is shouting out at me."

Chapter 35

LYNNE

"THE FASHION SHOW is set up for next Friday," said Lynne. "Girls, the Sari Shop is opening their doors to us on Sunday. We need to be there at two o'clock to try on saris and choose three to model at the show. Is everyone okay with that?"

Except for Jaya and Kiri, everyone nodded. Kiri still grieved over her son's death. She tried returning to work but was not too productive. Chandra recommended she take a few days off. Jaya slowly recovered from her first procedure and looked forward to taking her first plane ride to Delhi for more extensive work. Chandra recommended taking a flight over the bus and suggested that Lynne accompany her.

The other girls looked forward to the show. It gave them something positive to think about as they distributed the flyers Jaya made.

Cheerful conversation spread through the café between the girls and their customers. Everyone wanted to know the details which resulted in the selling of more tickets than they expected. Chandra decided the venue needed to be moved from the café to a larger hall a block away.

Chandra walked into the café pleased to see how well everything was going. Lynne approached her with details of Jaya's scheduled operation. Chandra said, "Good thing you girls didn't leave for Varanasi yesterday."

"Why's that?"

"You haven't heard? There was a terrible accident yesterday afternoon. A 164-foot section of concrete from a flyover bridge under construction collapsed onto the highway below."

"Oh no! How did that happen?" asked Lynne.

"The beams constructed in between the columns of the flyover bridge were not tied with cross beams. Plus they think the mix of cement was not good."

"Oh wow, we were there just last weekend. Anyone hurt?"

"Fifteen people reported dead and ten injured. Some of those involved were bridge workers, but the others were in cars crushed under the weight of the concrete blocks."

"Oh, those poor people," said Lynne.

"This morning the news reported two were American girls visiting the country for a couple of weeks. They were with their host family in one of the cars."

Lynne's face paled. "Do you know anything about those girls? You know, where they're from and why they were in India?"

"No, why?"

"Hmm . . . this is a long shot for sure, but the two girls sitting next to me on the plane were from Long Island and were staying with a host family. I mean . . . what's the probability, right? Besides, they were staying in Delhi."

"These two girls were also staying in Delhi but were returning from visiting the ghats in Varanasi. Do you know their names?"

"No, not really. I didn't interact much with the girls. They were behaving quite spoiled on the plane complaining about their seats not being in first class, hating the plane food, and wishing they weren't on the trip."

"So why did they sign-up?"

"I don't know for sure, but I could guess. I think the girls' parents wanted to reset their priority button. You know, give them a taste of how some people live."

Chandra shook her head. "So send them to India?"

Lynne shrugged her shoulders. "I listened to them as we flew over here and pretty much felt sorry for their host family. It might sound a little crazy, but I've been thinking about them. You know, wondering how they've adjusted to life over here. I hope they weren't the two killed."

"Turn on the TV. It's been on the news all morning."

"I'll watch later. I need to check with Jaya to make sure she's all set for our trip to Delhi tomorrow. She's staying at the house with Naomi and me. This way we can leave for the airport together—less complicated."

Several hours later, Lynne and Jaya took the bus to Lynne's house. They walked in to find Naomi watching TV.

"Have you heard about the bridge?" Naomi asked.

"Chandra told me. She said two of the fatalities were Americans."

"Yeah, they're reporting now that both were college students living with a host family for a couple of weeks."

Lynne sat down in the empty chair. "I'm wondering if they were the same two girls sitting next to me on the plane."

"Most likely not," said Naomi. "I mean, what are the chances?"

"Are they showing photos?" asked Lynne.

"Not yet. Too soon, I guess."

"Not to change the subject, but would it be okay if you rehearsed the runway walk with the ladies?

"Me? Are you serious? Do I look like I have experience with that?"

"It's easy, Naomi. I've seen it on TV. Let me show you."

Lynne jumped up, paused with her face looking forward, chin up, right hand on hip, slowly walking with one foot directly in front of the other. After several paces she hesitated, looked from right to left, turned and walked back to where she started.

Naomi and Jaya bent over laughing.

"What's funny?" Lynne asked.

"You," said Naomi. Both girls got up and imitated Lynne's runway walk, exaggerating the hip and head action.

"I didn't look like that."

"I wish I had my camera," said Naomi, "it was too funny."

Lynne didn't mind being the brunt of the joke, especially since she delighted to see Jaya lose herself in the fun.

As the girls laughed, a picture of two girls flashed across the TV screen. Lynne caught a glimpse and immediately stopped to listen to the woman announcer:

"Two American college girls, Shelby Jessup and Kimberly Bentley, were on an exchange program from New York. They were two of the several people killed as the bridge collapsed onto the car they were riding in."

Lynne covered her mouth with both of her hands as she listened to the reporter. "It is them! It's the two girls that sat next to me on the plane. Oh, how awful!"

"Are you certain?" asked Naomi.

"I am. Everything matches. Although I didn't have much interaction with them, I did learn they were from Long Island and were freshmen in college. I feel terrible about how I totally ignored them on the plane."

"Why?"

"They had this snooty attitude. It kind of rubbed me the wrong way, but never would I wish this upon anyone, especially those two girls."

Chapter 36

KASI

"HOLD ONTO THE walker. You need to get out of bed and walk."

"It hurts too much," said Kasi to the nurse.

"I'll be right next to you. The more you walk, the stronger you will become and the sooner you can return to America. Where in America do you live, Kasi? New York? Los Angeles?"

Kasi lost her footing and almost fell onto the floor. The nurse caught her and helped her to stand.

"I don't think I can do this," Kasi cried. "Please, I want to stay here with my family. I don't want to go back to New York with him."

The nurse looked at her. "But why?"

"I can't say right now. Please, don't tell my husband I said that, okay? Don't let me be alone with him."

The nurse looked into Kasi's eyes and saw the desperation. "Okay, stay calm. It's not good for you to get so worked up. No one will force you to go anywhere you don't want to go."

"Thank you. I want to be with my family."

Although puzzled, the nurse nodded her head and helped Kasi maintain her balance as she struggled to walk down the long hallway.

"Well, look at you. I see you're becoming much stronger."

Kasi froze in her step. It was Keith.

The nurse looked behind her and saw Kasi's husband standing there. "Hello, uh . . . when did you arrive?"

"Just got off the elevator. How is my wife doing this morning?"

"A little better—right now we're trying to get her out of bed so that her muscles don't deteriorate."

"Here, let me help."

Kasi stared into the nurse's eyes. The nurse returned the look to let Kasi know she understood. "You know, it's still quite soon. I think it's better if I walk with her for now. Perhaps in a couple of days."

Keith looked displeased but said nothing as the three walked along the hospital corridor. "I heard she has first degree burns?"

"Yes, she's in quite a bit of pain, but once that subsides, Dr. Kallawat can work his magic. For now, the idea is to keep her moving so her muscles don't lock up, right Kasi?"

Kasi nodded her head as she avoided Keith's eyes.

After a full length of the hallway and back, the nurse took Kasi back to her room where the nurse positioned her in a recliner next to the window. She pulled the heart monitor over and hooked it up. "Here's a buzzer. Just press this button if you need anything, okay?"

Kasi nodded. She stared out the window hoping to avoid eye contact with Keith. He bent over and kissed her on the top of her head. She stiffened.

"Is something wrong?" he asked.

"Something wrong? I just spent the most harrowing days of my life—kidnapped, raped, beaten, and tortured. Sorry if I'm not greeting you with a cheery smile."

Keith sat on the edge of the bed. "Look, I didn't mean it

that way, Kasi. You're acting differently towards me. What's going on?"

"I don't want to talk about it now, Keith. I asked you to come with me to my cousin's wedding so you could meet everyone in my family. They all wanted to meet you, but you chose to stay back in New York to work. Maybe this would not have happened if you came along. Then again . . . maybe it would have."

Keith looked deeply into his wife's eyes. "I hope you aren't holding me responsible."

"Keith—now why would you think that?"

"I mean, you know—just because I didn't return with you."

Kasi wanted to scream and ask why his cell number was on Hari's missed call list, but she decided otherwise. She didn't want him to become suspicious. It was better to keep him off-guard, but doing so was difficult.

"Tell me about this Hari guy. Wasn't he the man your family had chosen for you to marry instead of me?"

"Yes."

"How do I know this whole kidnap thing wasn't a set-up?" asked Keith.

Kasi was shocked. What was he insinuating?

"Are you serious, Keith?"

"Oh, maybe you came back to meet up with him. Huh? Now that I think about it, you weren't that anxious for me to go with you."

"Keith, I asked you on several occasions, but you made it clear it wasn't a good time to leave work. Plus, why would I want to meet up with Hari? That's simply crazy."

"There is something I've wondered about, Kasi. Perhaps you returned to see Hari and used your cousin's wedding as an excuse—a pretty poor one at that."

Kasi tried to get out of the recliner, but the pain held her back. Instead, she shook her fist at him. "How dare you say that to me."

"Look, see how upset you get over a simple discussion? Could that result from feeling guilty?"

"Guilty? Guilty of what?"

"Perhaps you were dissatisfied with your life in New York. Maybe you wanted to see this Hari fellow, so you got in touch with him."

"How could I do that?" Kasi asked.

"Easy—there I was working hard to pay the bills. What were you doing? Nothing. Absolutely nothing. Maybe you got ahold of him and told him to pick you up at the airport. After a while, hmm . . . maybe things didn't go as well as you thought they would. Hari no longer owned a business. He no longer could offer you a comfortable life, so you decided you wanted out. Maybe this Hari was not happy with that decision—rejection is bad but being rejected twice can be intolerable."

"Get out of here. I don't want you here. Just leave," Kasi shouted.

Her voiced reverberated throughout the hospital, so much that the nurse came running in. "What's going on here?"

Keith shrugged his shoulders and gave a confused, pathetic look. "She's over-reacting. Could it be the medication she's on?"

The nurse went over to calm Kasi down. "I think it's best you leave now."

"I'm her husband and have every right to be here."

"I don't want him here," Kasi cried. "Make him go away."

The nurse walked over to Keith and said, "I'm sorry but

you'll have to leave." She put her hand gently under his elbow. "Please leave quietly, or I'll call security."

Keith tightened his brow. "This is not right. I'm reporting you to the head administrator."

"That's your privilege, but my first responsibility is to the patient. She's distraught over your conversation."

Keith picked up his jacket and stormed out of the room.

"Are you alright?" the nurse asked Kasi.

"Now that he's gone—yes," she said, crying into the sleeve of her hospital gown.

"I'll get you a cup of tea," the nurse said. "You need to rest."

After the nurse left, Kasi was alone with her thoughts. She rehashed the story Keith composed about her relationship with Hari. Surely, no one would believe that. Why would Keith think Hari didn't abduct her, but that she willingly stayed with him? How did he know Hari was no longer a successful businessman? Her family didn't even know that. How did he?

Enraged, Keith raced through the hospital corridor and slammed a food cart into the wall before he pushed open the door with such force that it nearly knocked over two young women—one with a severely disfigured face.

Chapter 37

LYNNE, KASI, & ALLISON

AFTER A SHORT plane ride, Lynne and Jaya arrived at the Delhi Hospital. They were to meet up with Dr. Lalit for Jaya's second procedure. As they entered the second floor, the door flew open nearly knocking them over. A man rushed past and hurried out the door.

"What was that about?" Lynne asked, approaching the reception desk.

"Someone in a big rush?" asked Jaya.

The receptionist stood up behind her desk as the door swung back and forth. "He appears upset about something. What can I do for the two of you?"

Just as Lynne was about to speak, Jaya stepped forward. "I'm Jaya Gowda. I'm supposed to see Dr. Lalit regarding a second reconstructive procedure."

"Yes, we are ready for you. Please take a seat and someone will take you to your room."

Lynne quietly smiled. She was thrilled that Jaya took the initiative on her behalf since that would not have occurred a few weeks ago. Getting her started with these procedures was crucial because eventually, she'll need to start doing things for herself. Depression robs a person of initiative. Hope returns the gift.

Shortly, a woman came by and asked Jaya to follow her. "The procedure you'll undergo is a little more extensive than the last one, so you'll be staying here for a couple of days."

"Dr. Lalit's office mentioned that to us," said Lynne.

"This floor of the hospital is primarily for burned victims. Here we are—Room 204. You'll have a roommate. The bed closest to the door is yours."

Lynne and Jaya stepped inside and saw a young woman sitting in a recliner by the window. Lynne thought she looked familiar. *Could this be the same person whose picture had been broadcasted on television the past several weeks as missing and was recently found wandering in the fields outside of Delhi?*

"Kasi, you have a roommate," said the nurse. "This is Jaya Gowda."

Kasi nodded to the new girl. "Namaste, please come in."

The nurse handed a hospital gown for Jaya to change into. As Jaya left to go into the bathroom, Lynne sat on the edge of the bed. A few awkward moments of silence transpired as both girls smiled and then stared at the floor.

"Are you an American?" Kasi finally asked, breaking the tension.

Lynne perked up. "Yes, I am. I'm from New York State, not the city."

"I lived in New York City for a couple of years, but I don't plan on returning."

Lynne was convinced. *She looks like the person shown on TV, and she just said she lived in New York City.* "How did you like New York?"

"Very nice place but busy. I plan to remain in India with my family."

"I see."

"What happened to your friend?" asked Kasi.

"Jaya was a victim of an acid attack. She's here to get reconstructive surgery on her face. Dr. Lalit is her surgeon. Have you been involved in acid attacks as well? The nurse told me this floor was primarily for burned victims."

"No, I had a pot of soup fall on me. Your friend will be happy with Dr. Lalit."

"Is he your doctor, too?" Lynne asked.

Kasi said, "No, he's my brother, so I'm a little biased."

"Your brother? Now that's a coincidence. He seems to be a very compassionate person. I know Jaya feels comfortable around him."

"Has her experience not been good with men?"

"No, the trouble had been with her father. He's the one who threw the acid at her because she didn't obey him. He pretty much intended to ruin her life. I'm hoping she'll realize she can adjust and take a different path. Hopefully, your brother's skill will work wonders on her as it has with some of the other girls at the café. How about you?"

"My father is a kind man. Right now, I'm having problems trusting other men."

"I'm sorry to hear that," said Lynne.

Before any further conversation could take place, there was a soft knock on the door. Lynne got up to answer it. Standing in front of her was the woman she had met at baggage claim upon arriving in India.

"Hey, aren't you the person that was on my plane from New York?" asked Lynne.

"Yes, I didn't expect to see you here. Your name is Lynne, right? I still have your card and planned on getting in touch with you about the work you're doing in Agra, but things have been busy here in Delhi. How is it going?"

"I've been busy as well, but it's a good busy since I love

what I'm doing. The ladies at the cafe are inspirational. I don't know how I would handle things if I had to endure what they go through day after day. They help me more than I help them."

"Why are you at the hospital?" asked Allison.

Lynne pointed to Jaya as she came out of the bathroom and climbed into her bed.

"This is one of the girls from the Mukta Café. She's here for reconstructive surgery, right Jaya? I'm just accompanying her." Jaya covered up part of her face with the sheet of her bed.

"Allison, is that you?" a voice called out from the recliner.

"Yes, it is. I've come to see you. Excuse me, Lynne, I have to say hi to my friend over there." Allison walked past Lynne and hurried over to Kasi. "How are you doing? I've been so worried about you." She gave Kasi a soft hug.

Kasi started to cry. "Right after I left the airport, everything turned bad. I heard from my brother that you were very helpful with the investigation."

Allison said, "Reports of your disappearance were continuously being broadcasted on TV. I happened to be standing outside the terminal and saw the exchange you had with some man. I believed what I saw could be helpful, so reporting it to the police was something I had to do."

"I also heard you followed Hari to the house."

"Yes, I saw him at the soup kitchen. I was there getting a tour when I spotted him in line. I'm so happy to see you're doing better. Things of this sort don't always have a happy ending."

"Thank you, Allison. Not sure how happy of an ending it is, but at least I'm alive."

"Are you okay?"

"With time, I will be fine—physically. It's everything else I need to deal with."

Realizing Kasi needed an unbiased friend, she asked, "Are you able to walk around?"

Kasi nodded. "I'm supposed to walk several times throughout the day."

"Well, come on. Let's get some exercise." She helped Kasi out of her recliner and hooked her apparatus to the walker. "I saw this once on TV," she joked.

Leaving the room, Allison asked, "Lynne, will you be here when we return?"

"All day for the next couple of days."

"I'll talk to you later. Right now, I need to get this girl moving."

Once out in the corridor, Kasi told Allison everything that happened to her. "I feel that outside my family, you're the only one I can trust."

"What about your husband? Have you been in touch?"

"He's here in India but, Allison, I'm worried that he's somehow involved."

Allison stopped short upon hearing this. "Kasi, I had the same thoughts."

"What do you mean?"

"Well, I happened to be with the police when they broke into the house you were in. One of the officers found a phone number scribbled on a piece of paper inside a duffle bag. I noticed it had a Manhattan area code and quickly memorized it until I could write it down. Once I had time, I dialed the number and your husband's voicemail came on."

Kasi described her own encounter with the phone number. "I saw it as a missed call on Hari's phone. It's Keith's cell number, Allison."

"Is there a reasonable explanation for this?"

"Not any that I know. I mean, how did Hari know I was coming to India, much less the exact time of arrival?"

"You think Keith was in on it?"

Kasi teared up. "Yes, and I don't know what to do about it."

"Have you seen Keith?"

"He was just here. He wasn't happy when I told him I wanted to stay in India and that I wanted him to leave the hospital. He pretty much lost it."

"So you never hinted of your suspicion?"

"No, I almost did but I stopped myself."

"I think you need to speak to Detective Mahor about this. He's the man in charge of your investigation."

"I've met him. I wanted to be somewhat certain before I dragged Keith into this, you know? Right now, the search is on for Hari."

"If Keith is involved, maybe it's smart not to let him think anyone is suspecting him. He could lead us to Hari. I do think you need to talk to the detective. Maybe they would put a tag on him."

Chapter 38

KASI

THE MORNING SUN started to creep into the room as an orderly wheeled Jaya out of her hospital room. Lynne followed as far as the operating room, but then was instructed to sit in the visitors' waiting room for Dr. Lalit's post-operative report.

It was a restless night for Kasi; she had only been asleep a few hours when the room's activity awoken her. Behind a privacy screen, Kasi laid in bed with her eyes closed. A few minutes later, the screen moved. Sensing someone standing there, Kasi opened her eyes and saw Keith. With her heart wildly palpitating, she knew this had to be a time to remain calm—calmer than she was the previous day.

"Hello Keith, you're here early."

"I need to speak to you," he said.

"Keith, I have to apologize for the way I treated you yesterday," she said, choking on her words. "I've gone through a lot since arriving in India. I think my emotions just boiled over."

Keith's angry, tensed features softened. He sat down in the chair next to the bed. "I understand. When do you plan to return to New York?"

Kasi swallowed hard. "First I need to get better and maybe visit with my family. My family canceled my cousin's wedding until next weekend, but I've told her that I couldn't attend. She understands. Where are you staying?"

"I'm at a hotel not far from here."

"Which one? You know, in case I need to get in touch with you."

Keith fidgeted in his seat. "Oh, can't remember the name. Not familiar with all those Indian words. Just call my cell phone."

Kasi noted that was strange—hotel names were not that confusing. India, having once been governed by Great Britain, had been profoundly touched by the English language. Instead of questioning his answer, she decided the right tactic at the moment was to accept it. No sense stirring things up now.

Kasi closed her eyes hoping this would send a cue for Keith to leave. She watched as he paced in and out of the room, continually looking at his phone. The door opened and a nurse walked into the room.

"Namaste. How are you doing this morning, Kasi?"

Kasi opened her eyes and signaled an okay to the nurse.

She started to tidy up the area and pulled out a wash pan from the bottom drawer of the bed stand. Turning to Keith, she asked, "Would you mind stepping out of the room for a minute so I can tend to Kasi?"

"I'll be outside." As he walked out of the room, his phone rang. "Hello? Hold on. I need to take this elsewhere."

The phone call ignited Kasi's curiosity as she wondered who would be calling him in India. Would it be Hari? No matter how hard she strained her ears, she couldn't hear any of the conversation. She wanted to get out of bed and go to the door, but the nurse was busy treating her wounds as she lay on her side feeling disturbed over what Keith and possibly Hari might have been discussing. Maybe it wasn't Hari. Is she becoming paranoid? She needed to figure out what to do about this complicated situation. It was apparent—they needed to locate Hari.

"Hey, where are you?" Keith asked. "I've been trying to get a hold of you for several days now."

"Where am I? I'm hiding. I am so messed up because of you. I have nowhere to go and no money for anything."

"Hari, I just gave you money. What happened to that?"

"Gone, everything spent mostly on your wife."

"Why did you need money for her?"

"Food—she had to eat."

"Well, you no longer have to feed her. By the way, you certainly blew your chances."

"You never said I had to kill your wife. Kidnap and hold onto her for ransom was what we agreed. I risked a lot."

"What did you have to risk?" Keith asked.

"Everything. Once I picked Kasi up, it was over for me. She'd tell the police who did this. There's no way I could stick around. I need the money you promised to get out of here."

Keith shook his head. I overestimated the money I thought her family had. It turns out they live on a modest income."

"What about her brother? Isn't he a doctor?"

"Yeah, but up to his neck in debt. Ransom will not work."

"So you changed the plan without telling me?" asked Hari. "You know, that's not how it works. If you wanted her gone, you either find someone else or do it yourself."

"You had the perfect opportunity to finish the job," Keith said in a low voice. "She seriously scalds herself with a fallen pot of soup. Something that could be proven was accidental. So what do you do? Nothing. All you had to do was pour more boiling water on her, enough to shut down her systems."

"Finish the job? After she takes a cast iron pan and slams it over my head? You know, I blacked out. I still have a headache. I should be dead, the way she whacked me. Uh, why are you whispering over the phone?"

"I'm at the hospital acting like a concerned husband. Stop yelling or I'll have to hang up on you!"

"Look, this was all of your doing, but nothing happens to you. Meanwhile, I'm hiding out in the woods with no money. I can't even go to the soup kitchen because someone will recognize me. Exactly what do you suggest I do, Keith?"

"Let's be reasonable about this, Hari. What has happened is not at all what I planned."

"Here's something to think about—either give me the money promised, or I let the police know about you. They already know about me. But you? You're walking around free, at least for now."

About to explode, Keith's face turned blood-red. "Okay, give me two days and I'll have your money. Where should we meet?"

"I've come up with a plan. You can have your two days, but that's it. Go to the Jantar Mantar. It's an observatory south of Connaught Place. You know, one of those stargazing places. You can't miss it. Once through the gates, look for the Prince of Dials which is a large Sundial. Any trouble, ask someone where the Samrat Yantra is. Once you find it, look for the west tower and the steps leading up to the top. On the 13th step, look over the edge on the left, and you will see a narrow shelf-like structure. There will be a note taped on the underside of that ledge telling you where to meet me at 10:00 that night."

"Look, I have to go," Keith whispered. "There's this woman who is sitting out here in the hall staring at me. Not sure, but she appears to be listening in on our conversation. She's coming over to use the water fountain. Hey, I'll talk to you later."

As Keith headed back towards Kasi's room, two people pushing a stretcher reached the room and carefully transitioned Jaya onto her bed. Bandages covered her head with only a few open areas for her eyes, nose, and mouth. Dr. Lalit followed behind the stretcher to give Jaya's post-operative report. Hearing the procedure had finished, Lynne left the visitors' room and headed down the corridor. Without realizing it, she once more bumped into the guy who almost knocked her over as she entered the building the day before. She glared at him, but he paid no heed. She wondered who that jerk was. She didn't have to wait long to learn it was Kasi's husband.

Chapter 39

LYNNE, KASI, & ALLISON

HEARING KASI'S CONCERNS over Keith bothered Allison. She decided to return to the hospital to make sure Kasi was doing okay. When she got to Room 204, the floor nurse asked if she would wait outside while she changed Kasi's dressings. Allison took a seat in a chair not far from the room and immediately looked at her cell to see if there were any messages. The door to Room 204 opened and a man hurried out while answering his phone. Allison wondered who he was, but then thought perhaps it could be Kasi's husband, Keith.

No matter how hard she strained her ears, she could not distinctly hear his end of the conversation. At one point she overheard him say, "You had the perfect opportunity to finish the job."

Finish the job? What job? That doesn't sound good. Am I over-thinking this? Is my imagination working overtime? Maybe he's chastising someone over a job at work?

Allison looked away once she realized her stares were becoming noticeable. She looked down at her phone as though involved in texting someone. Every so often, she glanced over in his direction. He certainly wasn't happy about something. She wished she were closer. Allison stood up and walked over towards the water fountain with the pretense of getting a drink.

"Give me two days and I'll have your money. Where should we meet?" the man asked.

Allison worried about this conversation. It didn't sound like he was up to any good. *Money? Where will they meet? Could he be talking to Hari? I need to be sure this is Keith, and then I better get in touch with Detective Mahor.*

After a drink at the water cooler, Allison walked by the irritated man hoping to hear more, perhaps where he was meeting this other person. Unfortunately, he hung up and headed towards a chair outside of Kasi's room. A stretcher appeared and made a turn into the room. Keith started to follow it but was asked to remain in the hall a few more minutes while they assisted the patient to her bed. Following the stretcher, Lynne smiled and said hello to Allison who stood by the door not far from this man—that same rude man who almost knocked Jaya and her over.

As they waited, the man looked at his watch, grumbled a few words under his breath, paced back and forth two or three times, and then left the building.

Allison turned to Lynne, "Did you know who that was?"

"Yes, Kasi's husband."

After settling Jaya in her bed, both ladies were allowed in the room. Jaya was awake but in a stupor.

"How are you doing?" asked Lynne.

"Tired—very tired."

"I won't bother you. Just wanted to let you know I'm here if you need anything."

Jaya nodded.

Meanwhile, Allison approached Kasi and asked if everything was okay. "Was that Keith who was just here?"

"Yes, has he left?"

"I believe so. He seemed agitated."

"He's always agitated. I don't want to return to New York with him, Allison. I want to stay with my family."

"Does he know that?"

"Yesterday I had a little melt-down and announced that bit of news. He turned into a crazy person, so this morning I apologized and told him it must have been the medication."

"Why did you say that?" Allison asked.

"If he was involved in my abduction, I don't want to tip him off on my suspicions. What am I going to do?"

Allison didn't want to tell Kasi what she overheard out in the hall. No sense in escalating her fear; she had enough of it already.

"Kasi, I think I should talk to Detective Mahor about your suspicions. How do you feel about that?"

"But what happens if he's not involved, Allison? This could be a big problem."

"Not as big as if he *is* involved and you say nothing."

"Let me talk to Lalit about this, okay? He should be coming in soon to talk to Jaya about her operation."

Allison nodded, opened her purse and pulled out a magazine. "I thought you might like to read this. I bought it the other day. When I returned to my room, I noticed it wasn't in English."

Kasi smiled as Allison handed her the magazine. As bad as things have been, she needed that little bit of humor.

"Allison, remember when I told you about the bangles?"

"Yeah?"

"I broke two more   my silver bangles."

"Oh, tell me again—what does the silver symbolize?"

"It stands for strength."

"How did it happen, Kasi?"

Kasi turned her head to the window and then looked back

at Allison. "Hari became angry and we got into a scuffle. That's when the bracelets broke."

Allison understood the meaning behind this and the superstition that Kasi attached to the bangles. "You know, Kasi, there is no one I can think of who has more strength than you. Just because the silver bangles broke, doesn't mean your strength is gone. You still have it, Kasi. Don't give up."

Kasi shook her head in agreement. "I feel so deflated, you know? I no longer trust my judgment. I knew I didn't want to go through a marriage with Hari. That turned out to be a good decision. There was something about him that I didn't like. He seemed too pushy; you know what I mean?"

"Yes, authoritative."

"Keith had me fooled. But then again, maybe I used him as a way to escape from marrying Hari. I never understood why my parents thought Hari was a good match."

"Do you think Keith wanted Hari to hold you for ransom?"

"I asked my brother about that, but Lalit said no one contacted the family about a ransom. I don't know what Keith's motive would be."

"But Hari didn't kill you. Don't you think he would have done it right away?"

"Maybe. Maybe Hari wanted the opportunity to punish me for not marrying him."

"Well, you're safe now. Look, I'll let you get some rest. I saw Keith leave before I came in. At least I think that was him."

"Was he on the phone?" asked Kasi.

Allison nodded.

"Then that was probably Keith talking to someone about me."

Lynne followed Allison as she walked out of the room. "Allison, how is it going with Kasi?"

"She's having a tough time. Not only is she emotionally upset over what had happened to her with this Hari, but she's also distraught that her husband may be involved. That has to be pretty demoralizing."

"Well, if you ever want me to talk to her, just let me know. Jaya and I should be leaving here as soon as she gets discharged."

"Before you leave, I need to sit down and talk to you about your work at this women's café. It sounds like something I could use in my documentary on Indian women's issues."

"Hey, we're holding a fashion show in two weeks. How about coming up to see it? You can bring Kasi with you. Talking to the ladies at the café might be good medicine. It certainly could be a diversion."

"You may be right. Not sure if Kasi will be up for the trip, but do count me in."

Chapter 40

ALLISON

"WELCOME BACK, ABHA!" everyone in the office yelled.

"Oh, what is this? What's going on?"

"Just a little welcome back surprise that Allison put together," said Mr. Arun.

"That's so nice. Thank you, everyone. I feel so welcomed."

"We all missed you, Mr. Arun said. "No one here knows how to run this office better than you."

"For sure," Allison added.

"Look at all this," she said, pointing at the display of sweets on the table normally cluttered with file folders, newspapers, notepads and other office materials. "Where did everything go?"

"Oh, over there in a little . . . er . . . I mean a big pile," said Riya, one of the assistant editors of the newspaper.

"You're gone one week and the place is falling apart," said Vihaan, a copy editor.

"This is so nice," Abha said as she looked at the balloons, cake and tea. "I never expected anything like this, Allison. Thank you."

"I've been learning about your customs so I thought I would show you a little of ours. In the United States, we always look for an excuse to have a little party. The return from your wedding trip certainly merited one. So cut us a piece of cake and tell us all about your holiday. But before you do, I have to tell you that I had the best time at your wedding. I never experienced anything like that before."

"Your weddings are different in America?" asked Abha.

"Not even close. Here you go," Allison said, handing her a cake knife. "Cut the cake. We've been looking at it all morning."

"Tell us about what you did," said Riya.

"As you know, Jay and I traveled to Rajasthan to stay near the Ranthambore National Park. We stayed at this beautiful place near the park in Sawai Madhopur. The countryside is so beautiful there. It was nothing at all like Delhi. No busy traffic, no smog or horns blaring. Just many lakes and beautiful forests, so peaceful."

"Did you go to the tiger sanctuary?" asked Riya.

"Yes, my most favorite part. We rode in a canter all through the forest and saw all kinds of animals grazing and roaming around. Monkeys were everywhere. We had to be careful because they would jump in our vehicle and steal things right from our hands. They tend to be more aggressive than the monkeys we have here in Delhi. We saw antelope, deer, jackals, crocodiles and even a tiger."

"You saw a tiger?" asked Allison. "To see a tiger in the wild had to be a fantastic experience. What was it doing?"

"It was near the end of our safari, and the driver stopped near a waterhole in this secluded area. We saw the tiger laying down on a flat rock tucked into a hill—much like a cave. The driver turned off the cantor's engine, and we sat and watched this beautiful animal until he stood up and walked over to the waterhole. He had his front legs stretched forward so that he could easily bend over to drink the water. It was a moment I will never forget."

"Do you have a photo?" asked Mr. Arun.

Abha pulled out her phone and searched through her pictures. "Here, look at this."

"What a gorgeous animal," Allison said. "I don't see how anyone could kill such an exquisite animal."

Abha said, "Usually for either money or bragging rights. That's why the national park is such a treasure because hunting is not allowed. The tigers come out even in the daytime because they have no fear of humans driving around in their safari vehicles."

"I imagine they're used to seeing people," said Vihaan.

"They are. None of the animals seemed to pay much attention to us except for those crazy monkeys."

"Did you know that Ranthambore was once the hunting grounds for the Maharajas of Jaipur?" asked Vihaan.

"The naturalist told us that," said Abha. "The whole park was fantastic. Dry areas were mixed in with a forest environment. I certainly wouldn't take a walk around there. You never know what might jump out at you."

After everyone drank their tea, ate their cake and listened to Abha's many stories, they decided to return to work to get the paper out the following morning.

Allison stayed behind to put the snacks away and return the table to its usual disarray. As she washed the last dish, Abha came by to personally thank her for the welcome back party. "Allison, have you ever heard of the Women's Project outside of Ranthambore?"

"No, I haven't, but it sounds like something that would interest me. Tell me about it."

"To discourage poaching, a woman started this workshop

to bring an alternative livelihood to ex-poacher families. This workshop created job opportunities for the people, and a means for the local villagers to sell their crafts. The idea is pretty basic—a few shed-type buildings and a lean-to. There's also an outdoor canopy offering protection for both the people who arrive for lunch and the women who sat on mats as they embroidered, stitched, did beadwork and hand block printing."

"Sounds like what we used to call a quilting bee."

"Yes, exactly. The women chat and exchange stories as they put together these amazing products." Abha went to her desk and pulled out a green cloth bag with a tiger stamped on front. "I bought this so you'll remember your time with us in Delhi."

"A gift for me? That is so nice of you, Abha. What is it?"

"Open and see!"

"Okay. Hmm . . . feels firm but squishy." Allison opened the package to find a turquoise sack-type purse. On the front was a block print of the elusive tiger.

"Oh wow, what a treasure. Is this purse handmade?"

"Yes, here let me show you." She pulled out her phone and found the pictures of the Conservation Center. Allison browsed through to see the women at work just as Abha had described. "Here is a photo of the woman who made this purse."

Allison saw the lady sitting with three other women. She had on a lime green sari and a white veil over her head. What made this photo so beautiful was her lovely smile.

"Could you send this photo to me? I would love a copy."

"Of course. Here is the email address of the organization if ever you want to send a note telling Divya that you received the purse. That would make her happy."

"An excellent idea. Of course, I will do that." Allison gave Abha a big hug. "Thank you for such a wonderful gift.

So glad everything went well with the wedding and that you returned happy and content."

"So, anything happened while I was gone?" Abha asked.

Allison laughed. "Sit down. I have lots to tell you. So where shall I start?"

Chapter 41

KASI

"YOUR NECK AND shoulder seem to be healing quite nicely," said Dr. Kalawat. "It won't be much longer before I discharge you from the hospital."

Lalit said, "Now that's good news, Kasi."

Kasi said nothing.

Dr. Kalawat left the room leaving Kasi's brother behind. "Kasi, can you tell me what's up with you?"

"What do you mean?"

"You need to talk to someone who can help you deal with all that you've been through."

"I'm scared, you know, not knowing where Hari is. He's really unhinged."

"The police are looking for him. It's like he just disappeared. By the way, we've asked Keith if he would like to stay with us. We have the room, but he insisted on staying at the hotel."

"No, don't ask him."

"Why's that?"

"I don't trust him anymore."

"Are you still thinking he's involved with Hari?"

"Yes, that's the problem I have. The only person who seems to believe me is Allison. She actually came to the same conclusion before I even brought it up. Don't you think that's revealing?"

Lalit said, "You know, Keith is going to think you should be at the hotel with him after you leave the hospital."

Kasi's eyes flared. "No, I'm not doing that! I want to stay with you and Rani. Maybe you can ask Dr. Kalawat to tell Keith that it would be a good idea for me to stay at your house to prevent complications with my injuries."

"That would not be the case."

"But Keith won't know. It will sound more official if it comes from Dr. Kalawat and not you."

"You're really serious about this, aren't you?"

"Are you finally realizing that? I do not want to be alone with him—not at all."

"If you're certain, maybe you should talk to the police about his possible involvement."

"I've already decided to do exactly that. Allison contacted Detective Mahor and he's due here this afternoon."

"What happens if Keith shows up?"

"I'm meeting Detective Mahor in a private conference room. I've already shared some of my thoughts with the head nurse. If Keith does show up when Detective Mahor is here, she's going to tell him that I'm at rehab."

Lalit listened but offered no suggestions which was good because once Kasi made a decision, no one could ever talk her into doing otherwise.

Kasi pointed to the empty bed next to her. "Jaya left this morning. Whenever I feel sorry for myself I think of the troubles others have. Will Jaya be able to regain any of her facial expressions?"

Lalit said, "The surgery went well but this is only the second procedure. I see many more operations in her future."

"Well, she loves *you*. I know she isn't looking forward to years of reconstruction, but her spirits have lifted knowing there is something that can be done."

"Hope is a powerful medicine."

"Yes, it is. I don't say this often, Lalit, but I'm proud you're my brother. You give so much of your time and talent to people who literally would have no one to turn to."

Lalit patted her hand. "Thanks. Hey, I need to leave—you be good, okay?"

"Please ask Dr. Kalawat to tell Keith he recommends I stay with you. Rani won't mind, will she?"

"Of course not. Just don't know how agreeable Keith will be?"

"Well, don't offer to have him stay at your place. I want to be around him as little as possible."

"You are married to the guy, Kasi."

"Not sure how this will end."

"If it comes out that he had nothing to do with your kidnapping and there is a perfect explanation as to why his number showed up as a missed call on Hari's phone, will you return to New York?"

"No, absolutely not. He has a nasty side to him, Lalit. A side he rarely shows to anyone. I've experienced it the past two years and no longer want any part of him. If the last few weeks have taught me anything, it's life is too valuable to just squander away the days."

"You've always cut your losses whenever you've realized you made a mistake."

"And a mistake I made."

"What mistake did you make?" a voice asked from the room's entrance. It was Keith.

Lalit and Kasi stared at each other. How much had he

heard? Lalit said, "Hi Keith. We were just rehashing our earlier days, remembering the times when we were kids."

Kasi smiled and played along. "Yes, can't go through those years without making a few mistakes."

"Remember that time you went to the bazaar instead of school?" asked Lalit.

Although Kasi had no idea what he was talking about, she responded, "Yeah, that wasn't a smart thing."

Lalit laughed. "Especially when our parents found out."

Keith never smiled or commented. He simply looked from Kasi to Lalit back to Kasi.

"When does Dr. Kalawat come to see you?" Keith asked.

"He's already been here."

"Any mention of when you can leave India? I have to get back to New York."

Lalit said, "She's to undergo several weeks of rehab."

Keith walked over to the other side of Kasi's bed. "We have rehab centers in New York."

Lalit said, "Yeah, but that long plane ride back to America may not fare well with my sister at this stage of her recovery."

Keith said, "We'll see. Working long distance is good for only so long, you know. Right now, I have something important to tend to. I'll be back later this afternoon to see how you're doing."

Keith walked out of the room. Kasi and Lalit said nothing. Lalit quietly walked to the door to make sure he was gone and then said, "If he's at all involved, we can't let him leave India. Extradition is tricky and takes a long time."

"I can stall only so long," said Kasi, "it's important I see Detective Mahor this afternoon."

"Jantar Mantar Observatory, just south of Connaught Place," Keith said to the driver as he entered the cab. The traffic was heavier than usual. Although he followed Hari's instructions of being at the large sundial before crowds of tourists showed up, he failed to recall the early morning congestion. Jammed between a rundown bus and a motorized rickshaw, Keith had little choice but to view the activity on the other side of the window. It was typical of what he remembered seeing while working in India three years ago.

Congestion was a good description—bikes, kiosks selling everything from mops, cameras, hubcaps, food and condoms. Alone in a dried up field stood a sad-looking tree stripped of its leaves but supported by broken concrete slabs heaped haphazardly around the base of its trunk. Goats, sick-looking dogs, a slow moving train, women squatting on stone slabs washing dishes, and the back of a man peeing against a wall. The homeless in Manhattan had little to complain over when weighted against some of the situations in Old Delhi.

After what should have been a 20-minute ride turned into an hour, Keith exited the cab and approached Connaught Place. A series of colonnaded shops, banks, and restaurants ran along the perimeter of the busy traffic circle. Just as Hari described, the Observatory was a short distance from this business center. After entering the site, he saw several reddish colored structures strategically placed within walking distance of each other. Looking for a sign that pointed the way to Samrat Yantra, he easily found the massive Sundial.

A small group of tourists listened while their guide described how the sundial worked. Keith hid behind a fairly large tree and listened to the woman explain how these 13 architectural instruments were built in 1719. After the group left the Prince of Dials, Keith looked around and saw no one nearby. Now was the time to climb the steps and look for the instructions that should be near the 13th step.

"There it is!" he said under his breath. He skimmed the slip of paper he ripped off the small ledge. Printed in scribbly letters, he read:

> *Meet me on Saturday at the Red Fort just before midnight. I will be close to the main entrance near the Lahore Gate. Come with the 670,000 rupees we agreed upon. Police will be contacted if you don't show up. Be assured, this is neither a threat nor a warning. This is how it is.*

Keith chucked the note to the ground. "670,000 rupees? Where does he think I'm supposed to get 670,000 rupees? Crazy fool. This foolishness needs to end."

Chapter 42

LYNNE

"HI NAOMI, I'M back," said Lynne arriving late that evening.

Naomi was resting on the couch semi-involved in the latest Bollywood production. "Hey! How did everything go?"

"The operation went well, or so Dr. Lalit said. What are you watching?"

"Some Indian soap opera. Don't quiz me on what it's about since everything is in Hindi."

"You must be bored."

Naomi laughed as she turned off the TV. "Yeah, not sure what's happening but there certainly is a lot of drama centered on the daughter. I think her family is upset she doesn't want to go along with an arranged marriage."

"That sounds familiar—much like the girl that was in the hospital room with Jaya."

"How's that?"

Lynne went on to explain how she ran into this woman journalist that was on the plane coming over to Delhi. "Yeah, I'm in the room with Jaya, and she arrives to visit this Kasi in the next bed."

"You ran into a person you met on the plane at the hospital?"

"Yeah, she was sitting near me; plus, we had an interesting conversation at baggage claim. She wondered why I was in India and when I told her, she gave me her card and said she would like to come and visit the café."

Naomi said, "I mean, how often does that happen?"

"Yeah, crazy, huh? I have another crazy coincidence. You know Jaya's doctor?"

"Dr. Lalit?"

"Well, his sister is the same girl?"

"The journalist or the patient in the room with Jaya?"

"Oh, the girl occupying the other bed in Jaya's room. She went missing after arriving at the airport. All of Delhi was looking for her. They found her walking on this deserted road outside of Delhi with half her body burned from hot soup.

Lynne picked up her duffle and walked into her room.

Naomi got up and followed her. "Don't stop now. Hot soup? You have my total attention. Explain."

"Well, from what Allison said . . . "

"Allison? Who is Allison?"

Lynne put her duffle on the chair and gasped. "Allison is the journalist, the lady on the plane. So okay, Allison told me this guy Kasi was supposed to marry abducted her from the airport and hid her away for several weeks. I don't know how she got away or the circumstance behind being burned with soup. I didn't get a chance to have much of a conversation with her. She pretty much stayed by herself behind a screen when she wasn't going to rehab. I did notice she was depressed. I guess some awful stuff happened to her."

"Now how did this Allison lady know Kasi? Were they traveling together?"

"No, they sat next to each other on the plane."

Naomi shook her head in disbelief. "When I'm on a

flight, I never know anyone much less get involved with their lives after landing."

Lynne smiled. "Yeah, it's pretty crazy how things worked out. So, how're the preparations going for the fashion show?"

"Good. I practiced the walk with the girls on the runway which ended up being pretty hysterical."

"Why is that?"

"When I demonstrated the walk, they sat there and laughed at me. So I told the girls to do it their way!"

"Are they excited?"

Naomi answered, "Very much so. Most of the tickets are gone, and we still have a week to go before the show."

"That's fantastic! I'll have to give the go-ahead to Allison."

"Why is that?"

"I invited her to come see the show and talk to the ladies. She's in India putting together this documentary on social change in India with an emphasis on women's rights."

"This should fit right in," Naomi said.

"That's what I thought. Oh, is it okay with you if I offer the third bedroom to Allison while she's here?"

"Not a problem with me. You might want to pass it by Chandra."

"I will. By the way, if the hospital discharges Kasi, Allison hopes to bring her up. She already spoke with Kasi's brother who thought it would be a great distraction for her."

"That room has two beds," Naomi said, "so they could both stay in there."

"Yeah, much homier than a hotel room. What are you thinking about, Naomi? You have this devilish look on your face."

"Oh, not much . . . er . . . okay, I'm thinking if Kasi stays here, we might find out more about the hot soup."

The days passed quickly, and Jaya began to feel more comfortable. She went to rehab at the Agra hospital twice that week which got her out of the house and amongst people. They removed the bandages except for a small one covering her left ear. Lynne convinced her to come into the café that afternoon to help with some last minute preps for the fashion show. Not entirely comfortable with mingling with the afternoon customers, she stayed in the back room putting together small net bags of mints with the Sari Shop's business card attached. The café was to close in two days to give everyone the time to set things up at the event center down the road.

"One hundred tickets—all sold," announced Naomi.

"One hundred tickets translates into one hundred little bags of mints," laughed Jaya.

Lynne smiled to see her involved with life—now to keep it going.

"Jaya, remember the girl that was in the hospital room with you?"

"Yes, I do—Kasi."

"Well, she's being discharged from the hospital and will be back with her family."

"Will she be staying with Dr. Lalit?"

"That is the plan, but I mentioned the fashion show to Allison and she hopes to attend. She wants to bring Kasi with her."

"They're coming all that way to see the show?"

"There's more to it than that. Allison wanted to come and visit the café, so I suggested a good time to come would be for the fashion show."

"That was a good suggestion. By the way, what's your opinion on these favors I'm putting together?"

Lynne picked one up and looked at it. "Very nice. You're doing an excellent job," she said, putting it back on the table. "I like how you gave special credit to the Sari Shop in exchange for letting us model their clothing."

"Without their contribution, there would be no fashions to model," Jaya said, smiling.

It warmed Lynne's heart to see Jaya smile. "Do you think you could spend some time with Kasi during the show, Jaya? That might make her feel welcome and put her at ease. The others will be busy with the show."

Lynne noted the look on Jaya's face. It was an 'I'm on to what you're doing' kind of look. Jaya picked up the material needed to make a new favor. "Looks like I will now need 102 favors."

Chapter 43

KASI

"YOU WILL BE coming with me, right?" asked Keith in a stern voice.

"It would be much better if Kasi went to Lalit's house to finish her recovery, Keith."

"Why is that?" Keith asked Dr. Kalawat.

"We have to be careful of infection. Hotels are often receptacles of germs from the many people who stay there. Not always are they thoroughly cleaned." It was apparent to Kasi that Lalit had spoken to Dr. Kalawat and that he must have agreed to this arrangement.

Keith said nothing. He didn't like being in a vulnerable position. Much like the dominant wolf who meets up with an alpha from another pack, one has to succumb. Submitting was not a natural behavior for Keith. He looked at his watch. "It's late—need to leave. I'll pick you up in the morning and take you to your brother's house."

Keith kissed Kasi on the forehead and headed out the door before she could say otherwise. After he left, Kasi said, "Did my brother ask you to tell Keith I couldn't stay at a hotel?"

Dr. Kalawat nodded. "I don't like deceiving people, Kasi, but your brother said it was important. I had to believe him. I don't know what's going on, but I know Lalit wouldn't ask me to do this favor if it weren't important."

A few minutes after Dr. Kalawat left, there was a knock on the door. Kasi froze. Certain that Keith had returned, she got out of bed and locked herself in the bathroom. The door to the room opened and the nurse said, "I don't know where she's at, Detective. She was here a short while ago."

"I'm in the bathroom," Kasi yelled. Quickly, she unlocked the door and came out. "I'm relieved you're here, Detective Mahor."

The nurse left and the detective walked into the room. "Your friend, Ms. Wagner, said it was important I speak to you about some information you needed to share."

"Did Allison tell you anything?"

"No, she wouldn't. She said you needed to be the one to tell me, otherwise it would just be hearsay. So I'm here. What is it? Do you know where Hari Chubney is?"

"No, I don't and that frightens me. Come sit down, Detective Mahor. I have to tell you what I think is going on. Kasi went on to recap how Hari fell asleep, and she picked up his phone from the floor and noticed a missed call from Keith. Kasi stopped and looked at the detective who sat, blank-face, across from her.

"Don't you believe me?"

"Why would you ask that?"

"I thought you would be surprised."

"Well, your information is useful—another piece of the puzzle we're trying to put together, but we've suspected your husband to be an accomplice."

"Really?"

"When we checked out the cabin you were in, we found a Manhattan phone number on a piece of paper in Hari's duffle."

"Allison told me about that, but I didn't realize you knew."

"Well, not at first. Not until I called the number and your husband answered."

"Are you going to arrest Keith?"

"Not yet, need a little more time—a few more things to check out before we can do that. Right now it's speculation."

"But all the time you spend waiting, I'm frightened he might do something to me."

The detective said, "He's not aware we're onto him. You need to act normal around him, or he'll become suspicious. You know what I mean?"

Kasi nodded her head. "But it's hard on me—emotionally."

"Of course, I get that."

"When he left this evening, he said he would pick me up in the morning to take me to my brother's house. How do I get out of that?"

"That's the other thing I wanted to talk to you about. Ms. Wagner mentioned that she wanted to take you to Agra."

Kasi squirmed. "I don't want to go. I want to stay at my brother's house."

"I realize that but by going to Agra, we'll get you out of town, and Keith won't know where you are. The hospital is prepared to make up a story that you had an emotional breakdown, and they transferred you to a quiet sanctuary that can meet your emotional needs."

Hari's note said to go to the Red Fort and look for him by the Lahore Gate before mid-night with 670,000 rupees. Keith laughed every time he thought about that request. After a quick bite to eat and a stop at the hotel, he opened the room's safe and pulled $200 from an envelope. This amount was much lower than the amount Hari requested, equivalent to 1200 rupees. Keith couldn't come up with the sum they originally agreed upon. Perhaps this will buy more time with Hari.

"Pull over here," Keith said to the driver about a mile from the Red Fort. He got out of the cab and watched the driver take off. Waiting a few minutes, Keith looked around the deserted street. Seeing no one, he started the mile walk to the Red Fort. As he came upon the Lahore Gate, he noticed a figure in the shadows.

"That you, Hari?"

"You got my money?"

"Yeah, I brought your damn money, but we need to talk first."

"I see no reason to talk. I'm not killing her. Never killed anyone and don't plan on getting myself hung over something that benefits you."

"You won't get caught. People believe you've left the country for Pakistan," he lied."

"How do you know that?"

"I overheard two police officers talking in front of Kasi's door."

"So they aren't looking for me?" Hari asked.

"Not anymore." Keith hesitated and looked at the ground.

"I'm still not killing her. Not killing anyone, but we did have a deal. I kept my end, so where's my money?"

Keith handed over an envelope. Hari looked inside and counted 1200 rupees. "There aren't 670,000 rupees here. Hell, not even close. I want the money we agreed upon a few weeks ago. You know, I stuck my neck out for this."

"Don't have that kind of money and never will. Twelve

hundred rupees is all you'll get; don't ask for any more money. There is none. The pot is dry. Understand?"

"We'll see about that," Hari threatened. "Tomorrow morning I think I'll make a little phone call to a certain detective friend of mine."

"You do and they'll identify your location."

Hari laughed, turned around and started walking towards his vehicle. Keith ran up to him, grabbed him by the neck and the two tumbled to the ground. Hari punched Keith in the gut causing him to double over. As Hari started to stand, Keith bit him on the ear with such force that he tasted blood. Hari spun around and slammed Keith's head into the ground. Keith reached for the concealed knife inside his jacket and swiped it across Hari's neck. Hari fell over releasing his grip on Keith.

"There you go, Hari. Next time, don't mess with me. Then again, there won't be a next time, will there?"

Blood pooled around Hari's head as he attempted to stand up. Keith reached into Hari's coat and pulled out the money he had just given him. "You won't be needing this anymore." With a malicious show of mercy, he pierced Hari's body a second time, puncturing his chest cavity inches away from his heart. Hari gasped, slowly closing his eyes as the blood continued to drain from his arteries.

"I hate to see a man suffer. Have a good cremation, my friend."

Keith saw Hari's car keys laying on the ground. He grabbed them, raced over to the car parked by the side of the road, and drove the several miles to the hotel.

Keith planned to buy time with Hari until he could get out of the country without raising any suspicion. Realizing this was not going to happen, he had no other choice but to kill him. He once heard the first time was the toughest. Killing Kasi would not be as difficult.

In the eerie shadows of the night, the full moon silhouetted the scene near the Lahore Gate. Alone and rapidly leaving this empty life, a dying man dragged his heavy body over to a nearby wall. With an unsteady hand, he used his blood to write the letters K E I on the wall. Unable to finish, his body seized with a sudden jolt and Hari gave up the struggle.

Chapter 44

ALLISON

"HI WES, WERE you able to get that information from the insurance company?"

"Yes, as a matter of fact, I did. The agent said Keith took out a policy on his wife several months ago."

"Really? Now that's interesting. How much?"

"Yeah, it was a million dollar policy."

"Wow! I need to give this information to the detective on the case."

"Allison, are you doing any work on the documentary or spending most of your time playing Amanda Stretcher from the TV series, *Writing About Murder*?"

"Why would you ask that, Wes? Of course, I am. I'll soon be leaving for Agra to check out this Mukta's Café that helps rehabilitate women who were victims of acid attacks."

"That sounds good, but the buzz around the office is whenever you go on an assignment, you become involved in some pretty . . . hmm, how shall I put it? . . . sticky situations."

"Who is saying that?"

"It isn't any particular person, Allison. You have that reputation, my friend, and now you're telling me about a kidnapping with possible suspects being an ex-suitor and her current husband. Like, who gets involved in stuff like that?"

"That's what happens when doing this kind of work, Wes. You meet up with some pretty questionable characters.

Besides, my results have been award winning. We did earn the Best Documentary category for *The Orchid Bracelet*, didn't we? Oh, that's right, you weren't here for that."

"You made your point, Allison. I'm not second guessing your tactics. I just don't want to hear you're in jail or in a ditch somewhere, you know?"

"Nice one. Would you be saying that if I were a man?" Allison asked.

Wes said, "Yes, as a matter of fact, I would. Now be careful over there. We all think highly of you and don't want anything to happen."

"I understand, but I am careful and I'm really not in any conceivable danger."

Wes said, "Conceivable? That doesn't sound too convincing. What is it you're not telling me?"

"Oh, you're reading too much into it, Wes. I'm more worried about Kasi; that's why I'm taking her to Agra."

"Kasi? The girl they were looking for?"

"Yep, turned out she was abducted but got away. Right now we're hiding her from Hari. No one knows where he is."

"Kasi? Hari? Agra? For the benefit of my sanity, I refuse to ask for clarification."

Allison laughed. "Probably a good idea, Wes. Namaste."

"Allison, what are you doing here?"

"I've come to pick you up. We're going to visit the ladies at the Mukta Café."

"That's in Agra. I can't go there. Keith's coming to take me to Lalit's house."

"There's been a change in plans. Lalit and Detective Mahor want you to leave Delhi as soon as possible."

"But why?"

"You may be in danger. Now come on, let's go before Keith gets here. We cleared everything with the hospital."

"Is there some trouble with Keith?"

"Kasi, I thought you were afraid of Keith and didn't want to be alone with him?"

"I don't. I'm just wondering what this is all about. You know, why the sudden change in plans?"

"You knew about the café."

"Yes, but I thought it was an option."

"Look, give me your bag. We need to get out of here. There's a taxi waiting outside to take us to the airport. I'll explain more as we make our way."

The two women got into the elevator and pushed the first-floor button. Ten minutes later Keith showed up at the hospital. He walked into Room 204 and saw an aide making up the empty bed.

"Do you know where my wife is?"

The aide shrugged her shoulders and continued stripping the bed.

Keith left the room for the nurses' station. "Excuse me, but where's my wife? I'm supposed to pick her up this morning."

An aide looked up. "Oh, she's gone. Left a short while ago."

"With who?" asked Keith.

"I saw her leave with her friend from New York."

Baffled, Keith said, "She doesn't have any friends here from New York."

"Well, she left with some lady. Maybe she's not from New York, but she's American."

"Damn!" Keith said, hitting his fist on the counter.

"Please, sir, this is a hospital ward with sick people in it," said the head nurse who happened to be walking by. "Do not cause a problem."

"Cause a problem? When are you people going to understand she's my wife and I have certain rights?"

The nurse looked directly into his eyes. "Mr. Beckham, she may be your wife, but Mrs. Beckham made a note on her health proxy that only her brother had access to her medical affairs. We have to abide by that. That is how we do it here. I'm sure you have the same policy in America."

"Well, we'll need to get that proxy changed, won't we?"

After Keith stormed off the floor, the two women looked at each other.

"Did I say something I shouldn't have?" the aide asked.

"The head nurse, nodded. "No information is to be released to Mr. Beckham."

"I'm so sorry. I didn't know that."

The head nurse picked up the phone and immediately called the police headquarters.

"Detective Mahor, Mrs. Beckman's husband was here to pick her up and left quite upset when he found she was gone. He was not happy . . . Yes, Mrs. Beckham left with her friend from America . . . No, we didn't say anything about where she was going. If I had to make a prediction, I would say he may be heading towards Dr. Joshi's house. He took off in pretty much of a rage . . . Yes, I'll call if he returns. Bye."

"Uh, is my wife here?"

"Hello, Keith. No, she's not," Rani answered through a half-opened door.

"Do you know where she is?"

She shook her head. "I have no idea."

"I was to pick her up at the hospital and bring her here, but she already left. Has Lalit heard from her?"

"Keith, I don't know where she is. Lalit was scheduled to be in surgery all morning, so I doubt he heard from her. Maybe she took a cab?"

"No, the nurse said she left with some friend from New York."

"Well, that wouldn't be us. How did you get here?"

"Rented a car to pick up Kasi. That reminds me, do you think Lalit would let me use his car for the next couple of days? Too expensive holding onto this one."

"I don't know, Keith, you'll have to ask him. He does use it to get to work. When are you leaving India?"

"Soon, I hope. Just waiting for Kasi to be given the okay to travel. Her doctor and that damn hospital have control issues."

"They're just looking out for what's best for Kasi."

"And I'm not? Is that what all you people think? That I'm not looking out for her best interest? I want to get out of this country."

"I didn't say that, Keith."

"But you inferred it."

Rani took a deep breath. She sensed he was on the verge of a major meltdown and didn't want to be part of it. Kasi told her he could be explosive.

"Well, I know you need to get back to work so once she's feeling better and is capable of riding in a plane for over fourteen hours, she'll fly back. I mean, she did come alone. She can return alone."

"Oh, here we go again. Blaming me for letting Kasi travel alone."

"No one is blaming you for anything. I made the point because she's been located and is on the path of recovery. Right now, she has her family to watch over her until she's well enough to return to New York."

"So you don't know where she is?" he asked again, trying to look inside the house."

"No, she certainly isn't here. I'll give you a call when I find out more, okay?"

With that, Rani quickly closed and locked the door. She hurried to a window and peered around the edge of the curtain. Keith stood next to a Toyota as he looked up and down the road. Rani knew Kasi was flying to Agra but was instructed not to mention that to anyone. She didn't like the drama this whole situation had put her family in and worried about how it would play out. Relieved that Keith refused Lalit's initial invitation to stay with them, she wondered how Kasi coped the past two years being all alone in a large city with this crazy person. As the weeks dragged by, the family noticed how unhinged Keith could get. His behavior fluctuated so much that it frightened her to be left alone with him. Rani reached for her phone and dialed the number Lalit had given her.

"Allison, this is Rani. I'm Lalit's wife. He gave me your number in case I needed to speak to Kasi. Is she with you?"

"Yes, we're at the airport all set to board. Is there a problem?"

"I thought I would let you know that Keith was here at the house looking for Kasi."

"I hope you didn't tell him anything, Rani."

"No, I said I didn't know where she was. Keith's eyes had this wild, alarming look."

"Did he threaten you?"

"No, but at times seemed irrational and very defensive."

"Did he say where he was going next?"

"No, but he asked to borrow our car. Lalit lent it to him a few times when he first arrived. He told me he currently had a rental, but he couldn't keep it because it was too expensive. I don't think any of that story is true."

"Why's that?"

"The car he drove to the house looked too battered to be a rental. Now that I think about it, it looked a lot like the one they showed on TV as the type of car that picked up Kasi at the airport."

"What do you mean?"

"It was a Toyota. What color was the one Hari had?"

"Silver . . . a silver hatchback," said Allison.

"That's what he had—a silver hatchback."

"Allison, is something wrong?" Kasi asked, overhearing the conversation.

"No, just a problem at work."

Allison rose from her chair to talk privately to Rani. "Okay, I can talk better now. It's probably not a good idea to let Kasi know Keith may be driving Hari's car."

"So you think the car might belong to Hari?" asked Rani.

"If not, it sure is a wild coincidence."

"Allison, why would he even think of picking Kasi up from the hospital in the same car used to abduct her? That's insane."

"Better yet, if it is Hari's car, how did he get access to it? I mean, where is Hari?"

Chapter 45

ALLISON

"DETECTIVE MAHOR HERE, what's up, Yash? You're calling late."

"I'm at the Red Fort near the Lahore Gate. A call came in about a male stabbed to death lying in the bushes. Got here about ten minutes ago. Looks like a homicide."

"What else do you have?"

"A couple from Britain were headed towards their hotel when they spotted a partially exposed body from under the brush," said Yash. "They moved closer to get a better look and saw the body of a man. They immediately called us. The scene is pretty gruesome."

"How's that?" asked Detective Mahor.

"Someone slit the guy's throat and finished the job by penetrating his chest cavity. Blood is everywhere. He definitely bled to death."

"Any signs the victim is homeless?"

"No, usually they have all of their stuff with them. My opinion? I'd say this was the result of a fight and not an incidental killing."

"You think the victim may have known his attacker?" asked the detective.

"My first impression—yes. It's too gruesome to have been done by a stranger. If someone had him staked out, they would have done their thing and quickly left. The trampled grass and bushes at the scene looked like there was a bit of a struggle between the two. Someone was mighty pissed and had it out for this guy."

"Any identity?" asked Detective Mahor.

"Yes, the license says Hari Chubney."

"Hari Chubney? Are you serious?"

"I thought that would be of interest to you. That's why I called you in the middle of the night instead of waiting until morning. Here are a few other items for you. There are several bloody footprints on the ground. Plus it appears the knife broke off when it went into the chest cavity. Part of it is still in the body while a section of the damaged handle is on the ground."

"Anything unique about the knife?"

"It's pretty dark out here; but under my flashlight, it appears to have a pearl handle. Certainly not a knife meant for killing someone," said Yash.

"Sounds too much like an amateur. Okay, Yash, have the area cordoned off. Call for an investigator. I'm coming right over."

Upon arriving that afternoon, Allison and Kasi settled into the house with Lynne and Naomi. Lynne took Allison over to the café to meet the ladies while Kasi remained with Naomi to recuperate from a long, stressful day. She would meet everyone the following morning.

"Ladies, I want you to meet Alison Wagner," said Lynne, standing in the center of the café's kitchen. "She's from New York and is in India to learn about some of the problems women continuously face. So don't be shy. She wants to hear your thoughts and have you share your experiences with her. She knows you're busy but whenever you have a few minutes, go over and have a chat."

The girls swarmed around Allison displaying their friendship and warmth. They were as anxious to talk to her as she was with them. Allison's previous assignment involving the investigation of the brothels of Vietnam and Cambodia sobered her as she helped free young women and children. Still, that experience didn't prepare her for the shock of seeing Jaya's face for the first time at the hospital. Allison was strong, or so she always thought. Now today, feeling the full-impact of meeting the other women at the café made her extremely angry to think what one human being can do to another. The control that person lorded over a woman took her breath away. Something needed to be done. The world needed to know and Allison was determined to bring it to their attention.

It wasn't only a matter of vanity, the face is a personal thing. Lovely or unattractive, it's what people first see when they look at you. It's how you are identified and set apart from your sister, cousin, or friend. People find you on a crowded street corner or notice you in a photo by your face. To have someone intentionally abuse that part of your body, distort and mangle it by throwing acid was inconceivable.

How Allison personally felt was secondary and she never wanted her feelings to supersede those of the victims. She never wanted them to feel uncomfortable or self-conscious resulting in the need to cover their scars with a scarf. These women displayed a different kind of beauty to which only self-confidence could contribute. Allison hoped, in time, she no longer saw the distortions, the scars, the pasted-on skin; but instead, could cut straight to the whole person.

The café had several hours before closing, so it was business as usual. Allison sat at a corner table, ordered a pot of tea and sweet roll, and observed. Customers entered and left. The conversations were natural, never forced. People ordered from the menu, ate, paid their bill—all normal restaurant behavior. Allison opened her journal and jotted down a few notes. She knew she would never have this rare moment again because tomorrow would be different and the day after that a little easier. The initial impact would ease. It had to. That had to be the secret of this place.

"Namaste. May I sit down?"

"Oh yes, please do," Allison said, closing her journal. "I would love to have your company. Can I pour you some tea?"

"No, thank you. I wanted to come over and thank you for your visit. It means a lot to all of us. How do you know Lynne?"

"Well, it's a little crazy, but I met Lynne at baggage claim when we landed in Delhi. We were on the same flight from New York. We got talking, and she told me she was heading up this way to work in your café."

"That is crazy. How do you know Jaya?"

"I happened to be visiting a person who was in the same hospital room as Jaya. That's also how I reconnected with Lynne. She was there, as well."

Lynne told me a little about Agra and the café. I thought I would come up and bring Kasi with me. Kasi was the patient in the bed next to Jaya. You'll meet her tomorrow at the fashion show. But enough about me. What about you? Like, what's your name?"

"Oh, yes! I'm Kiri. This is my first day back at work."

"Were you on holiday?"

"No, we had a bad rainstorm, and the roof of my house caved in killing my son. Chandra let me take off time so that I could properly grieve."

"Oh Kiri, how terrible. How are you coping?"

"One of the girls is letting me stay with her until workers repair my house. I have such good friends. So many have come together and helped with the repairs. I'm fine on those days. I get depressed when I'm alone. The walls whisper to me. I miss greeting my son when he returns from school or hearing about what his day has been like—that part is difficult."

Allison reached over and squeezed Kiri's hand. "I've never been a mother or have experienced the love for a child as you have. However, I sometimes feel the loneliness that you talk about."

"I hope you have a child someday, Allison, if that's what your desire is."

Allison nodded her head. "Yeah, maybe someday. Right now, it most likely won't happen."

"You aren't married?"

Allison shook her head. "I was once and could have had a different life than I have now, but that didn't work out."

Kiri asked, "Regrets?"

Allison smiled, "Not too many. We were on different paths. You know, in America women have so many more options than women in India. That can be a good thing, but sometimes not."

"What do you mean?"

"More choices often lead to more confusion. When my grandmother was married, family was her whole life; but today, woman in America have so many opportunities. Women everywhere are striving to have equal status, you know? That is a good thing, but it doesn't come free. Nothing is free. The trick is to find a way to blend career and family with no harm to anyone. I've never had to do that. My time is my own and I don't have to share it."

Kiri agreed. "With me, I was married young as well. My husband was a pleasant man when we were first married but then became suspicious. One day when Kumar was maybe five, I took him to the park. I sat on a bench as he played with his ball. This man came along with his son, about the same age as Kumar. His boy watched as Kumar tossed the ball in the air. I told Kumar to share the ball with the boy. As they started to play catch, the man sat on the bench next to me. We started to have a conversation about our sons. My husband was on a bus returning home from work. From the window, he saw us together on that bench and became jealous. When Kumar and I returned home, he started arguing with me. He called me horrible names and started pushing me around. I tried to explain what happened, but his jealous nature refused to accept what I said. Kumar started to cry, so I took him in his bedroom to play with his toys. When I came out several minutes later, my husband was gone."

"Where did he go?" Allison asked.

"Later I found he went to the drug store and bought sulfuric acid. They sell it so easily in the store. He didn't come home until later that night. Kumar was already in bed sleeping. I tried to answer my husband's questions about the man in the park. I mean, I didn't know him. I told him he was a stranger, but he kept asking the same questions over and over. After a while, I stopped answering. I simply ignored him."

Allison put her hand to her mouth in anticipation of what Kiri would say next.

"He became furious, pulled out the bottle of acid and threw it in my face."

"Oh Kiri, how awful."

"It burned so badly. I could feel my skin melting as though it were butter."

Allison's eyes teared up. She moved her chair over to Kiri's and put her arm around her. "You've had a lot to overcome."

Kiri patted Allison's arm. "Thank you for listening. You know, I never experienced pain as bad as I did that day. That all changed the moment I heard Kumar died. You see, nothing will ever be worse than that."

"I just met you, Kiri, but I can see you are a strong person both inside and out."

"It's been through my work at the café that I became strong. Chandra has been a blessing to me. I call her my angel. She pulled me out of a bottomless pit twice now. I'm forever grateful to her and the other ladies."

"What job responsibility do you have at the cafe, Kiri?"

"I was a waitress at first, but then Chandra noticed I was good at math. So now I work with Naomi learning about doing the books."

"Oh, accounting?"

"Yes. Naomi is showing me how to do all of that on the computer. It was hard at first, but I'm starting to learn."

"I met Naomi this afternoon. She seemed to be an easygoing person."

"Yes, I've learned much from her. I will be sad to see her leave."

"That's right; she's only here for a few months—like Lynne."

"I'll be sad to see Lynne leave, too. Did you know she

and Naomi went with me to Varanasi to spread Kumar's ashes in the holy river?"

"I did not know that. That's a little distance from here, right?"

Kiri nodded. "Yes, I drove my brother's car. Those girls might be smart, but they are like baby chickens when driving a car in India."

Chapter 46

KASI, ALLISON, & LYNNE

"HELLO, MS. WAGNER, can I speak to Kasi. This is Detective Mahor."

"Is there a problem, sir?"

"Well, a little break in the case here. We found Hari. He was fatally stabbed multiple times. I need to tell her that as well as give her other information. Could you put her on?"

"Sure, hold on. Kasi is right here."

Allison handed her phone over to Kasi. "It's Detective Mahor. He wants to speak to you."

"What's it about?"

"He'll tell you. Go ahead, answer it."

When Kasi reached for the phone, Allison noticed her hand quivering. She thought perhaps she would mention that to Lynne at a later time. Maybe she could offer some help.

"Yes, Detective Mahor? Kasi here."

"Hello, Kasi. I'm calling with some news. I'm not sure if it will be on the news in Agra, but I wanted you to hear it from me and not from the TV."

Kasi's tremor escalated. She had difficulty holding onto the phone as she asked, "What's happening?"

"Late last night a couple from Britain discovered a body by the Red Fort that turned out to be Hari's."

"A body? Hari? Is he dead?"

"Yes, not sure if that's good or bad news for you, but at

least you don't have to worry about him tracking you down anymore."

"Was he shot?"

"No, actually he was stabbed to death. He lost quite a bit of blood from wounds in his neck and chest area."

"Do you know who did it?"

"We have a suspect in mind but need to check it out further. You see, they found Hari's body next to a wall where he started to write something using his blood. We think he was trying to tip us off as to who did this to him."

"What did he write?" asked Kasi.

"It doesn't look like he was able to finish writing it before he collapsed, but what we saw were the letters K E I . Does that make any sense to you?"

Kasi dropped the phone. It landed in her lap. Allison stood up and rushed over to her after she broke into heavy sobs. It was like the dam that carefully held all the fear, frustration, worry, and sadness suddenly burst. She could no longer hold up or pretend that all was fine. Upon hearing the sobs, Lynne ran into the room and asked what happened.

"The detective called to give Kasi news about the man who abducted her from the airport. They found him dead from several knife wounds. That's all I know. Lynne, could you take her into the bedroom?"

"Sure. Come on with me, Kasi. Let's talk about this."

"Kasi, are you there?" asked the detective over the phone.

"Detective Mahor, it's me, Allison. Kasi is having a little difficulty talking right now. What did you tell her?"

The detective repeated the conversation he had with Kasi. "I mentioned the letters written on the wall as being K E I ."

"Do you think he was trying to write Keith?" Allison asked.

"That's what we're checking out. Hari's injuries were so severe that he had to use every ounce of strength to drag himself over to the wall to write those letters. We believe he knew he was dying and wanted to tell us who did this to him."

"Do you know where Keith is?" asked Allison.

"No, not at this moment. Right now we're trying to keep this new information out of the press. We don't want to tip Keith off. The more confident he feels, the better chance he'll slip up."

Allison stood up and walked into the kitchen so not to be overheard. "I have something to tell you. Yesterday when we were at the airport, Rani called me. She's Lalit's wife. It seems Keith went to their house looking for Kasi. Rani said he was pretty worked up about her not being at the hospital when he arrived to pick her up. Keith asked to borrow Lalit's car since they lent it to him before, but Rani told him Lalit had used it to get to work. Keith told her he needed to turn in the rental because it was too expensive. After he left, Rani looked out the window and saw him getting into a fairly beat up Toyota."

"A Toyota?" asked the detective.

"Yes, she thought the whole story was a ruse. That no way would a rental agency lend out cars in that shape."

"Did she give any information about the type of Toyota?"

"Yes, a silver hatchback."

"Hmm . . . Interesting. Very interesting."

"That's what I thought. Isn't it possible that Keith may have gotten into a fight with Hari, killed him, and drove off in his car?" asked Allison.

"Sure looks that way. I need to stop by Lalit's house and speak to his wife," the detective said.

"Please keep us posted," said Allison.

"It might be a good idea if Kasi stays out of Delhi."

"I have to return to Delhi for work on Monday, but I'll make sure she remains here. It will not only be safer, but there's a lot of healing going on at this place."

Allison hung up the phone and decided to go into the bedroom to check on Kasi. When she spotted Lynne having a quiet conversation with her, she quickly turned around so as not to disturb them. The fashion show would be starting in four hours so she thought this would be an excellent time to jump in the shower and allow them the privacy to talk.

After Lynne took Kasi into the bedroom, she let Kasi cry thinking it was good for her to release all those pent-up emotions. After a few minutes, she started to calm down with only soft whimpers left in her system.

"Kasi, what's wrong?" asked Lynne.

"Did you know I was kidnapped and abused by the man I was supposed to marry?"

"Allison mentioned a little about that to me. Aren't things better now that you're with your family?"

"The detective on the case just called to tell me someone fatally stabbed Hari."

"Now you don't have to worry about him being loose, right?"

"When they found his body it was next to a wall where he managed to write the letters K E I using his blood."

"What does that mean—K E I ?"

"It could stand for the person who killed him. My husband's name is Keith. I've had suspicions over Keith's involvement."

"Why would Keith kill this guy?"

"I don't want to think about it, Lynne—I just don't want to think about it. I do know I am not returning to New York or my marriage. It had been deteriorating the past year, and now that I am here, I am not going back. I don't know what I'll do or where I'll go. I know I don't want to live with Lalit and Rani on a permanent basis, and I don't want to go back to my parent's home."

"Stay here," suggested Lynne.

"What?" asked Lynne.

"Stay here in Agra until you can figure it all out. You can continue to sleep in that extra bed. Allison will be heading back on Monday, but you stay here. She'll tell your brother where you are. He comes here on a regular basis to work in the clinic. You two can visit when he does. As time goes by, your head will clear, and you can decide what it is you want to do."

"I don't know if staying here is possible, Lynne."

"No need to make a decision now. Just consider it, okay? Now get dressed and come with Allison and me to the fashion show. It should be fun. The girls have been practicing and gearing up for this big event. We're raising money for the hospital to buy some expensive equipment that will benefit burn victims. All good stuff."

"Okay, but Lynne? If I stayed, I'm not sure what I would do here."

"Decisions don't need to be made right at this moment. Meet the girls and see what wonderful people they are. Each one of them has something that has dragged them down. They are reminded of their attack every time they see their reflection in a mirror. They learned not to let their scars control who they are. It wasn't easy, but they learned how to make a new life for themselves. So come and see what it's all about. Your hospital roomie will be there."

"Jaya? How is she doing?"

She gets a little better each day. Still has an upward climb with all the operations she faces. We're thankful for your brother. He's been a blessing."

"Yeah, Lalit is not only a skillful surgeon but a very compassionate man. Rani was lucky to have found him."

The event center down the street from the café started filling up as soon as the door opened. It's not often Agra has a fashion show, so there was lots of buzz in the air. Lynne and Kasi stopped by Jaya's house to pick her up as well as her mother. They got to the event center early and managed to grab front row seats.

"How do you like the way we set things up?" asked Naomi, greeting them at the door.

"Like Paris," Lynne joked. "You've done a great job."

"We have a sell-out crowd. The Sari Shop has been fantastic allowing us to come in after hours to try on clothing. The girls were excited over their total make-over—hair styled, make-up, manicures and pedicures, the whole spa treatment. You won't recognize them."

"Was all of that donated?" asked Lynne.

"Yep, the Taj Spa donated the spa time as well as the girls' manicures and pedicures. Kesh did the hair and make-up."

"I see we missed out on that one, Jaya," Lynne said giving her a wink.

"I was quite happy to cover for you in your absence," laughed Naomi.

"You had a make-over as well?" asked Lynne.

"Yes, doesn't it look like I do?"

Jaya and her mom laughed. "Yes, it does. I thought you look rather rested," said Jaya.

"Looking rested? That's not the look I aimed for, Jaya."

Kasi listened to the playful banter amongst the girls. How she missed that. Keith would not allow any spirited conversation. He thought of it as a waste of time. Kasi thought about how her image of the ideal man had changed. What was important three years ago was not high on her list anymore.

It didn't take too long for Jaya and Kasi to become acquainted. Lynne was thrilled to see the two girls quietly bond as they sat next to each other in the front row. She took two steps back to allow the friendship take root.

Once everyone was seated, Chandra came out on the raised platform that doubled as the runway and announced, "We are most grateful you all joined us this afternoon. The ladies from Mukta's Café have been hard at work putting this spectacular event together. As you know, we hope to have several events this year to raise money to purchase scar-removal equipment for the hospital. On your chair are a pad and pencil. If you see any particular sari that interests you, mark down the number. The Sari Shop will have it there for you to try on and will be offering everyone here a 20 percent discount all next week. I know several of you told me you're interested in purchasing an outfit for a wedding you'll be attending. Here's a great opportunity to do that. So, let the show begin."

The lights dimmed except for one spotlight centered on the stage. Lively music started to play and the curtain opened to show Salma dressed in a two-piece lime green silk sari that exposed her mid-rift. The bow neckline left part of her shoulders open. Across the front, the pallu fell over the left shoulder in the nivi style of draping while her long black hair fell loosely down her back. She looked beautiful. No one seemed to care about her scarred face and her nose being twice the normal size. What was miraculous was for the first time in a long time, Selma felt beautiful.

And so the show continued, one model after another. People applauded, cheered when they spotted a neighbor or friend, and celebrated life. Afterward, the girls came out to receive their accolades, had tea and cookies, and mingled with the audience.

Jaya took Kasi around the room and introduced her to the other women. They were becoming fast friends—Jaya with scars on the outside and Kasi with her scars on the inside. Lynne was pleased to see Jaya reach out to Kasi while Allison was thrilled that Kasi appeared more relaxed.

Allison approached Lynne and gestured toward the two girls. "I believe this place is already doing its magic."

Lynne said, "It's a new beginning for both of them. Although I find it amazing to watch, it's only a start."

Chapter 47

ALLISON

"ABHA, THIS PLACE I visited last weekend is amazing."

"How's that?" asked Abha.

"Let me tell you; these women are truly my heroes. After all they've been through, to get out of bed each morning and live their life? I don't know how they do it, but they do. No one displayed any negativity, and I give Chandra credit."

"Is she the founder of the organization?"

"Yeah, Chandra started the Mukta Café and had given these girls something they all needed—a reason to live. I decided to feature this woman in my documentary. Her story is the one to tell. Maybe I can get Wes' permission to fly her to New York."

"I bet you can, Allison. You seem to have this way of making things happen."

"Not too much of a secret, Abha. The key is to prioritize—not ask for everything, but when you sense someone or something is unique and special, pull out all of the stops."

"So why did you leave Kasi in Agra?"

"Pretty much for her safety. Her husband's behavior has been bizarre, and she's quite frightened of him."

"It's been all over the news that Hari was found at the Red Fort—murdered."

"Was anything else reported?" Allison asked.

"Like what?"

"Like the circumstances surrounding the murder or anything specific found at the crime scene?"

Abha got up and poured a cup of coffee. "Just that someone stabbed him leaving behind a knife with a pearl handle. What is it you know?"

"Not much more," said Allison, "except there was something else found at the scene that they aren't reporting. Using his blood, Hari wrote the letters K E I on the wall."

"Isn't Kasi's husband's name Keith?"

"That's what the police are going on. I think they're keeping that quiet to catch Keith off-guard. The less he knows, the better. By the way, what's this about a knife with a pearl handle?"

"Yeah, they found part of the handle laying in the bushes nearby."

"Hmm . . . I need to make a phone call, excuse me."

Allison went outside and quickly dialed Lynne's number. After several rings, Lynne answered.

"Hi, Lynne, Allison here. Is Kasi nearby?"

"Yeah, she's helping the girls at the café this morning. I must tell you that after only a few days, I've noticed a huge improvement in her."

"Really, how so?"

"She clicked with the ladies and their spirit is starting to rub off on her. I see her more relaxed and willing to join in."

"That's fantastic to hear. I hope to get out there again before I leave India. I do have something I need to ask Kasi but hope I don't cause her to regress. That's why I'm calling you."

"Sounds serious."

"It is. You know when the police found Hari's body, the letters K E I were found written on the wall, right?"

"Yeah, she knows that."

"We've assumed it to be a message and all the word lacked was a T H."

"Kasi has expressed concerned over that. What else do you know?"

"Well, it's reported that they found a knife with a pearl handle in the bushes. Could you ask her if Keith owned such a knife? Do you think that would be too upsetting for her?"

"If it's in the papers, we probably should say something to her. Let me put her on."

Lynne went into the kitchen to locate Kasi. Upon finding her, she told her Allison had a question she wanted to ask. Kasi nodded and went into the back room.

"Hi, Allison, what's up?"

"Hey Kasi, how do you like being at the café?"

"I love it here. It's been so long since I've experienced inner peace."

"That's wonderful to hear. You deserve it. How are your burns healing?"

"I'm still uncomfortable, but I feel less pain each day. Sometimes it's the inner scars that are worse than the ones you see. You know what I mean?"

"Yes, I do. I hope your relationship with the ladies at the café will help you along."

Kasi smiled. "It already has. I've only been here a short time, but the friendship they've shown has been overwhelming. Knowing what they continue to go through on a daily basis and seeing how well they handle their problems has helped me in my situation."

"I do need to ask you something that may or may not be troubling," said Allison. "Are you okay with that?"

"Yeah, this sounds frightening."

"No, no need for that. I just want to verify something. Do you know if Keith owns a knife with a pearl handle?"

"Yeah, he does. His father gave him that as a gift. He often has it on him. Why?"

Allison paused, trying to catch her breath.

"Allison, are you still there?" asked Kasi.

"Yes, I am. Look, I have disturbing news for you. The police found a broken knife in the bushes near Hari's body."

"Oh? Are you saying the knife has a pearl handle?"

"Yes, I'm afraid so."

The room started to spin, and a nauseous feeling overtook her. Kasi grabbed onto the table and sat in the chair nearby so not to fall.

"Kasi, are you okay?" asked Allison over the phone.

With a weak voice she answered, "Yes, I need a little time to process all of this. I mean, I had this crazy feeling that Keith had some involvement with my abduction. You know, the phone calls, the lettering on the wall, the insurance policy—all of that adds up. But the pearl-handled knife? That's the clincher. I mean, it's just too obvious. No matter how I feel about the guy, I did love him. I thought he felt the same. Boy, was I ever wrong!"

"Are you going to be okay?" Allison asked.

"Yeah, I believe I've suspected all along. It just seemed too obvious he was a part of this mess. What's going to happen now?"

"I need to call the detective and tell him. He'll probably want to contact you to identify the knife. I assume they'll want to pick him up before he leaves the country."

"Yeah, he's anxious to leave," said Kasi, "and now I know why. It has absolutely nothing to do with work."

Chapter 48

KASI

AS SOON AS Kasi finished her phone call with Allison, she called her brother, Lalit.

"What should I do, Lalit? I heard that it's been all over the news. Keith is most likely aware of that and even worse, he's mindful that I know he owns such a knife."

"The head nurse at the hospital said he'd been in on several occasions trying to locate you."

"Oh no! What if he succeeds?"

"No one is going to tell him, Kasi. No worries. Just stay where you are and try not to panic. You said Allison was getting a hold of the police? That should quicken the process once they have that bit of evidence." Lalit looked at his phone and noticed there was a call coming from Keith. "Look, I need to go—there's an emergency. I'll call you later today, okay?"

He quickly hung up and answered Keith's call trying to maintain some sort of normalcy in his voice. "Hey Keith, how are you doing?"

Not in the mood for small talk, Keith replied, "Fine— hey, where's my wife? No one at that hospital will tell me anything. You know, I am her husband. What the hell is going on?"

"Keith, relax. She had a bit of a breakdown. You know, everything she's been through with Hari. I don't need to spell it out for you, do I? She not only was abducted but tied up with ropes, raped, and dragged into shit-hole shacks for over two weeks. Right now, she wants to feel safe, get some rest and receive a little therapy."

"So why are all of you leaving me out of the process, huh?"

"Look, I don't even know where she is, okay?"

"Who does? Someone at the hospital said she left with an American. Who could that be?"

Lalit shook his head realizing that wasn't a good thing to tell this guy. He wondered who could have given him that information. The floor knew no one was to share information on Kasi's departure with anyone.

"I don't know anything about that," said Lalit. "I'll get in touch as soon as I find out anything new, okay?" Lalit wiped the sweat from his forehead.

"No, none of what's happening is okay," answered Keith. "I can't stay here much longer. I need to return to New York, and I plan on taking my wife. Do you all get that?"

"Sure, no problem with us, but Kasi may have something to say about that."

"What's that supposed to mean?"

"Oh, you know, when the time is right, and she feels well enough to make that long flight to America," he answered, trying to regain an ounce of friendliness in this irrational conversation.

Keith hung up on Lalit and decided to take matters into his own hands. He immediately stopped at a flower shop, bought a fresh bouquet of flowers and then drove over to the hospital. Once on the floor, Keith looked for the nurse's aide who gave him the information about the American woman. Putting on the charm, he smiled when he found her coming out of a patient's room.

"Hi, remember me? I'm Kasi Beckham's husband. She's doing so much better now. I'm thankful to all of you for that. So here is something I thought your floor might enjoy." He handed the flowers to the aide.

"These are beautiful. Thank you. I'll look for a vase and put the flowers on the counter at the nurses' station for everyone to enjoy."

Keith grinned. Everything was going just as planned. "You are welcome. I also would like to show my appreciation to that woman who picked my wife up last week—you know, the American woman? Could you tell me where I might find her?"

"Well, the only thing I know is that she's a reporter from America on some assignment. I think you might be able to locate her at the Delhi Newspaper."

"Wonderful—oh, do you know her name?"

The aide brought the flowers up to her nose and smelled them. "These are beautiful. So nice to have something cheery here on the floor."

Keith tried hard not to show his impatience. "Yeah, glad you like them. So do you know the name of that woman?"

"What woman?"

"What woman? The American woman!" Keith repeated.

"Oh, yeah—let me think about it. Could it have been Allison? Yeah, Allison—I've heard several people call her that. Don't know the last name."

"No problem—that's good for now." He made an abrupt turn and headed down the hall.

"Oh, thanks again for the flowers," the aide yelled to Keith who quickly disappeared into the elevator.

Keith got into Hari's car and drove over to the Delhi News. He had no idea what this woman looked like but decided to case out the place. Looking at his watch, Keith thought sooner or later people should start emerging from the building. He considered going inside but thought that would raise too much suspicion. The last thing he needed was to have everyone wonder why he was at the newspaper office. After a long afternoon of sitting, the door opened and two men walked out. Looking once more at his watch, he determined that the day shift should be ending soon. The door opened once more. This time two women emerged, busily chatting with no awareness of his car parked on the side of the road. Neither one looked American.

Several minutes later he spotted her. That had to be Allison. Her blonde hair and western dress made her stand out from the other women. She looked familiar but where had he seen her? He watched as she walked to the corner bus stop. Soon the bus arrived and she got on. Keith trailed the bus as it drove its route until the woman finally stepped off.

Keith hastily parked his car alongside the road and shadowed her until she reached her destination—an upgraded hotel. Several times she turned to look behind her, but he ducked behind the trees that lined the wide streets of New Delhi.

Keith knew this had to be the same person who left the hospital with Kasi. She looked familiar. Keith wondered where he saw her until he realized she was the person he spotted sitting outside Kasi's room at the hospital.

"Yes, that's it," Keith said aloud. "This is the same woman I caught listening in on my phone conversation with Hari."

Chapter 49

ALLISON

"HI WES, HOW is everything in New York?"

"Doing well, what's happening with you?"

"I have so much info on the ladies running the Mukta Cafe. What fantastic women! They were quite happy to share their personal stories and are okay with us featuring them and their café in the documentary. We need to give these women a voice and bring awareness of acid attacks to the public."

Allison walked over to the window and looked out at the rooftop before her. "That woman is doing her meditation."

"What woman?" asked Wes.

"Oh, you know, the woman I told you about when I first got here. I can set my watch by her. Every day at the same time she's on the roof doing yoga followed by meditation. I'm impressed by her commitment."

Wes said, "Yeah, not easy to do that; you know, make exercise a priority."

Allison's eyes went from the rooftop to the alley below. "Oh my Lord!"

"What? What's the matter?"

"This is insane, Wes. Kasi's husband, the guy I told you about? He's walking in the alley below my window. Like he's staking the building out."

"I don't like the way that sounds."

"I sensed someone following me when I got off the bus. I had nothing to base that on, you know, just a gut feeling. It seemed like someone was walking behind me; but when I turned around, no one was there."

"Do you think this Keith is onto you knowing where his wife is?"

"Maybe but I don't know how that could be a possibility."

"If there is more than one person who knows of a situation, there is always the possibility of a leak. Maybe you should return to New York."

Allison watched as Keith turned the corner disappearing from the alley onto the street. "No, not yet. I have to stay a little longer. Hey, no worries. I'll be okay. I need to finish my work here."

Allison ended her conversation with her editor and looked out the window. She no longer saw Keith, but that didn't mean he wasn't out there waiting for her.

"Hello, can I speak with Detective Mahor, please? This is Allison Wagner calling."

Allison paced back and forth waiting for the detective to answer. "Come on, come on . . . pick up."

"Hello, Allison, what's up?"

"Oh, hi Detective Mahor. I think Kasi's husband is following me. I felt someone was trailing behind when I got off the bus and walked to my hotel; but every time I turned around, no one was there."

"Why do you think it was Kasi's husband?"

"When I got to my room, I looked out the window and Keith was walking in the alley between the buildings. I have no doubt it was him. One other thing I wanted to tell you. I spoke with Kasi, and she said Keith had a knife with a pearl handle. It was given to him by his father, and he always had it on him."

"No, I didn't know that. I find that to be rather interesting. I think we might need to have you followed for your protection. Lalit had notified me that an aide at the hospital told Keith that Kasi left with an American woman. He must have learned that was you. You may be in a bit of danger."

Allison continued to pace. "I'm not above saying I'm a little concerned here. Sure, no problem accepting your protection. Do you think he suspects we know of his involvement?"

"Not yet," said Detective Mahor. "Remember, even though it looks that way, we are not sure of his involvement. We need to keep that masquerade going. It appears you are now in his crossfires. Are you okay with that?"

Allison took a deep breath. She wondered how she got so deeply involved. "Sure, I'm in. What do you want me to do?"

"I'll have a car trailing you as you make your way to work tomorrow. It'll be a forest green Honda. Look for it."

"Thank you. I will."

Allison kicked off her shoes, turned on the TV and called for room service to be sent up to her at 6:00. She decided a warm shower would help relax her.

"Hi there. I'm here to meet up with a colleague of mine from New York—an Allison Wagner. She's been staying here for some time now. Could you tell me her room number?"

"Yes, Ms. Wagner has been with us for several weeks

now. She's in Room 549. I'll give her a call to see if she's available."

"No problem, she knows I'm coming," the man said, hurrying towards the elevator.

The desk clerk said, "Wait!" He quickly dialed Room 549. It rang but no one answered.

The phone rang as Allison stepped out of the shower. She put a towel around her and rushed into the bedroom, but it was too late. Unconcerned, she decided if it were important, they would call again.

She dressed and started to dry her hair when she heard a knock on the door.

"Room service? You're early," she yelled.

A weak voice on the other side of the door said, "Sorry, madam."

Allison opened the door and stared into Kasi's husband's eyes. Her heart stopped, but she knew she needed to maintain a calm façade.

"Yes? I think you have the wrong room," Allison said.

Keith pushed the door open and forced himself into the room.

"Who are you?" Allison yelled.

"I believe you know who I am. I understand you know where my wife is."

"Who is your wife?" Allison asked.

"Look, no games here. I heard you left the hospital with Kasi. I want to know where she is. I am her husband, and I don't understand why no one will tell me her whereabouts."

"Let's remain calm, okay? Yes, I did pick her up from the

hospital. She's gone through a lot since arriving in India. Not only was she traumatized by being kidnapped and raped, but she's also recovering from first-degree burns. She's in therapy and doesn't want to see anyone—not her family, not you. Leave her alone and she'll contact you when she's ready."

Keith stared at Allison, not knowing whether to believe her or not. He walked around the room and started looking in drawers.

"What are you doing? Please leave right now."

"I'll leave when I find out where she is," he said.

"I don't know."

"But you do. You said yourself you picked Kasi up from the hospital. Where did you take her?"

"I did leave the hospital with her, but she wanted to go to some friend's house, so I put her in a taxi."

Allison was never a good liar. As hard as she'd try, her face gave it away. Today was no exception as Keith's eyes bore into her. He continued to walk around the room looking through her things.

"You better leave right now or . . . "

"Or what?" he asked. Out of the corner of his eye, he spotted a handwritten note:

Kasi

Mukta Cafe

Agra

"How amusing to see this so-called brave woman reporter not so fearless anymore," he said laughing.

As quickly as he arrived—he left, slamming the door behind him. Shaken, Allison dead-bolted the lock and called the police.

"Detective Mahor? He was here. Keith, Kasi's husband, he was here in my room. I thought it was room service and when I opened the door, it was him. He wanted to know where Kasi was. I told him I put her in a taxi to go to her friend's house. I know he didn't believe me. What frightens me more was this slip of paper that was laying on my desk had Kasi's name and the address of the café. I know Keith saw it because he immediately turned around and left. I fear that's where he's heading."

Chapter 50

LYNNE

"HI MOM, HOW are you doing?"

"Lynne, so glad to hear from you. How is everything going? Are you okay?"

"Things are going very well. I actually have such a nice situation. My supervisor, Chandra, has been awesome. She pretty much supports all my ideas."

"Tell me about what you've been doing."

"Well, I've been working with all the ladies, getting them to talk about their situation. It hasn't been easy, you know. They have such problems, both physical and emotional. Then there's me with none of those situations to draw from."

"I imagine all they want is a listening ear," Mrs. Fenton said.

"That I can do. When I first arrived, there was this person, Jaya, who was in a pretty bad place. She suffered extensive acid burns on her face. I encouraged her to see a plastic surgeon who specializes in burns. We went to Delhi for a while where he pretty much rebuilt most of her left ear. She still has quite a few more operations to endure, but the good thing is she's now willing to do the work."

"Why didn't she before?" asked Mrs. Fenton.

"Part depression, part money. I discovered this program that will cover most of her expenses with the rest paid by a government grant set up for acid victims. Trust me, what the government is issuing is a pittance when stacked up to what the expenses are for all of these operations. As for depression, she's starting to accept what happened which is the first step moving forward."

"It sounds like you're getting a lot from this experience, Lynne."

"Coming here was the best decision I've made. You know, I put aside the idea of going to India for several months before acting on it. The whole process of getting here seemed overwhelming, but something was gnawing at me to do it. I'm getting so much experience, Mom, not just in learning how to deal with people who have severe emotional and physical problems, but also the operations of a non-profit organization. Matter-of-fact, right now we are fund-raising for equipment that will minimize scar tissue. This one item costs between $150,000 to $200,000. We plan on donating it to the Agra clinic to be used not just for our ladies but any burn victim who needs it."

"I can see you throwing yourself right into the middle of that. Sort of reminds me of all the fundraisers you were involved in when in high school."

"Yeah, used that experience, for sure. We just put on a fashion show which was so cool. The models were the women from the café. To see them proudly parading up the runway made me cry. Naomi agreed she never experienced anything so emotional."

"Naomi is your roommate?"

"Yeah, we live in a house next to Chandra and her husband. It belongs to them. We have a pretty nice set-up. Naomi is an intern as well, helping a couple of girls learn how to manage the financial end of the business. The café is doing quite well and has gone from a small operation to a multi-level business that sells not only food but also merchandise."

"Where is Naomi from?"

"Israel."

"Really?"

"Yeah, we're making plans on connecting sometime after we graduate from college. Either Naomi will come to visit me, or I'll go see her."

"Or both?" Mrs. Fenton said.

Lynne laughed. "Yep, we thought of that as well."

"Sounds like you're developing some wings, Lynne."

"They've always been there, Mom. I only recently started noticing I have them, that's all."

There was a rap on the door. "Come in," said Lynne.

"Oh . . . Sorry," Kasi said, popping her head in the room. "I didn't know you were on the phone. Can I speak with you when you're finished with your call?"

"Definitely, be with you soon."

"Who was that?" asked Mrs. Fenton.

"That was Kasi. I believe I mentioned her in one of my emails. She's the person who was abducted from the Delhi airport and is now staying with us at the house."

"I was just going to ask you about her."

"Although she continues to have anxiety attacks, she's doing a lot better. I think she may decide to live here in Agra."

"Is the time going quickly, Lynne?"

"Yes, too quickly, I'm afraid. I still have so much more I want to do. I probably should say good-bye for now. Need to see what Kasi wants and don't want to use all my minutes. Talk to you again, Mom. Love you!"

Lynne hung up the phone and went to check on Kasi. She

found her on the couch in the living room reading a book. "What's up?"

"Hey, didn't mean to interrupt your phone conversation. Didn't realize you were talking to your mom."

"Not a problem. We were at the end of our conversation."

Kasi put down her book, picked up her bottle water, took a sip and looked up at the ceiling.

"What's going on?"

"I need to talk to you. I heard Keith learned that an American woman picked me up from the hospital. It's probably not going to be long before he figures out who that is and where I am."

"How will he figure that out, Kasi? I mean, he doesn't know Allison, right?"

"He'll find out. I know him. When are the police going to make an arrest? What's taking them so long?"

"I don't know. Maybe they want to be sure they have some solid evidence before taking the next step. Allison told me Detective Mahor is on top of things."

Kasi arose from the couch and started pacing the room. "You know, it won't be long before someone leaks the lettering on the wall. Keith will take off once he learns that. I want to know he's in jail. I can't sleep well unless I know that."

Chapter 51

LYNNE & ALLISON

"DETECTIVE MAHOR, I decided to fly up to Agra today so the car you were going to send for my protection won't be necessary."

"Will you be staying at the same place as before?"

"Yeah, there's an extra bed in Kasi's room. I have this urgency to be there. I'm concerned Keith is heading in that direction, and I feel responsible."

"Now how can you be responsible?"

"I had Kasi's address right there on the table. I know he saw it."

"Hey, not buying any of that. Keith Beckham barged into your room. Let it go."

Allison smiled. "Thanks, Detective Mahor. Sometimes I need permission to let things go. Anyhow, none of this changes my mind. I wanted to visit the café one more time before heading back to the states. Might as well make the trip now."

"Keep me posted," the detective said.

"Oh, we're starting to board. I will do that and once more—thanks."

"So Allison is coming back? She was just here about ten days ago. Do you know why she's returning?" Kasi asked.

"No, not really," said Lynne. "She left a voicemail saying she'll be here this afternoon and hoped it was okay to occupy the bed again. Maybe she needs to get additional information for her documentary."

Kasi shrugged. "Yeah, maybe. Hey, I'm going for a walk. My therapist said it was important to move my body to keep my muscles from tightening up. Do you want to join me?"

"Would love to but I'm working on a report I have to send to my advisor at school. It's due in a few days. Next time, for sure. Ask Naomi; she might want to go."

"I might want to go where?" asked Naomi, coming through the back door with her clean laundry.

"A walk? Want to go for a walk?"

"I believe I do. No rush to leave this morning. I'm taking the day off. Let me put this stuff in my room, change my shoes, and I'll be right with you."

A run-down, silver hatchback rounded the corner and slowly passed by the Mukta Café. He made a couple of passes before deciding to park the vehicle across the road. He looked at his watch. It was 8:00. The café's website said they opened at nine. He had an hour to waste. An hour goes by quickly when you're busy but can drag if waiting for something to happen. The driver of the run-down, silver hatchback wondered how things got so screwed up. It was supposed to be simple. Isn't that what he always believed? Make a plan simple. The more complicated and the more people involved, the higher the probability for something to go wrong. The plan he put together was simple. He contacted Hari, introduced himself and asked if he wanted to make some money. The guy was broke, lost his business, his house. He had nothing to lose and a lot to gain.

Keith had taken out a life insurance policy on Kasi a year ago—definitely enough time had passed so as not to draw suspicion. Hari was to pick Kasi up at the airport and figure out a way for her to be involved in an accident. Nothing complicated—a car wreck, hit and run, drowning. He didn't care. He needed something to occur and Hari agreed to do it.

Sometimes even simple plans get complicated. Little did Keith know Hari drank a lot. That most of the time Hari couldn't recall one day from the next. So did Hari remember what he agreed to? No, he did not.

Keith concluded that when Hari picked Kasi up at the airport, those taunting, hurtful feelings surrounding Kasi's rejection suddenly reappeared. It had been a couple of years which certainly was enough time to heal, but not if you're drinking and you lost your business, your house, and your money. His plan was destined to fail— doomed from the start.

And perhaps, there sat Kasi in his car looking beautiful with her black hair and dark eyes—dark frightened, vulnerable eyes. Keith fell for her, and so did Hari, but Keith won the prize. Hari didn't.

Keith looked at his watch once more—8:30. A half-hour more to wait. Too short of a time to go somewhere; too long to sit and think. The more he thought about his cunning plan, the more agitated he became. He punched the steering wheel.

"Damn you, Hari, why couldn't you follow the plan?"

Now Hari is dead. Keith killed him with the knife his father gave him—a knife he somehow lost. Keith had no choice but to kill Kasi. He needed that life insurance money. He was broke—like Hari. Living in Manhattan stripped him of his resources. Kasi proved to be a drain. The lovely, vulnerable lady turned into a depressed, moping creature. He couldn't take it anymore; until one day opportunity knocked on the proverbial door—her cousin's wedding. Kasi would return to India, he would remain in New York, and Hari would arrange the accident—a car wreck, hit and run, drowning. He didn't care how Hari carried it out. He just wanted it done and wanted it to be simple.

Chapter 52

KIRI

"CHANDRA, COME HERE and look," said Kiri. "There's this man across the street staring at the café. He looks like a Westerner. What do you think he's doing?"

"How long has he been there?"

"I would say for almost an hour. He sits and stares. At times, it looks like he's talking to himself. Do you think he's waiting for us to open?"

"Hmm . . . maybe. We'll find out soon enough. We open in five minutes. I wouldn't give it much thought. There's usually an explanation for everything. Are we ready to open?"

"Where's Lynne? Is she here yet?" asked Parvati, organizing the hostess desk as she awaited the doors to open for the first customer.

Chandra stopped wrapping silverware in the napkins and looked up. "She's not coming in today. Guess she has a report to work on for her professor at the university."

"That's something I wish I had the opportunity to do," said Parvati. "You know, go to college. Too late now."

Chandra continued to wrap the silverware. "Now why do you say that? That kind of thinking will get you nowhere."

Kiri asked, "Parvati, if you did go to the university, what would you study?"

"I would study to become a nursery school teacher."

Chandra smiled. "You never shared that before. When did you decide that?"

"Oh, it's something I've wanted to do but never had enough money."

"Parvati, they do give scholarships. Have you thought about that?" asked Kiri.

"Look at me," Parvati said, pointing towards her face, "what parent is going to want me for their child's teacher?"

Kiri and Chandra looked at each other. "Are you having a bad moment?" asked Chandra.

"No, I'm okay. Don't mind me."

Kiri said, "You know, I'm sure Lynne wouldn't mind listening to whatever is troubling you. Give her a call."

"I don't want to bother her if she has work to do."

Chandra said, "If you're having a problem, I'm sure she can take a half-hour break. Think about it." Chandra went over to unlatch the door and switch on the neon OPEN sign. "Okay, everyone, it's time. I'm opening this place now."

Kiri said, "That man is getting out of his car and coming across the street. Guess he was waiting for us to open."

The door opened and the man walked in. Parvati smiled and greeted him as she had done numerous times before with other customers. When he refused to look at her, she grew more self-conscious and pulled her scarf up around her face. "Do you need a table for one?" she asked.

"One is fine. Do you serve a full breakfast here?"

"Yes, we do. I'll get you a menu."

Parvati walked over to her stand and selected a menu written in English. She had come a long way since the attack made on her by some jealous school girls.

"Are you from England?" she asked.

The gentleman said, "England? Uh, no. I'm from America."

Parvati smiled. "We have an intern from America who has been working here for several months."

The man perked up. "Is that right? Where in the states?"

"Someplace in New York State. She always says she's not from the city. Where in America are you from?"

"Oh, I'm from New York as well, but I'm from the city."

Parvati laughed. "Wow, New York City, always wanted to go there. The first thing I'd do is visit Times Square."

The man, trying to decide on his breakfast order, was getting a little agitated with all this meaningless conversation. He could tell the café girl wanted to talk, but he had little use for chit chat. Besides, he thought her grotesque face was repulsive. He would not look at her but instead focused his attention on the menu.

Parvati sensed his reaction to her appearance and walked over to Chandra. "Maybe you should wait on him. I don't feel comfortable; I believe he feels the same. Besides, I have a phone call to make."

"Hello, Kasi, this is Parvati. Is Lynne able to come to the phone or is she busy?"

The man listened as he hid behind the menu. He lit up when he heard Kasi's name. He was now confident his hunch was correct. The address he saw in the American reporter's hotel room led him to his wife.

"Thanks, Kasi. Are you coming over to the café today? . . . Okay, have a good session with your physical therapist."

The door of the café opened, and Chandra greeted the two customers, sat them down and handed out two menus. She motioned to Parvati to continue her phone conversation, signaling she had everything covered.

"Hi, Lynne, Parvati here. Is it possible for me to stop by

the house later this afternoon? I have something I want to speak to you about . . . Great. Thanks!"

"What is Kasi doing today?" asked Kiri. "Sounded like she isn't coming in."

"She has a session with her physical therapist later in the afternoon, but right now she's going for a walk."

Kiri said, "Chandra, I spoke to Naomi earlier this morning, and she asked if I could stop by and drop off a ledger. It's a little slow here. Is it possible to go now?"

Chandra said, "Sure, go ahead."

Kiri grabbed the ledger and started out the door.

Chandra went up to the American gentleman to take his order. "So what can I get you?"

He put the menu down and looked at his watch. "You know, I'm running a little late for my appointment. I'll stop in later." He got up and rushed out of the café.

Chandra looked over at Parvati. "What a strange guy!"

Kiri waited for the next bus to Lynne and Naomi's house. As she stepped on, she noticed that the American man left the café and got into his car parked across the road. She wondered why he didn't stick around to order his breakfast since he waited in his car for the café to open. As the bus traveled its route, so did the silver hatchback.

Kiri got off the bus, looked around and saw nothing of concern. She continued the short distance to the house. Unseen, the driver of the silver hatchback did the same.

Chapter 53

KASI

"I HOPE I didn't slow you down, Naomi. I'm trying to walk faster, but the body won't cooperate."

"Not a problem, Kasi. I think the answer is to continue with your rehab and, in time, it will come back. Besides, I'm not in any rush. It feels good being outdoors."

"What are your plans for your day off?" Kasi asked.

"Well, I did my laundry, so that's done. Kiri is coming over with a ledger I left at the café. I hope to get that updated. Then I think I'll just chill out."

"Chill out? What's that?"

Naomi laughed. "It's an expression we use in America that means to do nothing."

"I like that—chill out. When I was in New York, I tried to do better with my American English, but I never heard that expression. Still more to learn."

"Kasi, your American English is excellent. I'm surprised to see how many people in India speak English."

"It's because of our past connection with England. For years, we were under their rule. But there is a difference between the English spoken in Great Britain and that in America."

"Yeah, like chill out! So here we are back at the house. Are you coming inside?" asked Naomi.

"I think I'll head on towards the market. There are a few items I have to pick up. See you in a little while."

Kasi waved good-bye and continued towards the store. As Naomi walked to the door, she spotted Kiri arriving with the ledger. "Hey! That was fast!"

"Yeah, things are a little slow, so Chandra said to get the ledger over to you now. Besides, it's such a nice day, and I was happy to get outside. Anything I can help you with while I'm here?"

"I need to put all that data on the computer. Let's go inside and we'll work on it."

Kiri started to enter the house but stopped to look around. "What's the matter?" Naomi asked.

"I don't know. Have you ever gotten the feeling someone was following you? I know it makes no sense, but there was this strange man that came into the café a short while ago. We saw him waiting out in his car for the café to open. He must have been out there for at least an hour. Then he comes in, looks at the menu and immediately leaves right at the time that I do."

"Maybe he didn't see anything he wanted to order?"

"For breakfast? Breakfast choices are pretty much the same. So as I'm riding the bus, I see him right behind us. We turn the corner; he turns the corner. I'm just wondering if he's here somewhere."

"Do you see his car?" Naomi asked.

Kiri looked around. "No, must be my overactive imagination. Let's go in. Hey, I hear Allison is coming today."

Naomi nods. "Should be here sometime soon. Lynne and I plan on taking her out to lunch. You want to come?"

"Sounds great but I'm heading back to the café as soon as we finish here."

Keith watched her as she left the market. He walked across the street and yelled, "Kasi, wait up."

Upon hearing his voice, Kasi's heart skipped a beat. She recognized the importance of playing out this charade. "Keith, what are you doing here?"

Keith ran over to her. "I've been looking all over for you. Why wouldn't anyone tell me where you were? I arrived at the hospital to pick you up and you were gone. Your family acted like they didn't know anything. What's going on?"

"Keith, no one but a few people know where I am. I needed to get away, go through my rehab and rest from all that has happened to me. I'm sorry if that caused you to worry."

"Uh yes, it did. I didn't know what was going on. Are you feeling better?"

"I'm getting there. How did you find me?"

"Oh, sort of a complicated story. I'll tell you later. You know, I haven't had anything to eat today. Is there a place where we can grab a bite?"

Kasi hesitated. Uh, I'm not hungry."

"Maybe a cup of coffee? You know, so we aren't standing here in the middle of the road talking."

Kasi said, "There is a small diner at the end of the block. I suppose we could go there."

The two walked in silence until they reached the restaurant. Once inside, Keith ordered eggs while Kasi got a mug of coffee. "Now that we are inside, please tell me how you knew I was in Agra."

"This hospital attendant mentioned it."

"Hmm . . . I don't know how anyone at the hospital would know where I went."

"Maybe Lalit mentioned it to someone?"

"Maybe, but I can't see him doing that."

Keith pushed his eggs around his plate as he thought about what she said. Lalit told him he didn't know where Kasi was. Now he hears that he did. *Why would he lie? Why would everyone be keeping Kasi's whereabouts from me?* He pushed back the urge *to* demand answers to those questions. *That wouldn't be smart at this point—not here, not in this diner.*

Instead, he said, "I see. No worries, Kasi. I only want to know if you're feeling better. When do you think we can return home?"

Kasi realized she better keep up this façade. "I'm not sure, Keith. I need to feel stronger; plus, I want to spend a little time with my family. You know, it's been a couple of years since I've seen them. The time here has not resulted in a joyful reunion. Excuse me. I need to use the restroom."

"Sure, go ahead."

As soon as Kasi left the table, Keith looked around and saw that no one was paying any attention to him. He reached into his jacket and pulled out a small bottle of ethylene glycol and carefully poured a little into her coffee. He took a spoon and stirred the mixture and then decided to add a bit more. Quickly putting the bottle away, he continued to eat his breakfast.

Kasi returned and said, "I really should be heading back, Keith."

"Oh, wait for me to finish my eggs. Besides, you still have your coffee."

Kasi nodded, picked up her cup and drank the coffee. "Pretty sweet."

"What's that?" Keith asked.

"The coffee, it's sweeter than I normally take it."

"Different places make it differently," he said. Trying to change the subject Keith said, "I'm sorry this visit back to India was so horrible for you."

Kasi took another drink. Not being able to process why he was acting so nice, she said, "I rather not talk about it right now. Maybe later, but not now."

Keith nodded. "Okay, what do you want to talk about?"

Kasi squirmed, trying to think of a topic. "How is your work coming?"

"I've tried to do whatever I could over here, but I've found it hard. With you missing, then in the hospital, and then I don't know where you are again."

Kasi bit her lip. Finishing her coffee, she said, "I'm sorry about all that, Keith. You do know I planned none of that."

Keith looked into his wife's eyes. He wondered what she meant by that comment—she planned none of that. Was that an innocent statement or a dig towards him? He had to resist reacting even though it was difficult. The breakfast done, he paid the bill, and the two left the restaurant.

Can I give you a lift back to wherever you are staying?"

"Uh, no. I'm feeling a little nauseous. The fresh air might be good for me," Kasi said, slurring her words. "I'm feeling somewhat dizzy. I think I'm going to pass . . . "

Keith caught her before she fell and helped her into his car. Once inside, he shook her, but she didn't respond. He called her name—no answer. He checked her wrist but could feel no pulse. Starting the engine, Keith drove to an abandoned building, stopped the car and dragged her limp body into an alley, leaving her slumped against a concrete wall.

With no hesitation, the silver Toyota hatchback left the scene and started its long journey back to Delhi. His plan completed. Someone will discover Kasi, drugged and over-dosed; her death considered a suicide. No one would suspect him—her worried husband hundreds of miles away in Delhi inquiring of her whereabouts. A simple plan was all that was needed.

Unfortunately for Keith, he never considered that the re-cipients of suicidal victims are often unable to collect on life insurance if the death took place within two years of taking out the policy.

Chapter 54

ALLISON

"ALLISON, I'M SO glad you're here," cried Lynne, running out to her.

"What's wrong?" said Allison, getting out of the taxi.

"I just received a call from the clinic. Kasi was found unconscious in an alley, and they think it was a drug overdose."

"What? What do you mean? Is she okay?"

"I don't know. Parvati and I were here talking when the phone rang. This all happened about five minutes ago. Naomi, Parvati and I are leaving for the clinic to find out what's going on. All I know is someone found her not too far from here."

"I'm going with you. Let me throw my bag in the house. Where are the others?"

"Right here," Naomi said, opening the front door. "I don't understand it. We had a nice conversation while we walked around town. I went back to the house, and she continued onto the market to pick up a few items. Kasi also had a physical therapy appointment this afternoon. It doesn't make sense that she would overdose on drugs during that short time."

"Look, I know Kasi isn't involved with drugs," said Lynne. "If she were, I think we would have figured that out by now. None of this makes sense. None of this."

"Hey, my taxi hasn't left. Let's get in and have the driver take us right over to the clinic."

When the girls reached the clinic, they practically ran into the building. Checking with the receptionist, she directed them to the emergency room. They were met by the floor nurse who explained how she was brought in by ambulance. Someone walking by stumbled upon her not far from the market. A small bag of groceries laid on the ground near her.

"You can't see her at this time. They're working on her right now. When she arrived, it looked like a DOA. She was pretty much out of it, but then we picked up on a weak pulse. We're treating it as a drug overdose. Something happened to this young girl."

Allison's face grew pale. She motioned to the girls to come over to the other side of the room. She explained how Keith had barged into her hotel room and demanded to know where Kasi was. "He started to rummage through my room and left immediately after spotting a note on the end table."

"What was the note?" asked Lynne.

"It had the name of the café and its location. I wasn't sure but had a gut feeling he put it all together. That's why I flew back here. I would have left last night, but there were no available seats on the plane until this morning. It had to be him."

Parvati listened intently. She didn't say a word until Allison finished. "Allison, what does Kasi's husband look like?"

"He's rather tall, thin, brown hair, glasses, an American. Why"

Parvati sat down. "It had to be him."

"What do you mean? Did you see him?" asked Allison.

This morning we saw a guy that fits your description

waiting in a car for the café to open. He sat there for most of an hour. The weird thing is once he sat down and Chandra was ready to take his order, he jumped up and ran out."

Lynne said, "That is strange. I wonder what brought that on?"

Parvati asked, "Do you remember when I was talking to you on the phone? That was when he was there."

"Yes, that was when you asked to see me," said Lynne.

"Not only that, Naomi asked Kiri to bring over a ledger that she needed. I mean, we were discussing amongst ourselves all of this as well as inquiring how Kasi was doing. He probably overheard us."

"Everything is coming together," said Parvati, "because when Kiri left, so did he. He must have followed her to the house. I can't help thinking we had a hand in this."

"Parvati, what would be the odds this guy would be her husband? We still don't know for sure," said Lynne.

"Allison asked, "Do you remember what kind of car this guy was driving?"

"I'm not good at car models. I couldn't tell you," said Parvati.

"Do you remember what color it was?"

"I think silver. Yeah, it was silver."

Allison looked at Lynne. "I'm calling Detective Mahor."

She went into a private conference room and dialed him up. As she was telling him everything that happened, Lynne came into the room.

"Sorry to interrupt, Allison, but I think you might want to know this. A nurse came out and announced Kasi didn't overdose. She had ethylene glycol in her system which is anti-freeze."

Allison repeated this information to the detective.

"It's a pretty popular concoction to use if you want to poison someone silently."

"Why's that?" Allison asked.

"It can easily be slipped into a drink when the victim isn't looking. If that's what happened, Kasi wouldn't have been suspicious. It's colorless and odorless, but does give off a sweet taste. The results would be stumbling, slurring of words, unable to concentrate."

"In other words, it would look like a drug overdose?"

"Possibly. A lot had to be poured into her drink for it to have such an immediate effect. How do you know it was Keith?"

"Several of the ladies in the café spotted someone of his description sitting outside waiting for the doors to open. Perhaps he was waiting to see if she'd show up."

"Was there was an encounter?"

"I'm not sure about that, but they believe he overheard one of the ladies mention Kasi's name. Kiri indicated she would be delivering a package to the house. When she left the café, so did this gentleman. The weird thing is he left without having ordered off the menu."

"Okay, let me give a call to the police chief in Agra. I'll ask him to send someone over to the clinic. Do you know how she's doing?"

"They're still working on her. So what about Keith? Do you have enough to make an arrest?"

"We'll grab him for interrogation. Meanwhile, see if you can get any information from Kasi. It would be helpful to find out who she was with after leaving Naomi. Could this Naomi be a possible suspect?"

"Naomi? Poisoning Kasi? Not at all." Allison smirked thinking about that suggestion. She decided it would be better not to mention to Naomi that the detective asked about the possibility of her being part of the plot.

"If this happened earlier this afternoon, he might be driving back to Delhi now," said Detective Mahor. "He probably will insist he was looking for his wife, but no one would tell him where he could find her."

Allison added, "Yeah, Keith being in Delhi and Kasi poisoned in Agra would make a good alibi, wouldn't it? He doesn't realize we know more than he thinks we know."

"After talking to the chief in Agra, I'll send two officers out to the Delhi airport just in case he shows up."

Chapter 55

KASI, ALLISON & LYNNE

"KASI, WE'RE ALL here—Naomi, Parvati, and Lynne. How are you feeling?" asked Allison.

"Oh, groggy. My stomach hurts. What happened to me?"

"You passed out in an alley. Do you remember any of it?"

"I passed out? I don't understand. Oh, wait . . . Keith, where is Keith?"

"Kasi, a detective is here to speak to you."

"A detective?"

"Namaste, Kasi. I'm a detective from Agra. I have a recorder. Is it okay if I ask some questions and tape your answers?"

"Yes, but why?"

"We think someone might have tried to poison you and that's why you passed out. Do you remember what happened after you left the market?"

Kasi held her head. "My head hurts so much. Yeah, I left the store and Keith approached me on the street. Keith is my husband."

"How did he know where to find you?" asked the detective.

"I have no idea, maybe the hospital?"

"So did you go somewhere with him?"

"I don't know. Wait, I think so. Yes, we went to a restaurant. Keith wanted to talk and hadn't had anything to eat. That's what he told me."

The girls looked at each other signaling with their eyes what everyone seemed to know. It had to be Keith who slipped poison into her food.

"Did you have anything to eat?" the detective asked.

"No, I wasn't hungry. Wait, I had a cup of coffee."

"At any time did you leave your coffee unattended?"

"Uh, only when I went to the restroom."

The detective turned off his recorder. "Thanks, Kasi. You've been quite helpful.

Allison and the detective left the hospital room. "I think we have enough here to warrant an arrest. I need to contact my chief as well as the detective in Delhi. Sure hope your friend makes it."

"Thanks, sir. We all do. Kasi's been through a lot. This episode is just one more hurdle. Good luck with finding him."

The sign on the wall read:

Gate 45
Departure to JFK
Boarding at 5:30 PM

A rather tall guy, dark hair with glasses, sat quietly in the seat nearest the wall overlooking the runway where a Boeing 787 readied itself for take-off. The flight attendant made the call for Zone 1 passengers to begin the process of boarding. The rather tall guy, dark hair with glasses, picked up his carry-on and made his way to the front. His ticket was about to be scanned when two police officers stormed in and approached the guy.

"Keith Beckham?"

The man looked from one officer to the other. "Yes, I'm Keith Beckham. What's up?"

"You need to come with us."

"Why is that?"

"We're bringing you in for questioning in regards to Hari Chubney and Kasi Joshi Beckham."

"What are you saying? I didn't have anything to do with Hari or my wife's death. I've had no idea where she was staying. No one would tell me."

"Oh, but you did know where she was, Mr. Beckham. Please come with us."

The two police officers pulled Keith's arms behind him and handcuffed his wrists.

"Hey, there's some kind of mistake here. I want to call the United States Embassy. It's my right. I haven't done anything. I haven't seen my wife in weeks."

"That's not what we heard."

"What do you mean?" demanded Keith, struggling as they hurried him amongst the other passengers behind a door that said "No Admittance."

"Your wife, Mr. Beckham. We never mentioned anything about her being dead, did we? Why would you assume that possibility, huh?"

The next evening everyone assembled at the Mukta Café after it closed. Lynne told all the ladies what happened the day before.

"Unbelievable," said Kiri. "It just never stops, does it?"

Lynne said, "The hospital is certain she'll recover. When

she gets out, everyone will need to support her both physically and emotionally."

"Of course," the ladies responded.

"When do you think she'll be well enough to leave the hospital?" asked Chandra.

"In a couple of days. Kasi's coming around quite nicely," said Lynne. "The hard part will be the emotional issues. I believe, in time, she will mend. She's a strong person."

"Just like all of us," added Parvati.

Lynne nodded. "Parvati, tell your friends what you're hoping to do."

"It's too soon."

"No, it's not. Remember what we discussed? If you set it as a goal, there's a good chance it will happen."

"Okay," Parvati looked at the group of women who had become her dearest friends. "Lynne and I will be checking out scholarships at the University of Delhi. I want to apply for admission."

Chandra said, "That's fantastic. What do you plan to study?"

Parvati's face brightened. "Early Child Education—I want to be a nursery school teacher."

"Tell them what you told me," Lynne said, nudging her further.

"Well, you see, I want to start my own nursery school. It seems like such a wild, far-fetched dream, but it's what I hope to do someday."

"You know, not too long ago I had this far-fetched idea," said Lynne.

"You had a far-fetched idea? Your ideas are never far-fetched," laughed Chandra.

"Hmm, maybe not," said Kiri, "with the exception of

having a bunch of ladies who are acid attack victims become models in a fashion show—that was kind of far-fetched."

"And don't forget the idea of getting free plastic surgery, that's a little nuts," added Jaya.

"Okay, okay . . . so I've had a few crazy ideas. But the one I'm currently thinking of happened a year ago."

"Tell us," said Kiri.

"Since you insist, I will. I found this brochure about some wonderful café that helped women become strong and independent. So strong that they overcame their physical disabilities and stood tall."

"That would be all of you," said Chandra. "What was crazy about that?"

"You need to let me finish. The crazy part was thinking this small town girl could figure out a way to travel to India and do her internship at the mentioned café. So you see, we can achieve if we at least try. Right?"

"Look here, everyone," said Naomi, waving a small paper bag in the air. "I have something Kasi wanted to give each of you."

"Kasi's giving us something? What is it?" asked Kiri.

"I don't know the meaning behind this gift. Kasi wouldn't explain, but she said Allison would know."

Everyone turned towards Allison who shrugged her shoulders and shook her head. "I have no idea what's in the package."

Naomi opened the bag and peeked inside. "Oh, wow!" She reached in, pulled out a note and a stack of bangles, all a variety of colors.

"There are bangles inside plus a note from Kasi."

"Read the note, Naomi," said Parvati.

Naomi laid the bangles on the table and unfolded the paper. She read:

"I have no further use for these bangles and hope you sweet ladies will accept them as a token of my appreciation for your friendship. Maybe someday I will begin to trust enough to allow myself to love again. When that happens, I hope to once again have a desire to wear the bracelets, but not now.

And now a few words to Allison. You've helped me so much in getting through this ordeal. I was only a stranger sitting next to you on a flight from New York, but that didn't matter. You stepped forward. Thank you for that. I hope someday we can have that lunch together. Until then, please know that no longer will I allow anyone to shatter my bangles."

In the back of the room stood the seasoned reporter who traveled to India to get information for a documentary on women's issues. Thrown into dangerous situations in Viet Nam, Cambodia, and Thailand—she always figured it out and ended up on top. Today, she took a back seat and quietly watched. Watched a group of women, not only find their way but know they no longer had an excuse to not. Realizing this made her cry. And Allison, no matter what was thrown at her, never cried.

"Allison, do you know what Kasi meant by not allowing anyone shatter her bangles?" asked Naomi.

Allison smiled and nodded. "Yes, yes I do."

BOOK CLUB
DISCUSSION QUESTIONS

1. The story focuses on Allison, Lynne, and Kasi. Which of the three women do you feel had the leading role? Why?

2. What are your feelings toward an arranged marriage? Do you think India will be able to continue this practice in today's society?

3. When did you realize who the master planner of Kasi's abduction was?

4. Cremations mean no ground burials, but they consume 50 million trees in India each year. Your opinion?

5. After reading this story, do you have a desire to travel to India? Why or why not?

6. Referring to a quote in the story: "Depression robs a person of initiative. Hope returns the gift." Comments?

7. There were several secondary characters. Which one would you be interested in further exploring?

8. Jaya had scars on the outside; Kasi had scars on the inside. Comments?

9. Kasi wrote in her note to the ladies at the cafe: "No longer will I allow anyone to shatter my bangles." What does that mean to you?

10. What does this quote from the story mean to you? "Determination and patience continuously oppose each other."

When I let go of what I am
I become what I might be.

Lao Tzu
(601 BC - 531 BC)

PREVIOUS BOOKS
BY AUTHOR

The Stolen Brooch

(Excerpt from *The Stolen Brooch)*

Once they reached the trailhead, the gravel road turned into a dirt path surrounded by thick bamboo. Steps were dug into the ground which made it a little easier for the trip down. An hour later, the two hikers heard the roar of cascading water.

"The sound is deafening but delicious," Allison said as she quickened her pace, eager to see what was up ahead.

** Finalist in the *2015 Next Generation Indie Book Awards* (Multi-Cultural)

Available online at Amazon, Kindle, and Barnes & Noble

www.outskirtspress.com/thestolenbrooch

The Poison Ring

(Excerpt from *The Poison Ring)*

Piles of dirt stood alongside the road and in the occasional empty lot. Wherever lay a patch of land, no matter how small, a vegetable garden was planted with perhaps a cow sitting in the center. Being lowered into this alien world with its diverse culture took time to process. No books, no photographs, and no personal descriptions prepared Liz and Sunita for their first encounter with Nepal.

** Finalist in the *2014 Next Generation Indie Book Award* (Multi-cultural)

** Finalist in the *2014 ForeWord Book of the Year Award* (Multi-cultural)

Available online at Amazon, Kindle, and Barnes & Noble

www.outskirtspress.com/thepoisonring

The Orchid Bracelet

Excerpt from *The Orchid Bracelet*

He was a seedy type of guy. He parted his hair on the wrong side of his head, a front tooth was missing, and he reeked of body odor. He went by the name of Mr. Swoon. There was nothing attractive about this man except for the wad of money he kept in his pouch. He used it as bait as he wandered into the village located in the central highlands of Vietnam where pine trees covered the hilly terrain. The area was scenic; but the village was poor. Mr. Swoon knew that. Actually, he counted on that.

** Finalist in the *2012 Next Generation Indie Book Award* (General Fiction)

** Finalist in the *2012 Foreword Book of the Year Award* (Multi-cultural)

Available online at Amazon, Kindle, and Barnes & Noble

www.outskirtspress.com/theorchidbracelet

Ride the Wave

Excerpt from *Ride the Wave*

Water is amazing. It's the place to be if ever I need to think. It doesn't have to be an ocean—a river or lake will do. Just being by it helps me sort out so many things. A month had passed since the accident and quite frankly, I can't free myself of the guilt. I knew I wasn't responsible. Everyone kept telling me that, but somehow the pain that took root in the pit of my stomach would not go away.

A YA novel available online at Amazon, Kindle and Barnes & Noble. (Ages 13-18)

www.outskirtspress.com/ridethewave

The Journey to Mei
Excerpt from *The Journey to Mei*

My alarm clock went off at seven. This is not unusual as it goes off at seven every school day. Normally, I groan, stretch, pull the pillow over my head and pretend the annoying blast of noise never happened. Today was different. I hopped out of bed and jumped into the clothes that draped over my desk chair. I was excited. Summer vacation would be starting in five hours.

The Journey to Mei is a story of international adoption. This book is a valuable resource that could be given to the adopted child to read and perhaps use as a tool to stimulate discussion. It's also a book that could be handed to the child's siblings, cousins, classmates and friends.

A middle reader available online at Amazon and Barnes & Noble. (Ages 8-13)

www.outskirtspress.com/thejourneytomei

A request:
If you've read and enjoyed any of these stories, a quick review written on Amazon or Barnes and Noble is always appreciated. With the publication of thousands of books each year, reviews are instrumental in alerting the reading public

of the book's existence. Word of mouth is also valued. Thank you and remember, the second best thing to traveling to one of those 'faraway places' is reading about it. I loved having you tag along as an armchair traveler. Namaste!

Freddie Remza

Check out my facebook page to see what I'm currently up to.

Freddie Remza's Saga of the birth of a novel

Groom at his wedding in Delhi, India.

Taj Mahal

Mahatma Gandhi's cremation site.

Soup kitchen workers

Soup kitchen workers

Camel in traffic

Village woman

Street scene

Woman weaving at a loom.

Chandri Chowk (covered bazaar)

Troupe of street monkeys.

Tiger at Ranthambore National Park.

Ranthambore National Park

Street scene

An Ashram (hostel) on the Ganges River.

Street vendor

Woman cooking.

Man making bangles.

A sadhu (holy man) at the ghats in Varanasi, India.